PRAISE FOR MA[illegible]

Best Friends Forever

"[*Best Friends Forever*] constantly pushes forward, asking readers to question every conclusion and warning them to never completely trust anyone . . . the characters are well drawn, speaking easily for themselves and standing out as unique people who feel real."

—*Kirkus Reviews*

"*Best Friends Forever* is a page-turner of a read, delving into the often-fraught world of female friendships and the wreckage left behind when they implode. The women at the heart of this novel are full of secrets kept from loved ones, each other, and, most of all, themselves. You may think you know how this story is going to end. But trust me—you don't."

—Amy Engel, author of *The Roanoke Girls*

"Friends or husbands? Who do women tell more truth? Give more allegiance? Margot Hunt shocks and astounds as she explores these tugs of loyalty in *Best Friends Forever*, a psychological thriller that kept me off balance even after I turned the last page."

—Randy Susan Meyers, bestselling author of *The Widow of Wall Street*

"*Best Friends Forever* is a clever thriller that asks how far we'll go to protect our friends. Margot Hunt will keep you guessing until the final satisfying twist."

—Alafair Burke, *New York Times* bestselling author of *The Ex*

"Margot Hunt's cleverly constructed thriller kept me guessing till the very end."

—Peter Swanson, author of *The Kind Worth Killing* and *Her Every Fear*

"Margot Hunt's richly drawn women wrap their hands around your throat and don't let go. A suspenseful page-turner that kept me puzzling over who did it until the last few pages. Fantastic!"

—Cate Holahan, author of *The Widower's Wife*

The Last Affair

"This gripping psychological thriller explores the reasons two marriages are unhappy and the ways vengeance-seeking women pursue their target."

—*Booklist*

"The action hurtles toward an astonishing conclusion. Fans of Paula Hawkins and Megan Abbott will be gratified."

—*Publishers Weekly*

LOVELY GIRLS

ALSO BY MARGOT HUNT

Best Friends Forever

For Better or Worse

The Last Affair

Buried Deep

The House on the Water

Tell Her Story

LOVELY GIRLS

A THRILLER

MARGOT HUNT

This is a work of fiction. Names, characters, organizations, places, events, and incidents are either products of the author's imagination or are used fictitiously. Otherwise, any resemblance to actual persons, living or dead, is purely coincidental.

Published by Thomas & Mercer, Seattle

www.apub.com

Amazon, the Amazon logo, and Thomas & Mercer are trademarks of Amazon.com, Inc., or its affiliates.

ISBN-13: 9781662504334 (paperback)
ISBN-13: 9781662504341 (digital)

Cover design by Amanda Kain
Cover image: © happycreator / Shutterstock; © LUMIKK555 / Shutterstock; © Lumina / Stocksy

Printed in the United States of America

For Sam

Live in the sunshine, swim the sea, drink the wild air.

—Ralph Waldo Emerson

PROLOGUE

Jessie Garner and Sylvia Chen met every morning at seven o'clock to walk the beach.

Despite both being in their late seventies, they made for an incongruous pair. Jessie was tall with long legs, an iron-rod posture, and a short shock of white hair she refused to color on the principle that aging was normal and everyone should get over it. Sylvia was of Chinese descent, had a sheath of shiny dark locks she was secretly extremely vain about, and was so much shorter than Jessie, she had to walk nearly twice as fast to keep up with her friend.

Although *friend* might be stretching it. The two women didn't have much in common, other than their fondness for early-morning exercise and a preference for walking with a companion. Sylvia occasionally doubted the latter. Jessie could be a handful. This morning, she was on a tirade about the condo board meeting that had been held the previous evening for the high-rise beachside building they both lived in. Sylvia was not on the board and so hadn't been at the meeting. You couldn't *pay* her to be on the board, especially after hearing all Jessie's rants on the subject.

"I proposed an amendment to the HOA rules that residents should be limited in the number of guests they can have at the pool at any given time." Jessie swung her arms forcefully as she walked, her hands fisted. "Last week, Elizabeth McNamara had all five of her grandchildren at the pool, and they were running around like little hooligans."

"I don't know," Sylvia said. It annoyed her that she always felt obliged to keep her tone mild and nonconfrontational around Jessie, and yet she always did. "I think it's nice when there are little ones around."

"Oh, please." Jessie snorted with disgust. "There's nothing pleasant about trying to enjoy a beautiful afternoon reading by the pool and having your peace and quiet ruined by a bunch of screaming snot-nosed kids. I can't believe the board voted my amendment down."

Sylvia stifled a sigh. She knew it wasn't worth getting into an argument with Jessie about kids playing in a pool, but still. Jessie always thought she knew everything about everything. It could be so tiresome. Was putting up with her bluster preferable to walking on her own?

The tide was out, and the two women were strolling on the wet stretch of sand the ocean had recently ceded. Jessie—always wary of stepping on a beached jellyfish—wore neoprene water shoes. Sylvia preferred to walk barefoot. She loved the feeling of the sand giving way under her feet while the cool water lapped up over her toes. The sun was rising in delicious ribbons of pink and orange. It was going to be a beautiful day, Sylvia thought. The forecast promised temperatures in the eighties, low humidity, and a gentle surf. On days like this, their South Floridian town was truly paradise.

"Look at that." Jessie pointed at a pile of charred logs midway up the beach. "Someone must have had a bonfire last night." She made a tutting sound, her tongue clicking against the back of her teeth. "I thought the police were supposed to be cracking down on that."

"I suppose they can't patrol every section of the beach. It's too much ground to cover."

"But how could they miss a fire? You can see them from a distance. I honestly don't know what we pay taxes for if they're not going to—"

"What's that?" Sylvia interrupted. She peered at something ahead on the beach. No, not *something*. It was *someone*. Was it a woman? The light was still dim enough that Sylvia couldn't immediately tell. No,

Sylvia realized with dawning horror as they drew closer. Not a woman. She looked younger than that. A teenager. And . . . was it possible . . . was what she was seeing true? And yet . . . Sylvia felt a lurch in her stomach, quickly followed by a growing horror.

"Is that girl *naked*?" Jessie exclaimed.

"I think so."

"This is unacceptable," Jessie huffed. "She's probably homeless and sleeping on the beach. I bet she's the one who set the bonfire." She took out her phone. "I'm going to call the police."

But Sylvia didn't hear her. Instead, she started walking faster and then began running toward the girl, her arms pumping, her splayed feet leaving deep imprints in the wet sand. There was something unnatural about the way the girl's body was lying, one leg bent behind her, the opposite arm splayed out on the sand.

It didn't look like she was asleep.

She looked like . . . and then Sylvia reached her. The girl's eyes were open, staring blankly up. Her lips were drawn back in a grimace, her teeth bared. Her skin had an unnatural bluish cast.

Sylvie retched and turned away, wrapping her arms around herself.

"Call the police!" she screamed back at Jessie. "She's not asleep! She's . . ." Sylvia looked back again and shuddered. "Oh, my God! I think she's dead!"

PART ONE

Before She Died

CHAPTER ONE

Video Diary of Alex Turner

August 1

I'm Alex Turner, and this is my video diary.

Alex held out her hand with a flourish, like a game show hostess. She sat on her bed, leaning back against a white-velvet-upholstered headboard, her long legs sprawled in front of her. Her duvet was covered in a cheerful print of oversize red and pink poppies. Alex flipped her braid back over one shoulder and looked uncertainly at the camera.

My therapist, Beatrice, suggested that I do this. Well, my ex-therapist. She's back in Buffalo, where I used to live before my mother suddenly decided she didn't want to live there anymore. She sold our house and moved us across the country to Shoreham, Florida. All without ever asking me if I wanted to move. And now I'm about to start my senior year at a strange high school in a strange town where I don't know a soul.

Alex shook her head and paused to take in a deep, shaky breath.

Where was I? Right, Beatrice. At our very last session, she said that I should start a diary and, you know, write down all the things I'd say to her in a session. But I hate writing, so she suggested that I could do a video diary instead.

I think she's hoping that this will help me remember what happened that day.

Alex hesitated, fidgeting with the end of her braid.

I've always wondered if Beatrice believed me. When I told her that I don't remember what happened. Maybe she thinks I'll say things here in this video diary that I wouldn't say to her. Because no one's ever going to see this.

But I don't feel like talking about that day.

Alex stared at the camera, her eyes wide and unfocused. Then she shook her head, as if to cast off a memory.

Although something did happen this morning. Something weird.

I went for a run, even though it was, like, a thousand degrees outside. I can't believe how freaking hot it is here. It was like running right into a wall of heat. I tried to focus on my music and putting one foot in front of the other. I ran until I wasn't sure where I was or how far away I was from home. I think I might have pushed it too hard because suddenly I got really dizzy. I stopped and had to brace my hands against my knees while I tried to catch my breath. Then I saw a park up ahead, so I headed there, hoping it would have a water fountain, which it did.

The water was warm and tasted terrible, but I drank it anyway and then splashed some more on my face and neck. I felt a little better, but I figured I should cool down before I ran home. I was looking around for somewhere shady to sit when I heard the sound of a tennis ball being hit. I hadn't even noticed there were tennis courts in the park. But then I saw them, off to the right of the parking lot. They were painted green and surrounded by a tall chain-link fence. There were some girls about my age playing there, so I sat down on a bench to watch.

There were three of them, although only two of the girls were hitting, baseline to baseline. The third was sitting off to the side of the court, bouncing her racket against the palm of her hand. They were good. Really good, actually.

One of the girls, who was tall and had dark hair, sent a ball flying out of the court. The blonde who was watching them laughed and said,

"Jesus, Shae, if you don't fix whatever the hell is going wrong with your backhand, Coach isn't going to put you on the lineup."

The girl called Shae said, "Callie just hit a good shot."

The blonde smirked at her and said, "No, she didn't. She pushed the ball like she always does, waiting for you to make a mistake, like you always do. That's how she beats you every time."

Callie was obviously the name of the third girl. She had strawberry-blonde hair and freckles. She rolled her eyes and said, "I don't push the ball, Daphne."

Daphne—the blonde—just laughed in a mean way and said, "Yes, you do. I don't blame you. You win by pushing. Well, not against me but against everyone else. You'll get second court this year for sure."

By this point, I'd figured out they were obviously all on a tennis team together. There are only a few high schools in town, so it was possible I'd play them at some point. I decided to take a video of them. I don't know why exactly. It's a weird habit I have. When I told Beatrice about it, she said that maybe it's how I process things. That's why she suggested the video diary.

Anyway, the brunette and the girl with the freckles started hitting again, and I held up my phone and started to record them. I didn't notice that the blonde who was with them had left the court and walked over to where I was sitting until she was suddenly standing right in front of me.

"What the fuck are you doing? Are you recording my friends?" she asked. She had her arms crossed, and she was glaring down at me, like I was a piece of shit she had stepped in.

I stared up at her, not sure what to say. I mean, I *was* taking a video of them. But even so, her reaction was so over the top. She was practically yelling at me.

And then she said, "Recording people is weird and creepy and probably illegal. Who the fuck are you, anyway?"

I told her my name and that I'd just moved here. And she snorted and said, "Great, just what we need. Another pervert hanging around the park."

My face felt even redder and hotter than it had when I was running. I managed to say, "I'm not a pervert. I'm a tennis player. I'm trying out for the team at my new school and was . . ." And then I trailed off. I had been about to say *checking out the competition*, but that presumed so many things. I didn't know if I'd ever play these girls. I couldn't seem to say anything right, and the blonde was just standing there smirking down at me.

"Good luck with that," she said. "I'm the captain of the Shoreham High School team, and we don't want a pervert on the team." Then she turned around and walked off, back toward her friends. When she reached them, she pointed in my direction, and all three girls turned to stare at me. I got out of there as fast as I could.

Here's the worst part. Shoreham High is my new school. I don't know a single person there, but somehow, I've already made an enemy. Maybe even three enemies.

Alex sighed deeply and tossed her braid back over her shoulder.

This can't be good. In fact, I have a feeling it's really, really bad.

She leaned forward toward her phone, her pale face in startling close up, and abruptly ended the recording.

CHAPTER TWO

Kate

I shouldn't have answered my phone as soon as I saw who was calling. I was out running the never-ending errands of the newly moved. Today's to-do list included spending a few hours online submitting address changes to my bank and credit cards and hiring a lawn-care service, and now I was headed to the store to buy a mop, kitchen cleaner, and garbage bags. I mentally added wine to the list. I was definitely going to need it after this conversation.

"Hi, Mom," I said after hitting the "Accept Call" button on my car's interface.

"Kate. Where have you been? This is the third time I've called!"

My mother's favorite opening gambit: a guilt trip. And I was already on the defense.

"I haven't gotten any messages from you," I said, careful to keep my tone neutral.

"I've called several times! Well, I think I called. I meant to. Anyway, *you* should have called to let us know that you and Alex arrived safely," she said.

"I sent you a text. A bunch of texts, actually. One when we got here, and when we closed on the new house, and another when the movers arrived," I pointed out.

"I don't read texts," my mother said.

Which . . . wasn't even true.

"You know how to text," I said.

"I didn't say I don't know *how*. I said I don't read them. I don't have time. I'm playing golf three times a week while the weather's still nice, and I'm in the middle of redecorating the guest room. Oh, and did I tell you I'm taking Thai cooking lessons? You have no idea how busy I've been."

This was just so typical of my mother and her limitless narcissism. I had, in the past month, packed up and sold our house in Buffalo, made the twenty-six-hour drive to Florida, and closed on our new house in the small beachside town of Shoreham, and then Alex and I had lived out of a hotel for a week until the movers arrived with our furniture. Now, I was trying to sort our lives into some semblance of order before school started for Alex. And all of this was made even more stressful by the fact that my seventeen-year-old daughter was so angry about the move, she was barely speaking to me.

"You're right, Mom. I have no idea how hectic life can be," I deadpanned.

"Don't take that tone with me," Mom said, as though I were still a teenager.

This time I couldn't suppress a sigh. "This really isn't a good time. I'm out running errands, and then I need to get back home. We're still unpacking."

"How's poor Alex doing?" My mother's tone switched to sugary solicitude, which was somehow even more irritating.

"She's fine," I said, although, of course, she wasn't. Alex hadn't been fine in months.

"I can't believe you moved her all the way across the country, away from her grandparents, just when she needs us the most." And the peevish tone was back.

I inhaled deeply and exhaled. My mother knew why we'd moved. I'd explained my reasons to her in detail. I wasn't going to get into it again. Not when I was doing everything in my power to keep it together.

"Mom, I have to go," I said abruptly. "I'll talk to you later."

I ended the call before she could respond, even though I knew I'd hear about it later. Why had I picked up? I'd broken my golden rule of never speaking to my mother unless I already had a glass of wine in hand, ready to anesthetize myself.

Other people had kind, supportive mothers who helped them when their lives shattered into pieces. I had the sort of mother who turned to me at my husband's funeral and said, "You have no idea how hard all of this has been on your father and me. Ed was like a son to us."

I glanced to the strip mall to my right and saw that one of the businesses there was a coffee shop.

Excellent, I thought, instantly cheered up at the thought of caffeine. I pulled into the parking lot.

The Roasted Bean was cute, with mismatched tables and chairs and a bookshelf off to one side stacked high with board games. I went to the counter, ordered an iced latte, and then took it to one of the smaller tables. I breathed in the delicious aroma of freshly ground coffee and blueberry muffins. The café was crowded. There was a group of young mothers sitting in leather chairs around a low table, each with a baby in a stroller or strapped to her chest in a sling. An attractive silver-haired couple sat at a bistro table by the window, having such a lively conversation, I wondered if they were on a first date. A group of teenagers was clustered at a table, all immersed in their laptops but also chatting among themselves. I was the only one sitting on my own.

The loneliness that hit me was so overwhelming, I thought it might swamp me, tipping me over like a small boat in a raging storm.

I wondered when I would get used to being alone. Other than Alex, I didn't have anyone in my life. No one I could call up and say, "Hey, I just need to hear a friendly voice," and then chat with about nothing or everything for a half hour. How had this happened? Was it a by-product of being a working mom, my attention ping-ponging from work crises to caring for my daughter? Somewhere along the way, I'd gotten out of the practice of having friends. I'm not exactly sure why. I always made an effort to be nice to everyone, even when I wasn't feeling particularly friendly.

Could people sense that? I wondered. Did they suspect that my warm nature and bright smile were just a facade?

Most of the people I knew back in Buffalo were say-hi-in-the-grocery-store sort of acquaintances. My mother was an emotional drain, and my father was emotionally distant. My one sibling, my sister, Lori, was seven years my senior and had fled to Seattle for college and never returned. We exchanged Christmas cards. I hadn't realized the extent to which I'd isolated myself until after Ed died.

Although it wasn't exactly like my marriage had fulfilled me to the point where I didn't need other people in my life. Ed and I had not been in a good place when he died. Quite the opposite.

Thank God he died when he did, a voice inside my head said.

Stop, I told it.

"Excuse me?"

I glanced up and saw that there was another single party at the coffee shop. It was a man who looked to be in his forties, probably about my age. He had dark hair lightly streaked with gray and was reading a hardcover book.

"Sorry?" I replied.

"You said 'stop,'" he said.

"I did?" *I did?* If I had started blurting out my inner monologue, I was in deep trouble.

"You did," he said.

"I'm sorry." I could feel my cheeks growing hot.

"Don't be." When he smiled, I noticed that he had kind eyes. They were dark brown and dipped down at the outer edges, which gave him a soulful look. "I haven't seen you in here before. Are you new to the area?"

"Really?" I asked.

"Was that cheesy?" he asked.

"A little." I softened the words with a smile and tucked a strand of hair behind my ear.

"I guess I need to work on my witty conversation starters," he said.

"You could come up with a list of offbeat yet interesting questions to ask random strangers," I suggested.

"You mean like, Have you read any interesting books or seen any good movies lately?"

"No, those are the worst kind of questions! It puts way too much pressure on the other person. I'd have to come up with something that makes me seem smart and witty. What if the last movie I saw was *Spider-Man*? What does that say about me?"

"Which Spider-Man franchise? Tobey Maguire, Andrew Garfield, or Tom Holland?" he asked interestedly.

"Wow, that went sideways quickly."

"Based on your answer, I deduce that you either have a thing for superheroes or you live with one or more teenagers. Probably the latter. But I think I can do better. Hold on." He paused, looking up as though contemplating the great questions of the world. Then his face lit up. "I know! Do you have any special talents? Or is that too high pressure?"

"No, that's good. But only because I have a special talent. I can teleport anywhere in the world just like that." I snapped my fingers.

"So you don't just have a thing for superheroes, you actually *are* a superhero?"

"Basically," I admitted. "But I don't like to brag about it."

He frowned. "That's not fair. When it was my turn, I was going to tell you about the time I won a bubble gum–blowing contest when I was a kid. But that's lame compared to actual superhero powers."

I shrugged modestly. "Sorry? But I mean, the bubble gum thing's pretty cool too."

He shook his head ruefully. "I know it sounds like it, but when the bubble burst, the gum got in my hair, and my mom made me get a buzz cut. I spent the rest of the summer looking like a skinhead."

"That sounds traumatic."

"You have no idea."

I laughed and then took a sip of my coffee. It made an empty slurping sound. I'd been so caught up in the conversation with this stranger, I hadn't noticed I'd finished my drink.

"Can I get you another coffee?" the man offered.

"Thanks, but I should get going. I actually am new in town, and I need to get back to my unpacking," I said, standing and shouldering my leather bag.

The man stood too. He was only a few inches taller than me, but he had a strong, solid build. He held out his hand. "Joe Miller."

"Kate Turner," I replied, shaking it.

"It was nice to meet you, Kate Turner. Maybe I'll see you around again sometime. If you decide to teleport back here," he said.

"Maybe," I agreed.

I could feel the smile lingering on my lips as I left the café. Maybe I had made the right decision moving us here after all. Where no one knew us. Where we could make new friends, create new memories. Exist in a space that wasn't crowded out by grief and regret.

Please, I thought. Please let things be different here. Please let me be different here.

CHAPTER THREE

KATE

Alex and I sat in my SUV, parked outside Shoreham High School, watching parents and students stream inside. Alex had been mostly silent on the drive over, and now she sat with her hands twisted in her lap, her long brown hair falling forward, shielding her face from my concerned gaze.

"We should go in," I suggested.

Alex raised one shoulder in a shrug. I wasn't sure what the shrug meant—yes, no, or indifferent. I pressed on.

"We don't want to miss orientation."

"We?" Alex's tone was caustic. "I don't care if I miss it."

"It's a new school, honey. They'll probably give us information we'll need. Like, who your guidance counselor is, and I don't know . . . where the cafeteria is located."

My seventeen-year-old daughter shot me a withering look. "I know where the cafeteria is located at my old school. You're the one who insisted we move here. Why don't you go find out all of this key information you think *we* need?"

I closed my eyes for a moment. It would be easy to snap back, but what good would that do? My child, who used to chortle with laughter at silly cat videos, who would sing loudly and off-key while she showered, and who'd always radiated with an optimistic determination, had turned into a completely different girl. Now she was anxious, edgy, angry. Always so, so angry.

But Alex had been through a lot. We both had. That's why I couldn't be reactive. I had to stay calm and measured and somehow get us through this transition.

"Let's just go in for a little while. If it doesn't seem helpful, we can always leave."

I unbuckled my seat belt and climbed out of the SUV. I wasn't sure whether Alex would follow me, so I was glad when a few beats later, her car door opened, and she got out.

We joined the tide of parents and students heading toward the school gymnasium. Alex fell into step beside me, although her arms were crossed over her chest and her shoulders were hunched over. Alex was a tall girl who'd surpassed me in height by the time she was in the seventh grade. Ed and I had joked about it, wondering which side of our completely average-height families she'd gotten the tall genes from. I wanted to tell her to stand up straight, to proudly occupy her space in the world, but managed to keep what I knew would be unwanted advice to myself.

The scene inside the gymnasium was chaotic. Alex and I both came to an abrupt stop as we took it in. There were dozens of tables set up in long rows, one for every school club or sports team imaginable, and most were surrounded by students and parents, waiting to talk to a coach or add their name to a sign-up sheet. Alex and I began to slowly circulate through the crowd. I pointed out a few clubs I thought she might be interested in, activities the old Alex would have enjoyed. A service club that walked shelter dogs. The school magazine. An a cappella choral group. She kept silently shaking her head.

"There's a table for the tennis team." I pointed. Alex looked over, her interest finally piqued. "Let's go check it out."

The table was adorned with a poster-board sign festooned with silver-and-gold glitter and **LADY PANTHERS VARSITY TENNIS** spelled out in bubbly red letters next to a cartoon of a panther holding an oversize tennis racket. Three teenage girls, who all looked about the same age as Alex, sat behind the table.

The trio was dressed in what I guessed was their team uniform—purple tank tops over short white tennis skirts. They were all thin and pretty, had long hair, and wore name stickers affixed to their team shirts. Callie, Shae, Daphne. Callie was freckled, with pointed features and long strawberry-blonde hair. Shae had smooth dark hair and large round hazel eyes. Daphne, who sat in the middle, was the most striking of the three. She had delicate features, navy-blue eyes fringed with thick eyelashes, and golden, expertly curled waves that spilled over her shoulders. They all sat with their legs crossed and exuded an absolute confidence that I had completely lacked at their age.

"Hi," I said. "I'm Kate Turner, and this is my daughter, Alex. She's new to the school this year, but she's an excellent tennis player."

"Mom, *stop it*," Alex muttered.

All three heads swiveled in her direction. I could feel my daughter shrinking back under the weight of their cool gazes.

"I remember you," Daphne said. She looked Alex up and down. "The spy."

Spy? I looked at my daughter. Alex had flushed a dark red.

"Anyway," Daphne drawled with a distinct lack of enthusiasm. "You'll have to try out. There are only two spots open, so it's pretty competitive. We have a really strong team."

"I know. You had a great record last year," Alex said, which surprised me. She'd been so against the move, so against relocating to Florida, I was surprised she'd bothered to research her new school's tennis team. I hoped it was a positive sign.

"Go ahead and sign up." Daphne nodded unsmilingly at a clipboard with a sheet of paper on it. "Tryouts are in a few weeks. Good luck."

Daphne's *good luck* was disingenuous at best and possibly even mocking. But Alex bent forward to sign her name, her hair falling forward over her face. I felt some of the tension in my stomach unclench. It was only a small step toward Alex establishing a foothold in her new life, but at least it was something.

And yet. This trio of teens unnerved me. There was something almost predatory in the way they watched Alex while she signed her name in loopy letters and then set the pen down on the table. And what had Daphne meant when she called Alex a spy? I wanted to wrap one arm around my daughter and move her away from their view.

Stop it, Kate, I told myself. Just because one bad thing happened doesn't mean there's danger lurking everywhere. They're just teenagers. Probably spoiled and self-centered, but certainly not evil.

"Daphne, what are you still doing here? You said you were only going to stay for an hour." A woman appeared beside me, standing in front of the table. "You're supposed to be working on your essay for your college applications."

"Jesus, Mom, school hasn't even started yet, and you're already riding my ass about applications?" Daphne rolled her eyes.

I glanced at her mother, wondering how she'd respond to her daughter's salty tone. She caught my eye and shared a wry smile. "Teenagers can be so charming, can't they?" She held out a hand. "I'm Genevieve Hudson. I don't think we've met."

I took her hand. "Kate Turner. My daughter, Alex, and I just moved to town."

Even if I hadn't just heard Daphne call Genevieve *Mom*, I would have known they were related. The resemblance was uncanny, from their heart-shaped faces and dark-blue eyes to the golden shade of their hair. Genevieve had the sort of slim athletic figure that would probably make even sweatpants look stylish on her. She was dressed up, though, more so than most of the parents, wearing an emerald-green sheath dress and nude high-heeled sandals. She looked like a cable news anchor.

"Welcome to Shoreham," Genevieve said. "Where did you move from?"

"Buffalo," I said.

"That's a big change. What brought you to Florida?"

I glanced at Alex, who was standing slightly behind me. She was slouching again and fidgeting with the ends of her hair. I suddenly realized that this was what was so unnerving about the girls sitting behind the table. Unlike most teenagers, who were always in motion, their energy in constant supply, these three were all sitting perfectly still. Not one of them was bouncing a foot or tossing her hair or touching up her lip gloss. They sat like a row of pretty dolls, staring coolly at us.

"We just needed a change of scenery," I said lightly. "And I liked the idea of living somewhere with an endless summer."

Genevieve laughed. "That's certainly Shoreham. Sometimes it does feel endless, though, especially this time of year. August is always beastly hot, but I swear it's worse than usual this year."

"I'll happily take the heat over six months of snow and freezing temperatures," I said.

"Hello, Kate Turner," a voice behind me said.

I turned and saw the man I'd met in the coffee shop standing there, smiling at me. I flushed, a bit embarrassed by how much I'd enjoyed talking to him.

"Hi, Joe," I said.

"All the places in the world you could teleport to, and you pick orientation night at Shoreham High?" he asked.

"It was between here or Paris. It was a tough choice, but orientation night won by a hair."

"Joe." Genevieve smiled at him and briefly rested her hand on his arm. "How've you been? I haven't seen you in ages."

"Genevieve. Always a pleasure."

There was a screech of a microphone that caused everyone to wince, followed by an announcement: "The orientation presentation is about to begin. Will everyone please begin to make their way to the auditorium. Thank you."

"I need to track down my son," Joe said, looking around. "I hope he didn't sneak out, the little scamp. It was nice to see you both."

Joe smiled at us, and then he turned and disappeared into the crowd.

"How do you know Joe?" Genevieve asked.

"I don't really. I met him briefly," I said. I glanced at Alex, who had her arms crossed in front of her. "I guess we should head in?"

"You go ahead," Genevieve said. "The orientation speech is really just for incoming freshmen and new students like your daughter. I'm in charge of the homecoming committee, so I had to supervise that table. Oh! You should join my committee. Parents are required to put in a certain number of volunteer hours at the school, and trust me, my committee is a hell of a lot more fun than most of them. Whatever you do, steer clear of the PTA."

"Why's that?" I'd been involved with the parent-teacher association at Alex's old school and had thought I'd probably do the same here.

"It's a total shit show. There are two factions who have been vying for power for years. I'm surprised an out-and-out war hasn't broken out yet." Genevieve shook her head. "It's a little terrifying how obsessive some of these mothers get."

"Well, thanks, I'd love to join your committee," I said impulsively. Alex wasn't the only one who needed to start getting involved.

"Give me your number."

I recited it, and Genevieve tapped my information into her phone.

"We're meeting Tuesday morning. I'll call you tomorrow with the details."

"Great." I turned to Alex. "We should probably go find a seat."

"Have fun," Genevieve said, before turning toward her daughter with undisguised impatience. "Come on, Daphne, time to go."

Alex and I followed the crowd leaving the gym and heading into the auditorium next door. The size of the crowd was overwhelming. If this was just the incoming freshman class, Shoreham High School was at least twice the size of Alex's old school in Buffalo. I could sense Alex tensing, recoiling at the sea of strangers.

"What did that girl mean when she called you a spy?" I murmured.

"Nothing. It was a joke."

"It didn't sound like a joke."

Alex let out an annoyed huff. "Just forget it. Who was that guy?"

"What guy?"

"The one you were flirting with?" Alex's tone was accusatory. I glanced around, hoping Joe wasn't nearby. I'd be mortified if he'd overheard. And I hadn't been flirting. Had I? I wouldn't even know how to flirt after so many years of marriage.

"Kate, over here!" a voice called out.

I saw Lita Gruen waving to me from a row of seats near the front of the auditorium. Lita lived next door to our new house and had stopped by the previous day with a basket of homemade muffins to welcome us to the neighborhood. I knew from our short chat that her son Aiden, the eldest of her three boys, was going into his freshman year at Shoreham High.

Alex and I headed over and took the two open seats next to Lita; a pleasant-looking man she introduced as her husband, Eric; and their gawky teenage son.

"I was looking for you earlier," Lita said once I'd taken the seat beside her. "But I saw you talking to Genevieve Hudson, so I steered clear."

"Why's that?"

Lita's eyes narrowed. "Genevieve is the worst person I've ever met."

"She seemed nice. Very friendly."

Lita snorted. "I've heard Genevieve Hudson called many things, but nice isn't one. She's a monster."

"Lita," Eric said mildly. "That's a little harsh."

"What? You know it's true. She's like the mean girl from high school who never grew up. And I've heard her daughter is just as bad. She and her friends have terrorized the school for years. I can't imagine how much worse they'll be now that they're seniors."

"Why don't we get started." A middle-aged Black woman wearing a royal-blue skirt suit was standing behind the microphone set up on the stage. "I'm Principal Thelma Hopkins, and I'd like to welcome you all to Shoreham High School."

Lita leaned over closer, too close, her breath hot and slightly sour in my ear. I had to fight the impulse to shy away from her. "I'm just telling you. You should really keep your distance from Genevieve Hudson. She's not a good person. In fact, she's an absolute nightmare."

CHAPTER FOUR

KATE

I heard the front door open and slam shut. A moment later, Alex appeared in the kitchen, sweaty and red faced. Her damp tank top clung to her.

"How was your run?" I asked, looking back over my shoulder while I stirred a sausage-and-marinara sauce that was simmering in a dutch oven.

"Fine." Alex poured herself a glass of water. She tipped her chin up and drank it all at once, then poured another.

"Why don't you run in the morning, when it's cooler out?"

"The whole point is to train when it's hot so I can acclimate to the heat. If I make the team, my tennis matches will be in the midafternoon," Alex said.

"I'm just concerned that you're going to push yourself too hard and get sick."

"Dad always said that strong people push themselves and weak people make excuses," Alex said.

It sounded like something Ed would say. He was forever lecturing Alex that she needed to work harder, train harder. He once forced her to practice side-to-side drills when she had a sprained ankle. When I found out, after they returned from the tennis courts, I was so incandescent with rage that the emotion frightened me. I had to go for a walk to calm myself and ended up staying out until the sun set. As I walked, I had fantasized about how much better off Alex and I would be if Ed died. I imagined all the ways it could happen. A sudden illness. A heart attack. A fall in the shower.

A car accident.

Had Alex forgotten how difficult her father could be and how unreasonably hard he'd pushed her? I wondered. Like the time she lost her match in an under-fourteen tournament and Ed made her go straight out to the practice court without a rest break. Or when he woke her up in the middle of the night to watch an Australian Open match live so he could lecture her on how to hit a swinging volley like Serena Williams. Or how he discouraged her from spending time with friends or on schoolwork because it distracted her from tennis.

Maybe it was too painful for her to remember. But I did. I remembered every moment when his coaching crossed the line from zealous to abusive. Even now, I hated him for it.

"I'm making baked ziti for dinner," I said brightly. "And garlic bread. How does that sound?"

I was not above bribing my daughter. And the old Alex would have been delighted at the carb fest, especially the garlic bread, which had always been her favorite. But this new closed-off Alex just shrugged.

"Fine," she said flatly.

"I thought we could watch a movie. We haven't had a John Candy marathon in a while."

"I'm not really in the mood for a movie."

"Maybe we can find a new series to binge. I've heard *The Marvelous Mrs. Maisel* is supposed to be great."

I felt like I was back in middle school and trying to convince one of the popular girls to be friends with me.

"I don't know. Maybe." Alex hesitated. "I need to talk to you about something."

"You can talk to me about anything." I could tell my overly enthusiastic demeanor was annoying Alex. She looked like she'd bitten into something sour and unpleasant. I decided to tone it down. "What's up?"

"If I don't make the tennis team . . . ," Alex began.

"You'll make it."

"Well, if I don't, I was thinking . . . I want to homeschool."

"Homeschool?" I repeated. I knew other parents who homeschooled, but always with younger children in elementary school. "You want me to teach you?"

Alex shook her head. "No, of course not. But Florida has an online virtual school that anyone in the state can enroll in. I already looked into it. All of the courses I need to take to graduate are on there."

It was a terrible idea. I knew it instinctively, even though I couldn't quite figure out how to mount the best argument against it. Alex was already too withdrawn, too isolated. Once school started, she'd be forced into spending time with other teenagers. My hope was that she'd make friends. Sitting home alone in her room and attending school virtually would only make things worse.

"What about your college applications?" I asked. "I don't think it will look good to the admissions offices."

Alex shook her head. "They won't care. All they look at are grades, test scores, and your personal essay."

"Don't you want to meet other kids?"

"Not really."

"Why not?"

"I don't fit in here," Alex said.

"Why would you say that?" I asked. Then I remembered the three girls manning the tennis team table at orientation. The girls with the cold eyes and pretty faces. When they looked at Alex, they'd reminded me of predators sizing up potential prey. I tried to shake this thought off. "I'm sure there are lots of nice, interesting kids who go to that school. You'll find the right group."

"I seriously doubt that," Alex said. "It doesn't even matter. I only have to get through one more year, and I'll be gone."

And with this pronouncement, Alex turned and walked off. I stirred the pasta sauce and blinked back tears.

Alex was right. In a year, she'd be off to college. All of the schools on her application list were out of state—New York University, Boston University, Tufts. Once she left, I'd see her only sporadically, on school breaks or over the holidays. My time with her was rapidly coming to an end.

When I was pregnant with Alex, Janice Fielding had thrown me a baby shower. Janice lived next door to my parents, and I'd known her since we'd moved into that house when I was five. The theme had been *pink*, from the flowers to the helium-filled balloons to the frosting on the cupcakes. When Janice handed me her present, wrapped in shiny pale-pink paper with an enormous bow, she patted my arm.

"You're so lucky you're having a girl," she said. "Boys leave, but girls always stay close to their moms."

Janice had lied to me.

I was about to lose Alex forever.

CHAPTER FIVE

KATE

Genevieve called a few days after orientation night to repeat her invitation to the homecoming committee meeting, which was going to be held at her house.

"It's a great group. I'm sure you'll love everyone," she'd told me over the phone.

I thought back to Lita's hostility toward Genevieve. Maybe there was some history between the two women that I didn't know about, an old slight that had festered over the years. Whatever it was, I wasn't going to worry about it. If I truly was going to start over, to forge a new life for Alex and myself, I needed to make friends. This was a great opportunity to do just that. Even if it was out of my comfort zone. Even if the thought of putting myself out there terrified me.

As I drove to Genevieve's house on the morning of the homecoming committee meeting, it struck me that there was a studied perfection about Shoreham, at least in the wealthier neighborhoods. The houses were all magazine beautiful, the yards perfectly landscaped, the cars brand new. I'd already noticed that many of the women who lived here were always dressed up and made up, even if they were just running to the grocery store.

It was almost too perfect, I thought.

I pulled into the Hudsons' driveway and stared up at the house, which was one of the more impressive ones I'd seen yet. It was large and white, with columns flanking the entrance. There were several other cars already parked in the driveway. I felt a flutter of nerves.

I drew in a deep breath, then climbed out of my car and headed toward the double front doors, which were painted a glossy black. I rang the bell, and a moment later the door opened, and Genevieve was there smiling at me. She was wearing a pink sundress that showed off her sculpted shoulders and slim figure. I suddenly felt horribly underdressed in my white button-down shirt and khaki shorts.

"Kate, I'm so glad you could make it," she said. "Come in and meet everyone."

I followed her into the house, taking in the soaring ceiling and winding staircase. There was a circular table in the foyer with a large arrangement of flowers in a crystal vase. As Genevieve led me through the house, the click of her high-heeled sandals echoed against polished marble floors. I followed her to a living room located just off the kitchen, which had a pair of low-slung white leather couches and bottle-green velvet armchairs surrounding a low rectangular coffee table. There were two women sitting there. One was so tiny, she was practically elfin, with nearly translucent pale skin and short blonde hair. The other had a friendly, open face and long, shiny dark curls that cascaded down her back. They both looked up and smiled when we entered.

"Girls, this is Kate. I've talked her into joining the homecoming committee." Genevieve raised one finger. "Don't say anything that will scare her off. We need all the help we can get."

"Hi, Kate. I'm Ingrid." The waiflike blonde rose and held out a thin hand that felt cold in mine when I shook it. "And this is Emma."

"Hey." Emma remained seated on the couch, her legs tucked underneath her. "It's great to meet you."

"You too," I said. "It was nice of Genevieve to invite me."

"Don't be so quick to call her nice," Ingrid said, sitting back down. "Just wait until we're up at two in the morning, covered in glitter and glue from making signs. Genevieve is very big on glitter. It's a sickness, really."

"That's one of my life rules. You can *never* have too much glitter," Genevieve said. "Would anyone like a glass of prosecco?"

"Me," Emma said, raising her hand.

"It's eleven in the morning," Ingrid said.

Genevieve rolled her eyes. "Don't be such a prude. Kate?"

I couldn't remember the last time I'd had alcohol so early in the day, but some part of me—perhaps my own inner seventeen-year-old—wanted to fit in. "Sure, why not?"

Genevieve headed into her kitchen and pulled a bottle of prosecco out of a massive stainless steel refrigerator. She unwrapped the foil from the top and used a pristine white kitchen towel to expertly pop the cork out of the bottle. She poured the sparkling wine into four champagne flutes, dropped a raspberry into each one, and then brought a glass to each of us, including Ingrid. Emma stood to accept hers. She was taller than I'd expected and had a statuesque figure.

"Let's make a toast," Genevieve suggested. "To glitter. And to making a new friend."

We clinked our glasses together, and I felt shyly pleased to have been included in the toast.

"How do you all know each other?" I asked.

"Lamaze class," they all said in unison and then laughed.

"That was years ago," Ingrid said. "Our girls are all seventeen now."

"Wow, you've known each other a long time," I commented. I felt another pang of loneliness. Why hadn't I made lifelong friends at my Lamaze class? Or even managed to keep in touch with my college roommate? But I knew why. I'd been unhappy for so long, it had been easier to lose myself in my work, in Alex, in the minutiae of life.

"We initially bonded over our mutual hatred of the Lamaze instructor," Genevieve explained. "What was her name again?"

"Harmony," Ingrid said.

"Oh, right. How could I forget that? She was so awful."

"'Embrace the pain. The pain is beautiful,'" Ingrid and Emma chorused together.

I laughed. "She didn't really say that, did she?"

"Yes, she did. She was one of those new age weirdos. You know the type. The kind who doesn't shave her armpits or believe in deodorant." Genevieve perched on the edge of one of the green velvet chairs and crossed one tanned leg over the other. "Needless to say, we all opted for drugs, so we were the class failures."

"And I had a C-section, so I was the biggest failure of all," Emma added.

"Our daughters were born within a few months of one another, and they've basically been best friends since they were babies," Genevieve said.

"Shae is mine, Daphne is Genevieve's, and Callie belongs to Ingrid," Emma explained.

"Callie would die if she heard you say that." Ingrid snorted. "Callie has been her own person since she was two and had strong feelings on what she would and would not wear to day care. I've never had any control over her."

"They all have . . . how should I put it? Strong personalities. Well, you met them the other night," Genevieve said to me. "Daphne, Shae, and Callie were manning the girls' tennis team table."

I hadn't exactly met them. The girls had barely spoken to Alex and me. But that wasn't unusual for teenagers, I reminded myself.

"Right," I said. "My daughter is trying out for the tennis team next week."

"It's super competitive." Genevieve's tone sounded like a warning. "We have one of the top teams in the state. Daphne is nationally ranked in the eighteen-and-under category."

I thought I caught a look passing between Ingrid and Emma, but I couldn't quite read what it was about.

"Alex is good," I said. "She practices a lot."

"I'm sure she'll do great," Emma assured me.

"We should probably get started on today's agenda," Ingrid said. "I have a one o'clock appointment." She glanced at me. "I'm a therapist."

"Oh, that's interesting."

"Really?" Ingrid lifted one narrow shoulder. "Mostly it means I spend all of my time listening to other people talk about their problems."

"But it must feel good to know that you're helping people," I said.

"In my experience, people are rarely actually open to change," Ingrid replied. "They want to complain, have me validate their feelings, and then take no action at all to improve their lives for the better." She shrugged again. "It's good for business."

"What do you do, Kate?" Emma asked. "Or aren't we supposed to ask that?"

"Why can't we ask that?" Genevieve replied.

"Doesn't it suggest that being a stay-at-home mom isn't enough?" Emma asked. "Like those women who go around calling themselves domestic goddesses to make it sound more glamorous."

"You don't call yourself a domestic goddess, do you?" Genevieve turned to me in mock horror. "I'm not sure we can be friends with you if you do."

"I don't." I laughed. "I promise."

"Thank God," Ingrid said.

"Although it is a good litmus test," Emma chimed in. "Like when the girls were little and we made a pact not to be friends with anyone who had those family stickers on the back of their car." She turned to me. "You know. Mom, dad, a boy with a soccer ball, a girl in a tutu. Gag."

"I promise I don't have those on my car either," I said. "But to answer your question, I had a consignment furniture store in Buffalo. I sold it when we moved here."

I felt a familiar pang when I thought of my beautiful store. It had been a warren of rooms that I set up in an ever-changing series of vignettes—a midcentury modern–inspired living room, a nautical-themed kid's room, a formal dining room. I always liked to imagine who would live in the room and then design it around the fictional person. I loved it when someone would come in and buy the whole room of furniture, wanting to set it up in their home exactly as I had in the store. It had been harder to let go of the store, with its happy memories, than it had been to sell our house.

"You should totally open one down here!" Emma raised both of her hands, palms facing outward. "We don't have any good consignment stores in Shoreham."

"I have thought about it," I said. "I'm just not sure what I want to do yet. I'm still in the unpacking-boxes phase at our new house."

"Where are you living?" Ingrid asked.

"On Collins Street. It's just down the street from that big old Victorian house with the pink shutters," I said.

"The Ainsley House," Emma said. "That's a bed and breakfast."

"Isn't that the street Lita Gruen lives on?" Genevieve asked.

"She's my next-door neighbor," I confirmed.

"Yikes. You need to watch out for her. She's batshit crazy," Genevieve said.

"I ran into her at Publix the other day, and she was a mess. She was wearing a stained shirt, and her hair was like a rat's nest, and worst of all—" Emma paused for effect. "She *smelled*."

"Gross," Genevieve said.

"I heard she's a hoarder," Ingrid said. "Like the kind they have on that television show, where they can barely move around their house, it's so packed with junk."

"You watch that show?" Emma asked, surprised.

"Don't judge me," Ingrid said.

"You should stay away from Lita," Genevieve advised me. "She's not the kind of person you want to be associated with."

I was frozen with discomfort. Genevieve's words were an echo of Lita's warning on the night of the school assembly. Clearly the two women didn't like one another. And yet the way the three women were talking about her, commenting on her appearance and mental state, seemed unkind.

"I don't know her very well," I said cautiously. "She brought us over a basket of muffins to welcome us to the neighborhood."

"I hope you didn't eat them." Genevieve shuddered. "I'd toss those right in the garbage."

"Is it just you and Alex?" Emma asked.

I was grateful for the change of subject, even if it was one with a land mine. "Yes, it's just the two of us."

"Oh, good, I'll finally have a single friend," Ingrid said. She stretched her thin arms over her head luxuriantly and smiled at me. "I'm divorced, and I swear everyone else in this town is married."

I smiled back. I knew that there was a question within her statement, but I wasn't ready to share my history with these women.

"Joe Miller was chatting Kate up at orientation," Genevieve informed the other two with a knowing tone that made me flush.

"He's cute," Emma said.

"You think so?" Ingrid mused. "I've always thought his eyes were too small."

"Oh, stop," Emma said. "He's very attractive."

"Ingrid is the pickiest woman alive," Genevieve told me as she topped off everyone's champagne flutes. "As soon as her divorce was final, every single man and quite a few of the married ones chased after her, but she had no interest in any of them."

"You wouldn't either if you knew half the things I've heard from my clients," Ingrid said. "I know far too much about what goes on in this town."

"Tell us more," Emma said, sipping her prosecco.

"You know I can't do that."

"You could use fake names," Genevieve suggested.

"And then we can guess who they are," Emma said, now laughing.

"Never going to happen," Ingrid said. She glanced over at me, and I realized how truly lovely she was. She lacked Genevieve's glamour and Emma's statuesque presence, but she had delicate features, large gray eyes, and that unusual pale skin that looked as if it had never been exposed to the sun. "They're incorrigible. They're always trying to get me to tell them stories about my patients."

"I imagine it's an occupational hazard," I said.

Ingrid's laugh was unexpectedly husky. "You have no idea."

"How's your daughter acclimating to Shoreham?" Emma asked. "Florida must be a big change after Buffalo."

"It's been difficult," I admitted. "New town, a new school. Although I'm hoping once school starts tomorrow and Alex gets on a schedule, that will help even things out."

"We're hosting an end-of-summer get-together at our house Friday," Emma said. "Why don't you come over and bring Alex? She can meet our girls."

I remembered how unfriendly their trio of daughters had seemed on the night of the school orientation. But maybe that was because of how crowded and zoo-like it had been that evening. They'd probably be more outgoing at a social event. And it would be good for Alex to meet some of her classmates.

"That would be great," I said. "Thank you so much. What can I bring?"

"Just yourself." Emma grinned at me, and I realized how much I liked her. I liked all three women. They were funny and engaging and so unlike what Lita had described.

"Mark and Emma always throw the best parties." Genevieve laughed. "After me, of course. Now, come on, let's get started on our committee work. This actually does have to be the best homecoming that school has ever seen, or else we'll never hear the end of it."

CHAPTER SIX

Video Diary of Alex Turner

August 10

Alex was curled up in an armchair upholstered in a navy-and-white ikat print, her feet tucked beneath her. She held her phone up in front of her, which caused the picture to be slightly off center. Three vertical lines appeared between her eyebrows.

I can only talk for a few minutes. Or record. Or whatever. This still feels weird, talking to no one. Talking to a camera. But I don't want my mom to overhear, so I need to get this out before she gets back from the grocery store. It's not like she eavesdrops, exactly. It's more like she hovers. Like she's always worried that if she's not watching me, I'll fall apart. And I really don't want her to hear what happened to me today.

Alex turned and looked over her shoulder, then back to the camera.

I thought I heard something, but I think it's just the next-door neighbors. Anyway, today was—dum, dum, *dum*—the first day of school. I've been dreading it. I've never been the new kid at school before. Back home, I was still friends with kids I'd gone to kindergarten with. I had no idea how today was going to go.

My mom got up and made breakfast for me, and okay, I know it sounds bratty to complain about that, but my mother knows I don't eat breakfast. I just bring a banana to school with me in case I get hungry before lunch. But this morning, there was my mom in the kitchen, standing at the stove, scrambling eggs. And even weirder, she was all dressed up in a sundress and wearing lip gloss. It was seven in the morning.

She was all like, "Hi! First day of school! I thought we'd have breakfast together before you go!"

I didn't want to hurt her feelings, so I choked down some eggs, and then she insisted on driving me to school, which was fine by me. I didn't want to ride the bus. Although that meant that I had to listen to her chirping about how she was sure I'd do fine and make new friends, blah blah blah.

Alex pantomimed shooting herself in the head, using her thumb and index finger as the gun.

Sometimes I think my mom believes that real life is like a John Hughes movie. That it's just a matter of time until I find a boyfriend like Jake in *Sixteen Candles* and everything turns into a series of cute teen montages. Walking in the park sharing earbuds so we can listen to the same music. Eating sundaes at an old-fashioned ice cream parlor. Going to prom wearing a corsage on my wrist. I don't know how it's possible that she's so completely and totally out of touch with what the real world is actually like.

Anyway. The new school.

Alex exhaled a long sigh and then shook her head. She picked up a yellow throw pillow and held it in front of her, clutching it to her chest like a shield.

Where to begin? First of all, it's huge. As soon as I passed through security and turned in to the first hallway, it was like walking right into a sea of people. There were surfer dudes and goth girls, band nerds and athletes, girls with blue hair and girls with the sort of long spiral curls that require a solid hour to style. And, obviously, I didn't know anyone. And it was so crowded, I couldn't figure out where I was going. I had English lit first period and had no idea where the classroom was. I actually wished I'd paid more attention at orientation.

I finally found where my classroom was and took the nearest open seat. I was all sweaty, and I know my face was probably bright red, and I was suddenly totally paranoid that everyone was staring at me. I glanced around, and I could not freaking believe who I had sat down next to. It was *Daphne.* The horrible girl that yelled at me in the park.

She was talking to the two girls I'd seen her with before. Callie, the girl with the freckles and stick-straight strawberry-blonde hair. And Shae, the tall brunette with the big boobs.

Daphne was complaining about how hot the room was. "This place is the same old shit show," she was saying. She kept tossing her ponytail back over her shoulder. "God, I can't wait to get out of here."

"I know, right?" Shae said. I can already tell she's basically Daphne's minion, bobbleheading along to everything Daphne says.

It seemed like they were annoying Callie, because she said, "It's only the first day of school. Are you two going to spend our entire senior year complaining?"

That made Daphne smile. "Probably," she said. "God, it stinks in here. What is that?"

"Axe body spray and desperation," Callie said without looking up from her phone.

Daphne laughed. Then suddenly, before I knew what was happening, her head swiveled in my direction. "Oh, my God. What are you staring at?"

And I just looked back at her, unable to speak. I tried to make myself say something, anything, but nothing came to mind. It was like that first day I saw them at the tennis courts. And the thing was, I *had* been staring at them. Eavesdropping on their conversation.

I knew before she even spoke that it was going to be bad. I just didn't know how bad. She looked me up and down, her eyes narrowing into slits, and she said, "Oh, my *God.* It's that pervert who was taking a video of you guys playing tennis the other day."

She was so loud, the whole class could hear. Everyone turned to stare at me. I could feel their eyes on me. It was like having bugs crawling all over my skin.

And Daphne didn't stop there. Instead, in the same loud voice, she said, "Do you guys think she's a lesbo? Maybe she was taking that video so she could jerk off to it later."

I wanted to die. Right then, right there. I wanted to be dead. And it's not because Daphne called me a lesbian. I mean, who cares if someone's gay? It was that she was making me out to be some sort of a creeper. Basically no one will even want to know me after this. It was the first day of school, and I've already been canceled at Shoreham High.

A tear streamed down Alex's cheek. She wiped at her eyes with one hand and then shook her head, looking angry and dazed.

And she wouldn't even leave it there. Once class started, I glanced over at Daphne. I didn't even mean to. I just couldn't help myself. And she was staring at me, openly, like I was some kind of a lab experiment. And then she smirked and mouthed the word *freak*.

I already knew she was awful. But it's way worse than that.

Daphne's *evil*. In fact, I think the world would be a better place if she were . . . oh, shit. My mom's home.

Alex looked over her shoulder and then turned back toward the camera. She fumbled with her phone, causing the picture to skew sideways, and a moment later, the recording ended.

CHAPTER SEVEN

KATE

On Friday afternoon, I stopped by the tennis club where I'd signed Alex up for a junior membership. She was out on one of the green clay courts, hitting against a ball machine. Every time it spat out a yellow ball with a popping sound, she'd run toward it, her racket angled behind her, and hit the ball with a whipping stroke that sent it explosively back over the net. I watched her through the wire fence for a few minutes, amazed by her power and absolute focus.

The machine finally ran out of balls. Alex turned it off and grabbed a metal basket. She began picking up the balls she'd scattered around the court.

"Hey, honey," I called out to her. "When you're done, we should get going."

"I'm not ready." Alex's tone was clipped. "I have to work on my forehand."

"You can practice more tomorrow. I told you we were invited to dinner at the Thackers' house. We can't be late."

"Tryouts are Monday, and there are eight girls competing for only two spots. The rest of the team has already been practicing for weeks. I have to be perfect."

"That's a pretty high goal to set for yourself," I remarked. "What happened to just doing your best?"

Alex shot me a look I couldn't quite read. I remembered a time when I knew all of her expressions, even knew what she was going to say before she spoke.

"Seriously, we have to get going, especially if you're going to take a shower first."

Alex ignored me and continued to pick up balls. I wondered if she'd load them back into the ball machine and start it up again, and if so, how I should react. Parenting had been easier when she was little and I could simply pick her up and carry her off when she refused to leave the playground when it was time to go. What could I do now? Threaten to take away her phone, even though as far as I could tell, she'd cut herself off from all her friends back home? Ground her, even though she never went out? Take away tennis, when it was the only activity she'd continued to show interest in after our lives had been tipped upside down?

But Alex saved me from having to solve that dilemma. She stored the ball machine and basket of balls in a wooden cupboard to one side of the court and then packed up her tennis bag. She was moving far more slowly than necessary, but at least she was coming. After taking her time arranging her rackets in the bag and adjusting her ponytail, she finally strode off the court.

"Let's go," she said, walking past me.

"It might actually be fun," I said.

"I don't like those girls. You know that."

I sighed. I did know. I wondered whether I should let Alex stay home and order a pizza while I went to the dinner party by myself. But wouldn't that make things worse for her, to hide at home? Wouldn't it give them a sense of power over her?

"I'll tell you what. We'll go for a little while, and then if it's not fun, we'll go home early," I suggested. "Deal?"

Alex gave me a long, measured look. "Fine," she said. "But if this sucks as much as I think it's going to, will you promise you'll never make me do anything like this again?"

I nodded. "Deal."

Emma greeted us at the front door accompanied by a pair of rambunctious golden retrievers. Alex leaned over to pet them, while I accepted a quick, warm hug from Emma. She was wearing a black strapless maxi dress and wore her long brown corkscrew curls loose down her back.

"I'm so glad you came. It's nice to have some new blood around." Emma smiled at Alex. "That's Scout who's licking your hand, and the other one is Atticus. My older daughter, Alyssa, was reading *To Kill a Mockingbird* when we got them as puppies. Just push them aside and come on in."

"Do you have any other children?"

"No, just Shae and Alyssa, who's away at college. FSU. Probably partying her ass off, but I try not to think about that."

"We brought you this," I said, handing a bottle of red wine to Emma as she escorted us into her house.

"Thank you so much! I'm sure we'll drink it tonight. It doesn't seem to matter how much wine I buy for these shindigs, we somehow always end up going through all of it. Come on back, everyone's in the kitchen."

I glanced nervously at Alex. Was I pushing her too hard, making her socialize before she was ready? Or was it good for her? I had no idea whether I was doing the right thing.

Emma's kitchen was bright and open, and there was already a small crowd gathered there, consisting of Genevieve, Ingrid, three men, and a lanky blond boy in his early teens who was sitting at the kitchen table playing a game on a computer tablet.

I didn't recognize two of the men, but the third was Joe Miller. He grinned at me, and I was startled by the flutter of butterflies in my stomach.

"Hi, Kate," Joe said.

"Hi," I said brightly.

I caught Emma and Genevieve exchanging a knowing look. Was this a setup? I hoped not. Joe seemed like a nice guy, but I was nowhere near ready to start dating. It was also embarrassing. What if Joe thought I'd asked my new friends to invite him?

Genevieve air-kissed my cheek, and Ingrid smiled a greeting.

"Kate, I'm so glad you came," Genevieve said. She linked an arm through mine. "This is my husband. Richard, this is our new friend Kate. We like her, so you have to be extra nice."

Genevieve's husband was a tall, good-looking man, although I guessed from the silver in his hair and beard and the deep laugh lines by his eyes that he was at least ten years older than his wife.

"I'm always nice," he said, shaking my hand.

"Sure." Genevieve laughed. "Right up until you're not. And this is Emma's husband, Mark."

"It's nice to finally meet you," Mark said. He was almost exactly the same height as his wife and boyishly handsome, with dark, thick hair and brows and a crooked grin. "Emma's already raved about you."

"She did?" I felt absurdly pleased at this. The warm reception was flattering. "This is my daughter, Alex."

Alex shyly shook hands with the adults.

"And that's our youngest, Jon," Genevieve said, gesturing toward the blond boy. He was so mesmerized by his computer game, he didn't even look up when she said his name. "He's a nationally ranked fencer in his age group."

"Wow, that's impressive," I said.

"His coach thinks he has the potential to make the Olympic team one day," Genevieve said. "Jon, put that down and come say hello."

"Good luck with that," Richard said. "I think it's surgically attached to his hand."

"Jon." Genevieve's tone was sharp enough that her son finally looked up from his device.

"What?"

"Where are the girls?"

"They're in the pool," Jon said.

"Did you bring a swimsuit?" Emma asked Alex, who shook her head. "You can borrow one of Shae's."

"No, that's okay." Alex shook her head again. "I don't feel like swimming."

"Maybe you can go put your feet in the water," Emma suggested.

The last thing I wanted was for Alex to get stuck alone with those three girls, away from the adults. I doubted they'd act up in front of us.

"Alex just had a long practice. She'd probably prefer to stay inside in the air-conditioning," I said lightly.

"Of course." Emma smiled kindly at Alex. "If you want, you can watch a movie in the den until dinner's ready."

I watched as Alex straightened her shoulders and raised her chin a few millimeters.

"I'll go sit by the pool," she said.

I felt a rush of pride and another emotion . . . hope. This was the first glimpse of the old Alex I'd seen in a long time.

"Jon, take Alex outside and show her where the pool is," Genevieve prodded him. "I'm sure you'd both prefer being out there with the girls instead of sitting in here with us."

"Right." Jon snorted, not looking up from his tablet. "As if I'd ever willingly spend time with those bitches."

"Jonathan." Genevieve's tone turned steely. "Don't use that word. And please get up and do as I ask."

Jon sighed heavily, but he finally stood and shambled out of the room. Alex, looking resigned, turned and followed Jon out of the kitchen, the two dogs bounding after them. A minute later, I heard glass sliding doors open and close.

"Kate, what can I get you to drink? I've got wine, red and white, or I can make you a cocktail," Emma said.

"A glass of white wine would be great," I said. "Thank you."

Emma filled a wineglass and handed it to me. "How's everyone else doing on drinks?"

"I think your husband needs a refill," Genevieve said, smiling at Mark.

"I meant guests," Emma replied. "Mark's more than capable of taking care of himself."

"I would certainly hope so." Genevieve laughed, resting one hand lightly on Mark's arm.

I glanced at Emma, wondering whether Genevieve's flirtatious behavior would bother her. Emma just rolled her eyes comically and refreshed Ingrid's wineglass.

"Thanks, hon," Ingrid said. "You might want to cut Genevieve off. We haven't even had dinner, and she's already all over Mark."

"She can have him," Emma parried back. "But full disclosure, Genevieve, he cuts his toenails in the living room. And leaves the clippings behind for me to vacuum up."

"Ouch." Mark tipped his head to one side, considering this. "Although, totally true."

"Alex is adorable," Genevieve said to me. "Is she ready for tennis team tryouts?"

"I think so. She was practicing today."

"That's good. She's up against some stiff competition," Genevieve said. "Her toughest opponent will be Stacey Yang, who has a wicked forehand. But she also tends to fall apart in big moments. If Alex plays her, tell her to target Stacey's backhand."

"I'm sure she'll appreciate the inside info."

"I'm glad to help. I know how hard it is to be the new kid at school. It would be great for her if she makes the team."

I felt a rush of warmth toward Genevieve, as well as Ingrid and Emma. They really seemed like women I could be friends with.

"Genevieve is a beautiful name," I said. "Is your family French?"

"Aren't you sweet? And, yes, I think I do have some French ancestors."

"But that's not why she's named Genevieve," Ingrid said, her voice dry. "She changed it when she was in college."

"Ingrid." Genevieve shot her friend an exasperated look. "For a therapist, you have absolutely no discretion." She smiled at me. "One thing you'll learn about Ingrid is that she's always brutally honest, with an emphasis on *brutal*."

"You'd rather I bullshitted you?" Ingrid asked.

"No, honey, never change." Emma slung an arm around Ingrid's narrow shoulders and gave them a squeeze. "We love you just the way you are."

"What was your name originally?" I asked Genevieve.

"Jennifer," she said. She shrugged. "But there were dozens and dozens of girls named Jennifer. I'm the only Genevieve."

We spent the next hour chatting over wine and a charcuterie platter Emma had thrown together. When the two married couples and Ingrid began to reminisce about a trip they'd all taken to the Keys, Joe turned toward me.

"How did you meet this gang?" I asked him. "Or is it a small-town thing where everyone knows everyone else?"

"Genevieve and I were neighbors back when my ex-wife and I first moved to town," Joe explained.

"What brought you here? Business?"

Joe nodded. "I'm a chef and had an opportunity to open up a restaurant with an investor. It's called the Surfside Grill. Do you know it?"

"No, but I've only been in town a few weeks."

"You'll have to come by sometime. I'll make you dinner."

"I'd like that," I said before I could think through what I was saying. Had he just asked me on a date? Or was he ginning up business for his restaurant?

"How are you settling in?"

"Good. Almost completely unpacked."

"That's impossible," Joe said. "I moved into a condo a few years ago, after my divorce, and there are still boxes I haven't gotten around to unpacking."

"I suppose that's the upside to having an obsessive-compulsive personality."

"What's the downside?"

"Keeping my spices in alphabetic order is a total nightmare."

Joe glanced over to make sure that the others were still chatting. He leaned closer to me and lowered his voice. "You do know this is a setup, right?"

I felt myself blush again. It seemed to happen with alarming frequency around Joe. "I did wonder."

"Wonder no more. And don't look now, but they're totally checking us out to see how it's going."

I turned reflexively, but none of the others were paying any attention to us.

"Ha! Made you look."

"Very mature. Did you know they were planning this?"

"No, but I'm not surprised. Genevieve hates my ex-wife, Kim. Hates her with the heat of a thousand suns. She'd love nothing more than to be the one who sets me up."

I thought of Lita and her feud with Genevieve and wondered how many similar conflicts Genevieve had around Shoreham. Was that odd or simply a by-product of Genevieve's strong personality? She certainly didn't shy from conflict, the way I always had.

"Would your ex-wife mind?"

Joe shrugged. "I doubt it. She's since remarried. But Gen would still count it as a victory."

"I think dinner is just about ready," Emma announced as she pulled a tray of barbecued pork out of the oven. My stomach rumbled, which surprised me. I hadn't had an appetite in months. Emma set it on the butcher block island next to large bowls of baked beans and coleslaw and a pan of cornbread. "Will someone let the kids know it's time to eat?"

"I'll go," I volunteered. I needed to take a moment after Joe's revelation to compose myself, and I wanted to check on Alex anyway. I wondered how she was getting along with the other girls.

I walked through Emma's house, which was smaller and less ostentatious than Genevieve's, but I preferred it. It felt more like a home, with its comfortable sofas, brightly painted walls, and family photos displayed on every table and shelf. There was a pair of sliding glass doors in the living room that led out onto a small patio and a pool with a waterfall feature, which trickled pleasantly in the background.

Daphne, Shae, and Callie were all floating on loungers in the pool, each wearing a slip of a bikini and large sunglasses, their lips painted the same glossy shade of cherry red. I was struck again by their unusual self-composure, each girl lounging like a contented cat. They were lazily tossing around a large beach ball, a childish activity that was a stark contrast to their studied young-sophisticate posing.

Jon was lying on a poolside lounge chair, his eyes again fixed on the tablet resting on his bent knees. I didn't see Alex anywhere.

None of the girls acknowledged me as I approached them and stood at the edge of the pool.

"Hey there," I said, addressing the trio in the pool. "Dinner's ready."

They ignored me, still intent on their game of tossing the ball.

"Oh, my God, you're like, totally splashing me," Daphne said to Shae.

"I totally didn't, that was Callie," Shae protested.

"Fuck you both," Callie replied, splashing a wave of water toward both her friends, who squealed and held up their hands to block the onslaught.

I blinked, startled by both their rudeness and their language.

"Girls," I said, my tone sharper.

This time I got their attention. The three teens went silent. They stared up at me from behind their sunglasses, expressions oddly blank.

"Dinner's ready," I repeated. "Your moms asked me to send you in. Where did Alex go?"

"She's over there," Daphne said, pointing.

I turned and saw Alex sitting in a bright-yellow Adirondack chair just past the pool, the two dogs lazing at her feet. She had worn her standard uniform of a T-shirt and jogging shorts. It was hard to believe she was the same age as the other three girls, who seemed like they were seventeen going on thirty-seven. Alex's feet were tucked up underneath her, and she was on her phone. I glanced at the girls again, who were still staring coolly up at me.

"Why don't you go get something to eat." I turned and walked toward Alex. Behind me, the girls went back to splashing one another, completely disregarding my instructions.

Mean girls. The words floated unbidden into my thoughts, and I tried to quickly dismiss them. I didn't know these girls. Maybe they were shy, or awkward around adults they didn't know. Moreover, I liked their mothers.

And yet . . . they didn't seem the least bit shy or awkward. They seemed unpleasant. No, it was worse than that. The way they had stared up at me without speaking had been openly hostile.

I hope something bad happens to them.

The wish appeared unbidden in my thoughts. And yet it was true. I wanted life to humble this trio of unpleasant, spoiled girls. To knock them down. To take away their unwavering belief that they were special.

I knew there was something wrong with me that I'd think such a thing. But I also knew I couldn't stop the bad thoughts from floating into my consciousness. The only thing I could do was to try to hide them behind smiles and niceties and hope no one ever figured out what I was really thinking.

CHAPTER EIGHT

VIDEO DIARY OF ALEX TURNER

AUGUST 12

Alex sat outside in a bright-yellow Adirondack chair. Two large golden retrievers were next to her, one resting his chin on the armrest of the chair. Alex stroked the dog's head. When she spoke, her voice was a whisper.

Current situation.

Alex flipped the camera view so it was pointed at the nearby pool, where Daphne, Shae, and Callie were floating on rafts. The three girls were chatting loudly, punctuating their conversation with occasional shrieks when they splashed one another.

"What do you think Coach is going to do with the lineup for the first match?" Shae asked. "I mean, obviously you'll get first-court singles, Daph."

"Obviously," Daphne agreed. She paddled one hand in the water, lazily spinning her raft around. "Other than that, I don't really care."

Callie splashed Daphne. "Thanks, that's very supportive of you."

"Hey! Come on, Cee. You know you'll probably get second singles," Daphne said.

"Probably," Shae said morosely. "I'll get stuck playing doubles."

Callie tipped her head back against her float. "I'm sure Coach will do whatever's best for the team."

"Oh, my God. You are so hot for Coach!" Daphne said.

Callie splashed Daphne again. "What? No, I'm not."

"You are so. You'd totally fuck him."

"Jesus, Dee. Stop screaming." Callie shushed her. "Our moms are, like, just inside!"

"Are you afraid Ingrid is going to find out you want to fuck Coach?" Daphne teased.

"She totally is," Shae said.

Callie raised her voice. "Will you two shut up."

"Make me," Daphne said.

The three girls began splashing one another again, screeching with laughter.

Alex turned the camera back on herself and rolled her eyes. When she spoke, her voice was a whisper.

I can't believe my mom made me come here. Sometimes I think I really do hate her.

CHAPTER NINE

KATE

Monday afternoon, I sat on the hard metal bleacher stands set up next to the high school tennis courts, watching Alex play her last opponent at the team tryouts. The temperature outside was almost unbearable, with the hot August sun blazing down and not even the hint of a breeze. The tryouts were down to three girls, and whoever won Alex's match was guaranteed one of the two open spots on the team. The loser of this match would play the third girl for the other spot. I was trying to exude a sense of quiet confidence—Alex wouldn't appreciate any open displays of concern—but my stomach was clenched as tight as a fist. Alex hit an ace to win her service game, and I exhaled loudly.

"Alex is only one game away now," Genevieve said. She was sitting on one side of me, and Emma on the other. Ingrid was perched behind us, wearing a giant straw hat to shade her pale skin.

"She's got this," Emma said. "She's playing great."

"And even better, Stacey's playing like shit," Genevieve murmured. "I told you she chokes under pressure."

"Harsh," Ingrid said.

"But true," Genevieve replied.

I knew it was wrong to root for a teenager to play poorly, but at the same time, I really wanted Alex to win. She needed a success to anchor her to this new life that she hadn't wanted or asked for. And it felt good to have allies with me, friends who'd come to cheer on my daughter to succeed.

They didn't seem upset that Alex and I had abruptly left the party Friday night. I could tell Alex was miserable, and I wanted to get her away from the other three girls. I'd made an excuse to cover our early departure, claiming I had an upset stomach. I think everyone had had so much wine by then, they barely noticed we were ducking out early. Everyone except for Joe. He'd held on to my hand for a few extra beats when we said our goodbyes.

"This is taking forever," Daphne said from behind us. She yawned loudly.

Daphne and the other members of the tennis team were lounging on the top row of the bleachers, also watching the tryouts. They had their legs stretched out and their bags scattered around them, and one of the girls—one I didn't recognize—was braiding each of the girls' hair in turn.

Callie, Ingrid's daughter, was the only girl not sitting with the team. She was standing with Coach Townsend at the side of the court where Alex was playing her match. Callie kept turning up to look at the coach, quick to laugh at anything he said, her arms entwined behind her back. Seth Townsend was tall and lean with shaggy dark-blond hair and high cheekbones. I glanced at Ingrid and wondered if she was aware of her daughter's obvious crush.

I looked back at the court just in time to watch Stacey hit a ball into the net and turn angrily, hitting her racket against one hand. As she did, her tennis skirt blew up in the wind, exposing the shorties beneath.

"Jesus, could she have a bigger ass?" Daphne asked loudly from behind us. Her teammates giggled.

I flinched at Daphne's words and glanced at Stacey, concerned that she might have overheard Daphne's ringing voice. But Stacey was already preparing to serve again and didn't glance toward the stands.

"It is true, though," Genevieve murmured in my ear. "Stacey takes after her mother, Nancy. They have the same build." She nodded in the direction of a pear-shaped woman standing by the fence, watching the match intently with her arms crossed over her chest.

"Genevieve, you're as bad as the girls," Ingrid chided.

"No, I'm not. She can't hear me."

"I manned a table with Nancy at the school bake sale last year, and I think she ate half of the cupcakes," Emma said, her voice low.

Genevieve and Ingrid both laughed, but I cringed at their harsh words. Even if Nancy couldn't hear them, it seemed petty and mean. The fact that there was an element of truth to their barbed comments—Nancy Yang was rather overweight and, in her oversize T-shirt and shorts, was nowhere near as attractive or glamorous as the three women flanking me—made it even worse. How could these women, who had been so kind and welcoming to me, be so casually cruel about others?

Alex lifted her index finger to indicate that the last ball Stacey hit had sailed long.

"It's match point for Alex," Genevieve said.

"That wasn't out!" Nancy Yang called out indignantly. "It was on the line!"

"Spectators can't make line calls," Coach Townsend said. From his bored tone, I guessed this wasn't the first time he'd had to admonish a parent for trying to interfere in a match.

"But she's cheating!" Nancy Yang insisted, her voice shrill and loud. "That's not fair! She shouldn't be able to cheat her way onto the team!"

I straightened in my seat, flushed with anger at this woman's ugly attack on my daughter. A moment earlier, I'd felt sorry for her. That was now replaced by a deep maternal rage. I looked over at Alex, worried that the catcalling had upset her, but she was cool and calm as she waited for Stacey's next serve. When the ball came toward her, she whipped her racket back and smacked a winner down the line.

"She did it!" Genevieve exclaimed. "She won!"

Emma squeezed my hand. "Good for her!"

I wanted to whoop but managed to contain myself. Alex would be mortified. My daughter walked to the net, looking composed, as she waited to shake Stacey's hand. Stacey, however, had thrown her racket back against the fence in a fit of temper, while her mother descended on Coach Townsend, still loudly disputing Alex's line call on the previous point.

"Yeah, like we'd want that hot mess on the team," one of the teenagers sitting behind us said.

"I don't blame her," Daphne said loudly. "Bad line calls piss me off too."

"Was that ball out? I couldn't see it," one of the other girls asked.

"Questionable," Daphne said. "Possibly shady."

I clenched my fists so hard, my fingernails cut into my palms. I hated that Alex's victory would be tainted in any way. I wanted this to be a moment of pure, unassailable joy for her. And anyway, the ball had been out . . . hadn't it? I was almost sure it had. And why wasn't Genevieve correcting her daughter? She seemed oblivious to Daphne's behavior.

Mean girls, I thought again.

Alex was still standing at the net, waiting to shake Stacey Yang's hand, but Stacey had instead stalked off the court to join her mother in shouting at Coach Townsend. Alex looked over at me and shrugged, obviously not sure what to do. Finally, she went to the bench at the side of the court to pack up her racket and other gear.

"Oh, my God," Emma breathed. *"Drama."*

"Leave it to Nancy to make a scene," Ingrid said.

Alex walked off the court and headed toward me. My heart swelled at the sight of my daughter, looking happy and confident for the first time in months.

"Yay!" I said, standing once she'd reached the bleachers. "You were fantastic!"

"She wouldn't shake my hand," Alex said softly, glancing back at Stacey.

"Don't worry about it." Genevieve stood and gave Alex a quick hug. "Congratulations, honey! We're so glad you made the team!" She turned. "Daphne, take Alex to Coach's office so you can help her find a uniform."

"Because that's my job?" I heard Daphne mutter. I glanced back and saw her rolling her eyes at Shae, and some of my joy at Alex's victory dimmed. I'd wanted her to win, of course. But that victory was going to keep her near this trio of girls.

That thought caused a sliver of icy fear to slither through me.

That night, while Alex was upstairs in her room, working on an English essay, I stood in our new living room, which still felt bare and unfamiliar. I hadn't had a chance to hang pictures yet, and I needed to purchase potted orchids and scented candles to warm the room up.

I stared out the front window onto the dark street. At our old home, back in Buffalo, I'd known all my neighbors by name, known who their children were, had watched their lives unfold over the years. Birthday-party balloons tied to mailboxes, graduation celebrations, receptions held after funerals. Here, I was still a stranger. Maybe I always would be.

I took a long sip of whiskey out of a heavy cut-crystal glass from the set Ed and I had been given as a wedding gift.

Ed.

Whiskey on the rocks had been his go-to. Drinking it now reminded me of when we were newlyweds and how it had tasted on Ed's breath when he kissed me. I liked remembering us back then, the way we were all those years ago. Before everything had gone wrong. I took another long sip of the whiskey, hoping that the alcohol would quickly numb me. I was feeling too much and needed it to stop.

"Mom?" I turned to see Alex standing in the doorway, backlit by the glow of the hall behind her. "Why are you standing here in the dark?"

"No reason. I was just thinking."

Alex flicked the switch on the wall, illuminating the austere overhead light that I'd already decided I hated and needed to replace immediately. It was yet one more item on the never-ending to-do list that came with moving.

"Why don't you ever cry?" she asked, her tone accusatory.

"Of course I cry."

"Not over Dad. You haven't cried once over him."

I inhaled sharply, as though she'd slapped me. "People express grief in different ways."

"Maybe. But normal people cry when their husband dies."

Alex and I stared at one another.

I thought about lying to her. Telling her that I missed Ed. That his death had unmoored me. That I cried when she couldn't see me. But Alex would know I was lying.

"My feelings about your father are complicated."

"You hated him," Alex said bitterly.

I shook my head. "No. I hated what he'd become."

"I miss him!"

"I know. I'm sorry."

"No, you don't get it. I miss him every minute of every day. And you don't even seem to care that he's dead!"

"Of course I care," I said. "And if you ever want to talk about him or talk about what happened, I'm always here to listen."

Alex shrugged. "I don't want to talk about it."

"Are you hungry?" I finally asked, groping for a topic that would defuse the tension. "Dinner will be ready in a few minutes. I made roast chicken and green beans amandine to celebrate your big win today."

Alex didn't speak. Her silence felt like an accusation. Maybe it was.

I rubbed the space between my eyebrows, a stress-triggered habit I'd picked up over the past year. "Why don't we just focus on what a good day we had today. I'm so proud of you."

Alex shrugged, but one corner of her mouth quirked up. "I still can't believe that girl wouldn't shake my hand after the match."

"That reflects on her character, not on yours."

"I know." Alex hesitated.

"What is it?"

"That ball was out. You saw it, right?"

"Yes, absolutely. Mrs. Hudson saw it too."

"Those girls think I cheated. Daphne and her friends. I heard them questioning the call."

"It was just because Stacey's mom was making a scene. You know how some people love creating drama."

"I heard Daphne say I cheated," Alex said flatly.

"But you didn't. And you know you didn't. That's all that matters."

Alex lifted one shoulder and let it fall.

"Well, I think it's great that you'll be on this team, and competing, and meeting new people. Maybe you'll make some new friends." I could hear how overly peppy my tone was. I sounded like a sitcom mother and wasn't surprised when Alex gave me a withering look.

"Like Daphne and her two minions?"

"Well . . . no," I admitted. "But there are other girls on the team, right?"

Alex shrugged and turned away. "I don't care about making friends. I just want to beat them all."

CHAPTER TEN

Video Diary of Alex Turner

August 24

Alex sat on her bed, cross-legged and hunched forward. She wore a maroon hoodie and gray running shorts. She looked pale, and her eyes were wide.

Oh, my God. I can't believe what just happened. I mean . . . did it happen? No, I know it did, I took a freaking video of it, but . . . oh, my *God.*

Alex shook her head from side to side. She ran a hand through her hair, which was loose around her face and damp from the shower.

Okay, so I should probably start from the beginning, right? Hold on.

Alex set down her phone, causing the video to veer wildly to a camera shot of her bedroom ceiling. When she picked the phone back up, she was lying on her bed, holding the phone up in front of her.

After practice today, Coach called a team meeting. Our first match is Tuesday, and he said he was going to put out the lineup. I was sort of nervous about it because I don't think he's paid much attention to me during practice. But I've won almost all my practice sets, both singles and doubles, so I thought I had a decent shot of making the lineup.

We were all crammed into his small office, which is next to the team locker rooms in a cinder block building near the tennis courts. Coach was standing at his whiteboard, holding a marker. There weren't enough seats, so I was leaning against the doorframe.

Coach said, "Here's the lineup for the first match," and then turned to write down the names in block letters.

I wasn't on the lineup. For singles, he put Daphne in court one and Callie in court two. And for doubles, it was Bella and Mackenzie in one, Shae and Leah in two, and Chan and Dena in three. Everyone started talking at once. Some people were happy, some were pissed off. I wasn't the only one who didn't make the lineup. There are fourteen girls on the team, and only eight can play each match, so six of us weren't playing. But still. Being left off the lineup for the first match of the year is humiliating. Back home in Buffalo, I played first-court singles every single match since I was a sophomore. I'd never been left off a lineup. Ever. And all I could think about was how disappointed my dad would have been in me.

Whatever my mom says, I know Dad just wanted the best for me. He thought I could be a champion. But I'm obviously not. I didn't even make the lineup for my high school team.

Alex's eyes filled with tears. She inhaled deeply and then exhaled, struggling to gain control of her emotions.

Anyway. I was standing there, and I could feel my face getting red, which I hate. But I tried to stay as calm as possible and kept looking right at Coach. He didn't look back at me. As far as I can tell, he barely knows my name, much less what I'm capable of on the court. And then I thought, well, maybe that's the problem. I've been to a full week of practices, and Coach hasn't seen me play once since I made the team. He spends most of his time watching the girls who made it onto the lineup. Like they're the only ones who matter.

Daphne was acting like she'd just won Wimbledon. She was smiling and tossing her hair around. And that idiot Shae, who worships Daphne, kept saying, "I knew you'd get first court. I just knew it."

Alex stuck a finger in her mouth and pantomimed that she was about to vomit.

Coach finally held up his hands and said, "Remember, this is just the first match. I'm sure there will be changes in the lineup as the season progresses. And everyone who wants to challenge for a spot will have the opportunity to do so."

After the meeting, everyone left. I headed back out to the courts with a hopper full of balls. I need to practice my serve, which is by far the worst part of my game. My dad would make me go out to the practice court after a loss. He always told me that I can't afford to have a weakness. I served until my shoulder hurt. It felt sort of good, like I was serving all of the anger right out of my body.

When I was done, I picked up the balls with the hopper and went to put it in the storage closet next to the locker rooms. Everyone on the team had left, but Coach Townsend's door was cracked open, and there was a light on in his office. I was trying to decide if I should go in and talk to him. And then I thought about my dad again. I knew what he would say, because he'd said it to me a thousand times before. *You need to fight for everything you want. No one's ever going to hand you anything.*

I could hear his words so clearly, for a moment, it felt like he was right there with me.

I decided okay, I was going to do it. I was going to go talk to Coach. I'd ask him about how the challenge system worked and see if maybe he'd watch me in practice one day. I hesitated at the door, trying to make up my mind whether to knock.

Then I heard a noise.

It was like a low moan. And then a sharp intake of breath. I thought for a minute that someone was hurt. Because it sounded sudden and urgent. But then I heard another voice. A female voice.

I suddenly realized there was a girl in there with him. And my first thought was Callie, probably because of what Daphne had said at the party about Callie having the hots for him. And at practice that afternoon Coach had been helping Callie correct her forehand swing. He'd been standing really close to her and had had his hand on her waist.

And now there was a girl in Coach's office moaning softly.

Oh, my God. I should have left then. Why didn't I leave then?

Instead, I took one step to my left, so I could see inside. And . . . it wasn't Callie.

Daphne was sitting on Coach's desk, her back to me. And she was completely naked. I could see her tennis tank top and skirt crumpled up on the floor. And Coach Townsend was standing in between her legs. His hands braced on her hips. And he was . . . inside of her. And Daphne was moaning and had her arms wrapped around the coach's neck.

They were having *sex*. I was *watching* them have sex.

Alex closed her eyes and put a hand over her face. She shook her head again and then lowered her hand and looked back at the camera.

At first, I was just trying to make sense of what I was seeing. I mean, obviously I knew what was happening. But they were doing it right there, in his office, where anyone could walk in and see them. Why would they take the risk?

I told myself to move, to get away before they realized I was there. But then two thoughts occurred to me. One, what they were doing was very, very wrong. And two, no one would ever believe me that it happened.

Before I knew what I was doing, I reached for my phone. I opened up the camera app, hit the red button, and started to record them. It was only, like, twenty seconds, but it felt like an eternity. Then I turned and slipped away before they saw me.

I'm not sure why I did it. Why I took a video of them having sex. It wasn't because I had some perverted interest in preserving the moment. I guess I thought there might come a day that I'd want proof that it happened.

Alex stared up at the camera, her eyes wide and unblinking. Then, she abruptly turned off the recording.

CHAPTER ELEVEN

Kate

"You weren't kidding about the glitter," I said.

"You thought we were joking?" Emma laughed. "Genevieve, did you buy out the craft store?"

"Pretty much." Genevieve tossed her blonde hair back over her shoulders. "I ran into one of the cheer moms there and saw her heading toward the glitter aisle. I beelined my cart in that direction and beat her there."

"Competitive glitter buying. Very mature," Ingrid commented.

"Maybe not, but we'll have the best signs," Genevieve said lightly. "That's all that matters."

We were in Emma's brightly painted kitchen, poster boards spread out over her long wood kitchen table along with assorted colored markers, colored printouts of the Shoreham High School logo, and many, many jars of glitter. Emma had lit a candle that smelled like apple cider, and we all had glasses of wine. The occasion felt festive, even though the four of us had only gathered to work on the homecoming signs that would be hung in the hallways of the school. I had no idea why we, the adults, were tasked with this chore instead of the students who would actually be attending the homecoming game and dance. But I didn't really mind. It was a nice change to have company in the evening. Alex disappeared into her room after tennis team practice every day, emerging only to eat dinner in near silence.

I was cutting out the logos—the snarling head of a panther—that we were going to glue onto the signs, while Emma and Ingrid were carefully spelling out PANTHER HOMECOMING in block letters. Genevieve watched us, a glass of white wine in hand.

"Are you going to actually do anything?" Ingrid asked, glancing up from her poster board.

Ingrid was wearing a loose cream linen tunic over matching pants. It was the sort of outfit that would make me look frumpy, but on Ingrid, it was effortlessly chic.

"I'm the glitter girl." Genevieve took a sip of her wine. "I'm waiting for you slackers to finally finish a sign so I can work my magic on it."

"We're working as fast as we can," Emma said. "Do you want the letters to be crooked?"

"No, I want them perfect," Genevieve said. "Everything has to be perfect."

Ingrid rolled her eyes at Emma, who smiled wanly. Ingrid frowned. "Are you okay, Em? You've been awfully quiet tonight."

Emma bobbed her head from side to side. "I'm fine."

"That's what you always say when you're not fine," Ingrid said.

"I'm just feeling a little down today. It's probably hormonal," Emma said.

"Where's Mark?" Genevieve sat down at the table and crossed one tanned leg over the other.

Emma shrugged. "Working late, supposedly. Who knows what he's really doing?"

Ingrid set down her purple marker and looked intently over the table at Emma. "What's going on? And before you accuse me, I'm asking as a friend, not as a therapist."

Emma's face suddenly crumpled, and she covered it with both hands.

"Oh, honey, what's wrong?" Genevieve stood and hurried over to put an arm around Emma's shaking shoulders.

"I'm not sure what's going on. Mark's just been so different lately. Maybe it's nothing, but I keep wondering if maybe it's *something*," Emma said. "For one thing, he keeps staying late at the office."

"Has work been busier than usual for him?" Ingrid asked.

"Maybe. That's what he says." Emma looked up, and I saw that her face was streaked with tears. "But he also made this weird comment the other day about marriage."

"What about it?" Genevieve asked.

"He said something like, maybe people aren't meant to be married forever. That maybe it's an unrealistic expectation."

"Where did that come from?" Ingrid asked.

"I don't know. It's not like we've ever talked about separating or anything like that. But then when I told him I was thinking we should take the girls to Europe next summer, he said it was too far away to plan."

"Well, it is only August." Genevieve squeezed Emma's shoulder and then went to pour her another glass of wine.

"I shouldn't," Emma protested. "I'm on a diet."

"It's medicinal," Genevieve said. Emma took the glass, and Genevieve sat down next to her.

"We always plan our vacations in advance," Emma explained. "I had the trip we took to the dude ranch in Wyoming this summer booked by this time last year."

"Is it possible he's concerned about finances and doesn't want to tell you?" Ingrid asked. "That could be a reason why he isn't comfortable planning a vacation right now."

"I don't think that's it." Emma shook her head. "He got a big bonus not too long ago."

I listened to the other three in silence. I didn't know Mark well enough to know whether a random mercurial comment meant nothing or everything. But seeing how upset Emma was, I wanted to do or say something to help. I wanted to connect with her, with all three of them.

I just wasn't sure how. I sensed that my default position of always being superficially nice while never saying what I really thought wouldn't work with this group.

"Have you considered marriage therapy?" Ingrid asked.

"You've always said marriage therapy is bullshit and never helps anyone." Emma sniffed loudly.

"You need to stop taking everything I say so literally," Ingrid said, which earned her a weak smile from Emma. Ingrid raised her hands, palms facing upward. "It can teach couples more effective ways to communicate."

"Hold on," Genevieve said. "How long has this been going on? Isn't it possible that Mark's just had a rough couple of weeks and you're overthinking it?"

"I don't know. I've been feeling this distance grow between us for a while now. At first, I thought I was imagining it, but now . . . I just don't know." Emma's eyes filled again, and another tear trailed down her cheek.

I reached out across the poster board and cutouts of paper panther heads cluttering the table and put a hand on Emma's arm. "Sometimes you can't fix it on your own. Even if that's what you want more than anything in the world."

It was the only thing I could think to offer.

"She's right, honey," Ingrid said. "It takes two people to make a relationship work. Mark has to be willing to meet you halfway."

"I have never met a man capable of meeting his wife halfway," Genevieve said.

"Come on, Gen. Richard worships the ground you walk on," Emma said.

"Oh, sure he does. Just as long as all of his needs are being met, preferably before he even realizes he has a need. But"—she stretched her arms out in front of her—"it's not like I didn't know that going into it."

"That's the main reason I left David," Ingrid said. "My happiness wasn't exactly at the top of his list of priorities." She paused and looked thoughtful. "It certainly came after fucking one of the doctors at his medical practice."

"Good riddance," Genevieve said with a wave of one hand. "He was never good enough for you."

"No, he wasn't," Ingrid agreed. She leaned forward and took a single almond from a small dish and popped it into her mouth. "But then, who is? I haven't found him."

"So, Kate," Genevieve said. I could feel the attention of all three women shift toward me, and my pulse began to thrum. I knew what was coming. "What's the story with Alex's father?"

My mouth went dry. I knew the question would come eventually. I closed my eyes briefly and drew a deep breath. "My husband died," I said, opening my eyes once the words were out.

It was blunt and had the benefit of both being true and frequently stopping further questioning. People were skittish about death, I'd learned.

"Oh, honey, I'm so sorry." This time Emma rested her hand on my arm.

"We suspected it was something like that, since you never mention him. But how terrible for you, and for Alex," Ingrid said.

"How did he die?" Genevieve asked.

I should have known it would be Genevieve. I'd already learned in the short time I'd known her that she never shied away from asking intrusive questions.

"A car accident," I said quietly. "Last October."

"Oh, my God," Genevieve said. "That's just . . ." Her voice trailed off. It was the first time I'd seen her speechless.

"Horrible," Ingrid said. "It's horrible."

"I've always thought that being widowed must be so lonely," Emma said.

"It is." I wasn't going to tell them the worst part, the real reason behind our move. But I felt like I owed them the partial truth. They'd been honest about their marriages with me. "But it's all a bit more complicated. The week before the accident, Ed and I had decided to file for divorce. We hadn't even told Alex yet. I'd just been adjusting to the idea, and then the accident happened, and everything changed so quickly. Suddenly, I was planning a funeral." And I was free, I added silently. I knew not to say that part out loud. "It was surreal."

"Does Alex know you were going to get divorced?" Emma asked.

"No," I said. "I didn't tell her. It seemed like it would just cause her additional pain at a time when she was already reeling."

Emma rubbed my arm, and Ingrid put her hand over mine. And for the first time in months, years even, I felt like I wasn't alone, just me against the world.

"I think Joe is perfect for you," Genevieve said. We all looked up at her. "You need a fresh start. And I know he's interested in you. He asked me for your number."

"He called and asked me to dinner," I admitted. "I said yes, but I didn't really think it through. I should probably cancel. I don't know if I'm up for it."

"Absolutely not," Genevieve said. "You have to go."

"She might not be ready," Emma said.

"Of course she's not ready. But that's all the more reason to go. And I'll help you look fabulous for your date." Genevieve set down her glass of wine. "Okay, hand me that poster, Ingrid. It's glitter time."

CHAPTER TWELVE

KATE

"This would look perfect on you," Genevieve announced, holding up a black one-shoulder jumpsuit.

It was so completely unlike anything I would ever wear that I laughed.

"No way," I said. "I could never pull off a jumpsuit or a one-shoulder top, much less the two combined."

"I'm serious," Genevieve insisted. "I'm too short waisted to wear it, but I can tell it will look great on you. Try it on."

We were at a very expensive boutique in downtown Shoreham called Lulu's. The shop had long racks along three walls, all filled with luxurious garments. There were white orchids scattered around and three-wick candles that glowed with the scent of lemon verbena. Every price tag I glanced at terrified me. Ed's life insurance policy meant that I was financially comfortable, but still. Blowing money on pricey clothes seemed ill advised. Especially a one-shouldered jumpsuit that I would never wear.

"Just try it." Genevieve practically pushed me toward the dressing room. She handed me a pile of garments she'd selected. A loose maxi dress, a satin tank top, white skinny jeans, a short dress in a tropical print. "And these too. Go on."

She relaxed on a white slipcovered sofa while I modeled each outfit for her. Genevieve rejected the first few outfits quickly. But when I tried on the jumpsuit, she gasped. "That's it! I knew it would be perfect on you."

I had to admit the jumpsuit looked better than I'd imagined. It was slimming and elegant.

"I don't know." I looked at my reflection in a trifold mirror, turning from side to side. Multiple Kates stared back at me. "It's not too over the top?"

"No such thing," Genevieve declared. "Now we need to do something about your hair."

"My hair?" I put a hand up self-consciously. I'd worn the same shoulder-length style for years.

"Trust me," Genevieve said, pulling out her phone. "I'll call my girl and see if she can fit you in this afternoon."

Two hours later, we were sitting in a café in downtown Shoreham with glasses of iced tea in front of us. The jumpsuit, zipped into a plastic garment bag, hung carefully over an empty chair. My hair had been cut into a sharply angled bob and felt lighter around my face.

"What's your plan with Joe for the evening?"

"I'm going to meet him at his restaurant," I said, feeling a fresh flutter of nerves. I was going out on my first first date in twenty-five years.

"Stop freaking out." Genevieve seemed to read my thoughts. "It's all going to be fine. Better than fine. Joe's great. I was so happy when he divorced Kim. She's such a bitch."

"Genevieve." I glanced around. "What if someone hears you?"

"If they know her, they'll agree with me," Genevieve said airily. "She's literally the worst."

"Why, what did she do?" I asked.

"She exists." When Genevieve saw my expression, she laughed. "I invited her and Joe to a party when they first moved here, and he was as lovely as could be. But Kim just stood there and barely made the effort to talk to anyone. Then Emma's husband, Mark, accidentally bumped into her and spilled a glass of red wine right down the front of Kim's dress, which was, unfortunately, white."

"Oh, no!"

"You would have thought from the way she reacted that he'd assaulted her. On purpose. Emma got a cloth and club soda to try and get the stain out, but Kim wouldn't let her help. Then she started yelling at Joe, 'We have to leave *now*! My Tory Burch is *ruined*!' She was so dramatic. It was hilarious. Once she'd left, we laughed until we cried."

And there it was again. Genevieve's casual cruelty. It made me uncomfortable, but—if I was being honest—I was also a little envious. Genevieve never tried to hide her thoughts or feelings. She was unapologetically herself.

"That doesn't sound like the sort of woman I'd imagine Joe with," I remarked.

Genevieve raised one eyebrow. "What sort of woman do you see him with?"

"I don't know." I blushed. "Someone a little less high maintenance."

"That's the perfect way to describe Kim. She's high maintenance on steroids. Needless to say, I never invited her to another party," Genevieve continued. "But that's not even the best part." She leaned forward across the table, her eyes gleaming. "She walks around like she has a stick up her ass. But it's all an act. She had an affair with her son's best friend's father. Jason Sherman. He owns a chain of hardware stores. Very wealthy."

"Oh, no."

"Oh, yes. Someone spotted them out together at a restaurant down in West Palm Beach and sent an anonymous photo to Joe and Jason's wife."

"Is that why Joe and his wife divorced?"

Genevieve nodded. "Both couples divorced, and Kim ended up marrying Jason. So I guess it was a happily ever after. Just not for Jason, who's now stuck with that humorless prig for life."

"Poor Joe." I knew how tough it was to have your marriage fall apart. I could only imagine how much worse it would be to have the photographic evidence texted to you. "What do you mean it was sent anonymously? He couldn't call the number and speak to the person who sent it?"

"I'm not sure. The story I heard was that they never found out who the tipster was. But whoever it was did Joe a favor. Now he gets to go on a date with you wearing that incredible jumpsuit."

I looked down and realized I had been shredding a cocktail napkin. I crumpled up the pieces in my hand. "I don't know what I'm doing. I haven't even told Alex that I have a date."

Genevieve sipped her tea. "Do you think she'd mind?"

"I don't know. She might view it as a betrayal of her father."

Genevieve patted my hand, which was still clutching the remnants of the napkin. "You get to have a life, Kate."

The waitress arrived then. She refilled our glasses. "Are you ready to order?"

"I'll have a garden salad with no cheese and the balsamic dressing on the side." Genevieve handed over her laminated menu.

"I'll have a BLT with a side of coleslaw." I smiled at the waitress. "Thank you."

"Where were we?" Genevieve asked once the server had left. "Oh, right. You having a life."

"I know. It's just that Alex and her dad were close. He was her tennis coach, so they spent a lot of time together."

"Your husband was a tennis pro?"

"No. Ed was an accountant. But he played tennis in college. And when Alex got old enough, he started teaching her how to play, and she loved it. Actually, I take that back. I've never been sure how much she loved tennis or how much she liked having her father's complete attention. I think the two things got tangled up for her."

"That sounds complicated." Genevieve looked sympathetic, and I nodded, grateful that she understood.

"Ed adored Alex. But he could be intense. I think he pushed her too hard."

"Isn't that part of the job of parenting, though? We have to push our kids to fulfill their potential." Genevieve tapped her hand on the table in emphasis. "If we let them do what they wanted, they'd spend all day watching YouTube videos."

I remembered Genevieve's obvious pride in Daphne's tennis and Jonathan's fencing. And I knew that she meant well. But I'd watched Ed push Alex past her limits and then push her some more. We'd argued about it constantly. He thought he could turn her into the next professional tennis star. I wanted her to have a normal childhood. He thought I was too soft on her. I thought his behavior bordered on abusive. The disagreement wasn't the only reason our marriage failed, but it had been a factor. I didn't want to have the same argument with Genevieve and possibly ruin our new friendship.

"You're probably right," I demurred.

"Speaking of tennis coaches." Genevieve leaned forward again, her head tilting toward mine. "What do you think of Coach Townsend? Because I think he's *yum*. I keep encouraging Ingrid to go for him."

"Really? Is she interested in him?"

"No. And she's always telling me I don't have any boundaries." Genevieve rolled her eyes comically. "I just want to live through my single friends. And I want to hear *everything* that happens tonight on your date with Joe."

The words *date* and *Joe* caused my stomach to wriggle with nerves.

"Oh, God. What am I doing? I'm too old for this."

"Nonsense," Genevieve said crisply. "You'll have a great time with Joe. You'll see. I'm almost always right."

CHAPTER THIRTEEN

Video Diary of Alex Turner

September 16

This isn't totally sketch or anything.

Alex turned her phone so the camera was pointing out the front window. She zoomed the picture in on Kate, who was walking down the driveway to where an Uber was waiting for her. Kate climbed into the back of a silver sedan, and a moment later, it drove off.

Why is my mother wearing that ridiculous jumpsuit? I have no idea. First, she picked me up from tennis practice with a new haircut. My mother has had the same exact haircut for as long as I can remember. Longer than I can remember, because it's the same in all my baby pictures. Then we got home, and she disappeared into her room for nearly two hours. Then she emerged all made up, like she was starring on one of those awful reality shows about rich housewives.

Alex switched the camera view so that her face was now centered on the video.

I asked my mom where she was going, and she flat-out lied to me. She said she was going to a meeting for the homecoming committee. But that's obviously bullshit. No one gets that dressed up to make posters. But why would she lie to me? What is she hiding?

Alex's brow puckered in confusion, but then she shook her head and shrugged. She sat on the leather sectional sofa and pulled her knees up in front of her chest. Her expression was serious.

In other news, I haven't told anyone about Coach and Daphne. Although that's not surprising, because it's not like I have anyone to talk to here. I thought about calling Beatrice to get her advice. I even dialed her number, but then I panicked and hung up before her receptionist answered. It's an adult having sex with a teenager. I wasn't sure if she'd be required to report it. If Daphne found out I was the one who tattled about it . . . I don't even want to think about what she'd do to me.

CHAPTER FOURTEEN

KATE

The Surfside Grill was elegant and airy, with exposed brick walls and white tablecloths. Huge windows along one side opened up onto the Intracoastal Waterway. The sun was dipping low in the sky, and the river was navy blue and dotted with whitecaps. A lone boat was passing slowly by, leaving a wide wake rippling in its path.

A pretty young woman with a wide lip-glossed smile and a sleek dark ponytail greeted me from the hostess stand. Before I could give her my name, Joe walked out and smiled warmly at me.

"Kate," he said, taking both of my hands in his. He looked me up and down, and I could feel myself blushing under the weight of his appreciative stare. "You look lovely."

"Thank you," I said. I glanced at the hostess, who was watching us avidly, like we were a particularly interesting zoo exhibit.

"And your hair looks nice," he said. "You changed it, right?"

"Oh." I reached up to touch my hair. The nape of my neck felt naked. "Yes, I had it cut. You look nice too."

Joe was wearing a sports coat over an open-necked shirt. He glanced down at himself. "I decided to forgo my chef uniform for the night."

"I see that," I said, using the overly bright voice that I knew grated on Alex's nerves.

I started to panic. Where had the easy conversation of our first few meetings gone? Would the whole evening feel this stilted and awkward?

"Why don't we sit down," Joe suggested.

I followed him past the long polished-wood bar and into the dining room. It smelled like garlic and fresh bread, and I inhaled deeply and tried to calm my nerves. Joe led me back to one of the tables by the windows that looked out on the water.

"This is beautiful," I said, admiring the view.

"One of the benefits of owning a restaurant is that I get to reserve the best table in the house." Joe grinned at me. "Would you like a cocktail? Because I could go for a cocktail."

"I would love a cocktail."

"I'll be right back." Joe headed to the bar, where he spoke briefly with the bartender. He returned a few minutes later. "I'm so nervous, I forgot to ask you what you'd like. But Rafe makes the best old-fashioned you'll ever have, so I ordered two of those. If you'd like something else instead, I can go back and change it."

"No, that sounds perfect." I smiled. "You're nervous too?"

"Terrified," he said. "This is my first date with a genuine superhero. I'm afraid if it doesn't go well, you'll laser beam me with your eyes."

I laughed. "I don't have that particular superpower, but now I sort of wish I did."

"So you can laser beam bad dates?"

"Obviously. And people who cut me off in traffic. It's a superpower with endless possibilities."

Rafe appeared with our drinks and set them in front of us. Joe waited until he'd left and then lifted his glass. I clinked mine against it and then took a sip. The bourbon was oaky and sweetened by the cherry juice.

"That is delicious," I said.

Joe smiled. "Rafe makes a good cocktail. You never told me how you ended up moving to Shoreham?"

"We took a family vacation here a few years ago and rented a condo over on the island. I got up every morning and walked the beach while the sun rose. I felt lighter just breathing in the salt air and being near the ocean. And I remember thinking at the time that I could be happy here."

I didn't add that it was the last family vacation we'd taken or that it was on that trip that I'd realized my marriage was damaged beyond repair. Alex and I had gone to the beach and shopped in the cute boutiques in downtown Shoreham. Ed and Alex had played tennis. And Ed and I had avoided being alone. He'd even slept in a separate bedroom, claiming his snoring would keep me awake.

"I had an almost identical experience," Joe said. "Only for me, we were driving from Jacksonville back home to Miami and stopped for gas just outside of Shoreham. I could smell the orange blossoms from one of the nearby groves. And that's when I knew I needed to get out of the city. Then the opportunity came up with this restaurant, to buy it with my business partner, Asa. I never looked back."

"You used to live in Miami? I've never been there."

Joe nodded. "There's a great restaurant scene there, and for a while I thought that maybe I'd be the next celebrity chef." He spread his hands and grinned. "I mean, can't you see this face on TV?"

"I definitely can. And you could produce your own line of reasonably priced cookware."

"Now we're talking."

"What changed?"

"My wife—now ex—was pregnant with our son, Sean. He's a freshman at Shoreham High School this year. And with a baby in the mix, the idea of living in a big city suddenly lost its appeal. For me, anyway. I think Kim always resented the move."

I flushed again, although this time because I remembered Genevieve's story of how his marriage had ended. The anonymous text sending him a photo of his cheating spouse.

"I'm sorry." Joe looked contrite. "I shouldn't have brought up my ex-wife. I told you, I'm a little nervous. I was fine until Genevieve called me this afternoon and basically threatened me not to screw this up."

"Wait, what?" I was startled. "Genevieve called you?"

"Yeah. It took me by surprise. It's not like she and I ever chat on the phone. But she called me out of the blue to tell me how great you are and to make sure you had fun tonight." He smiled again, this time looking embarrassed. "I mean, I didn't need her to tell me you're great. I already know that."

I felt a woosh of warmth and returned his grin. "I'm really glad I came tonight. But I suddenly feel like I'm in high school."

"But with really good cocktails," Joe pointed out.

"And in much nicer surroundings. My first boyfriend brought me to Friendly's and then told me he could only afford one sundae, so we had to split it."

"Smooth move." Joe smiled, and the corners of his eyes crinkled. "I was going to try the same thing, but it's harder to pull off when the date is in your own restaurant."

"Especially when your date has laser beam eyes."

"Good point. And just so you know, I wasn't comfortable with Genevieve's phone call either." Joe set down his glass and leaned forward, folding his hands, his elbows resting on the table. The first few buttons on his shirt were undone, and his skin looked tan against the crisp white fabric.

"I'm sure she was just trying to be a good friend, but it seems odd she'd call you."

It wasn't just odd. It was unsettling. I liked Genevieve, and I wanted to give her the benefit of the doubt that she was trying to be kind, wanting me to feel welcome in my new life. But I'd always maintained firm personal boundaries. I wasn't used to a friend intruding like this.

That's because you don't have any friends, a voice in my thoughts mocked me.

"Well . . . ," Joe began but then paused. "How close are you two?"

"I've only known her for a few weeks." Then, worried that I sounded churlish, I quickly added, "But she's been absolutely lovely. Very welcoming."

"Good, I'm glad. I just . . . ," Joe began but then stopped again and shook his head.

"What were you going to say?"

"I don't mean to keep bringing up my ex-wife, but I think I mentioned that she and Genevieve didn't get along." Joe lifted his glass, and the ice rattled softly as he drank. "Kim can be difficult. But she was convinced that Genevieve was out to get her. Our marriage was already in trouble by that point, and I was distracted with the restaurant, so I don't remember all of the details. But to say they didn't get along is actually an understatement. It's a good thing neither of them have laser beam eyes, because one of them would have ended up being vaporized."

I laughed. "That would be bad. And an abuse of superpowers."

"Like I said, Kim has her faults. But Genevieve can be tough. She and I have always had a friendly relationship, but that woman does not shy away from conflict."

"I'll try not to get on her bad side."

"Might be best not to," he agreed. "How are you doing with your cocktail? Can I get you another?"

I glanced down at my drink and was surprised to see that the glass was empty. "I need to pace myself."

"And mess up my plan?" Joe leaned forward and rested his hand on mine.

"What plan is that?" I asked, enjoying the warmth of his touch.

"To get you drunk enough that you'll tell me all about how you gained your superpowers. I want laser beam eyes and the ability to teleport."

I grinned at him. "I'll never tell."

"We'll see about that."

Once my nerves settled down, the rest of the evening was fun. I was pleasantly tipsy, and Joe was good company. Our conversation was easy, and we laughed a lot. It was nice to laugh. I hadn't done it nearly enough in the past few years.

On Joe's recommendation, I ordered the red snapper piccata, which was served with capers and a lemon-butter sauce spooned over it. I swirled linguine around my fork and used it to sop up the sauce.

"That was delicious," I said after I'd eaten every bite.

"Next time I'll cook for you," Joe promised. "I want to make dinner for you at my place."

There would be a second date. Pleasure curled through me at the idea. I wanted to see Joe again. Very much so.

"That sounds great. Will your son mind?" I asked.

"Nah, he's pretty laid back. But he spends half his time at his mom's, and he's always disappearing off to a friend's house." Joe paused. "What about your daughter? I liked her, by the way. When I met her at Emma's party."

"Thank you," I said. "She can be a little shy, especially around new people."

"It's always the shy ones you have to watch out for."

I knew Joe was joking, but I felt a shock of panic at these words. She's fine, I wanted to say. But didn't. Because it wasn't true. Alex wasn't fine. And I did have to watch out for her.

Ever since the day Ed died, Alex had been in danger. I just didn't know what form that danger would take.

"Are you sure you don't want dessert? I don't mean to brag, but our key lime pie is the best in town. Actually, I totally mean to brag."

I was glad he hadn't picked up on my emotional wobble. It gave me the time I needed to compose myself, to ignore the way my pulse had ticked steadily upward, to force myself to smile and meet his warm gaze.

"Thank you, but no." I checked my watch. "I should probably get home. But this was fun. I had a really good time."

Joe reached out and rested his hand on mine again. His touch was both comforting and exciting.

"Are you free for dinner Thursday?"

"Yes," I said. "I am."

CHAPTER FIFTEEN

Video Diary of Alex Turner

September 19

Alex sat in the passenger side of a car, the sun slanting down onto her face.

I only have a few minutes. My mom just picked me up from tennis practice, but she's talking to her new besties.

Alex turned her phone to show Kate standing in a loose circle with Genevieve Hudson, Ingrid Nord, and Emma Thacker. The four women were talking animatedly, gesturing with their hands and laughing.

Alex switched the camera back to face herself and rolled her eyes.

My mom looks like she's going to be a few minutes. I hope so. I have to get this out before I scream.

I walked into AP History today, and there was a paper on my desk. At first, I assumed it was left behind by whoever sat there in the last class. But then I looked at it. It was a printout of an article from the *Buffalo News*. About . . .

Alex took a deep breath, as if to steady herself.

About the accident. About my dad.

I stared down at it, trying to make sense of what I was seeing. It's not like I haven't read the article before. Of course I have. But here's the thing . . . my name isn't anywhere in the article. I'm a minor, so . . . whatever. And my mom's name isn't in it either. It just talks about my dad and . . . well, what happened. So why was it sitting on my desk? Who found it? And how?

Even if you knew my dad's name, it would be hard to find anything out about him. Edward Turner is a really common name. There's a bestselling author named Edward Turner, and a professor of biology at the University of Chicago. Same thing with my mom's name, and with mine. There are, like, multiple Alex Turners who post pictures of themselves in bikinis on Instagram. For someone to find that article, they'd have had to know what they were looking for. They would have had to search for *Edward Turner* and *Buffalo* and *car accident* just to find it.

I knew who was behind it. It was obvious. Daphne started cackling as soon as she saw me staring down at the article, and of course Shae joined right in, laughing just as loudly. I didn't hear Callie, but when I glanced back, I could see her watching me the way a python would look at a rabbit it's about to eat. I crumpled the paper up and threw it in the garbage, which just made them laugh louder. But then the teacher came in and class started, and I thought that would be the end of it.

I should have known better.

I was the first one out of the classroom after the bell rang. I wasn't running away from them, but I knew if I stuck around, they'd just start up again. I didn't want to deal with it. But now I wish I had said something. That I had confronted them. Because when I got to my locker and opened it up, a huge pile of papers fell out of it. Hundreds of pages spilling out everywhere. On me, on the backpack of the girl standing at the locker next to mine, all over the floor. Kids were stepping on them as they walked by, leaving dirty shoe prints on the paper. I grabbed one of the pages to see what it was, but I already knew. It was the same article about the accident. Hundreds and hundreds of pages of the same article. The news story of my dad's death was spread out across the hallway for everyone to see.

Almost angrily, Alex wiped away her tears with the back of her hand, as if their presence offended her.

I am not going to cry. I'm not going to give them the satisfaction of . . . oh, shit, here comes my mother.

Alex lowered the phone. She held it on her lap at an angle, aimed toward the driver's side of the car. The door opened, and Kate got into the car. She was still smiling, and her cheeks were rosy. But her smile faded when she looked over at her daughter.

"Alex, are you okay?" Kate asked. "You look like you're about to cry."

"Just go," Alex said. "Please."

"Honey, did something happen in practice?" Kate rolled down her window and waved goodbye to someone off camera. "Shae's mom is really nice. She invited me to walk that big bridge that spans the river tomorrow. I guess that's a thing they do here."

"Is she the one you told about Dad? About how he died?"

Kate turned to look at Alex. "What?"

"Now will you please get us out of here?"

Kate put the car in reverse and pulled out of her parking spot.

"What happened?" Kate asked once they stopped at the first traffic light out of the school parking lot.

"They found the article," Alex said.

"Who did?"

"Who do you think? The bitch queens. Your new best friends' daughters. There was a copy of the article about the accident on my desk in history class today."

"What? Why would they do that?"

Alex laughed without humor.

"Maybe because they're evil?"

Kate put on her turn signal and glanced over her shoulder.

"What are you doing?"

"Going back to your school. We have to tell someone what happened. Talk to the principal."

"Mom, no! God!"

"We can't let them bully you. This needs to stop. Now."

"Mom, seriously! No! It will just make everything worse."

Kate looked at Alex. Her expression was pinched, her eyes round with worry.

"Can we please just go home?" Alex begged. "Please?"

Kate hesitated but finally nodded. She switched off her turn signal and drove forward.

"How do you think they found the article?" Kate asked quietly. "Ed Turner is a common name."

"You must have said something."

"Alex. I would never have . . . ," Kate started to say and then abruptly stopped.

"But you did. You told them something."

"I just said your father was in an accident. I didn't get into the details."

"Well, someone went looking for that article. And they found it. And now everyone at school knows. What was the point of moving here? What was the point of our having a fresh start, if you were just going to tell them what happened?"

It began to rain. Not a light sprinkle but a sudden, violent storm. Rain pelted loudly against the car, and a crack of thunder sounded. Kate turned on the wipers, which clicked rhythmically back and forth.

"I'm so sorry, Alex," Kate said quietly.

CHAPTER SIXTEEN

Kate

The next morning, Emma and I walked the bridge that stretched over the Intracoastal Waterway. It was early enough that the heat of the day was still a few hours off, and a pleasant wind blew up off the river. Cars whizzed past us, leaving the smell of gasoline lingering in the air.

I hadn't been able to sleep the night before. I was so upset at Alex's story that her classmates had left a copy of the article about her father's accident on her desk that I'd spent the night staring into the darkness. Now, my limbs felt heavy, and my eyes were scratchy from the lack of sleep. The only thing propelling me forward was caffeine and anger. Had one of my new friends told her daughter about Ed's death? And why?

Emma was swinging her arms, her hands fisted. "Just think how many calories we're burning."

"I have to ask you something," I said.

Emma glanced at me. She was wearing a bright-pink racerback tank top over black leggings and mirrored aviator sunglasses. Her long dark hair was piled on top of her head in a messy bun. "What's up?"

"Alex told me yesterday that someone left the news story about her father's death on her desk."

Emma looked confused. "Why would anyone do that?"

Why indeed, I thought.

"I'm not entirely sure," I said. "But I think to upset her."

"That's terrible! God, kids can be so mean. I thought middle school was the worst age for that crap, but I think it's actually worse now that the kids are older. Or maybe it's just that the gossip is uglier."

"Here's the thing." I drew in a deep breath. What I had to say next was going to be deeply uncomfortable, but there was no getting around it. "You, Genevieve, and Ingrid are the only ones who know that Ed died. I haven't told anyone else."

Emma slowed and glanced at me, but I couldn't read her expression behind the mirrored sunglasses. "Could Alex have told someone? Maybe one of the girls on the team?"

I shook my head. "I don't think she's made any friends here yet."

"Well." Emma began picking up her pace. "I didn't tell anyone. Not even Mark, not that I see much of him these days. And Ingrid is always discreet. But Genevieve . . ."

"Yes?"

"I love her like a sister, but Genevieve is the opposite of discreet. I wouldn't be surprised if she told Daphne. I know they bicker a lot, but they're actually really close."

"I don't know Daphne very well." I didn't add that I hadn't liked what I did know of her. "Do you think she's capable of doing something like that?"

Emma didn't even hesitate. "Yes. Daphne is more than capable of doing that." She sighed and shook her head. "You have to understand, I've known Daphne since she was born. Shae grew up with her. Of course I'm extremely fond of her. However—"

Emma abruptly stopped speaking. I wondered whether she was going to continue, but we walked in silence for a few moments until we reached the top of the bridge. There, the wind was stronger, whistling by us. An osprey perched on the railing, looking intently down at the water below. When we got close, he suddenly spread his wings and took off, circling away.

"Please don't repeat this, but when the girls were born, we made a pact," Emma finally said.

"What kind of a pact?"

"That our daughters wouldn't grow up to be victims. That they would grow up to be strong and confident women. But sometimes Genevieve takes it too far."

"No one wants their child to be a victim," I pointed out.

"Of course not. But Genevieve had a rough childhood. She had an awkward adolescence. Braces, glasses, baby fat. Kids picked on her. And she swore that her kids would never experience what she went through."

"We all want to protect our kids," I said pointedly.

"I know, but I think Genevieve took it to the other extreme. I love Daphne, but . . ." Emma sighed. "She does have a mean side. For one thing, she's incredibly competitive. It's what makes her such a good tennis player and why she does so well in school. She always has to be the best. Always. In everything. Which means that no one else can be."

"That sounds ominous."

"It can't be easy having Genevieve as a mother." Emma held up her hands. "Don't get me wrong, I love Genevieve too. But she puts a lot of pressure on Daphne and Jon. It's not enough that they're healthy, normal kids. They have to be gifted—academically, athletically, everything. They have to be exceptional in every way."

"That doesn't excuse Daphne being unkind to Alex."

"No, I'm not saying it does. But if she did—and right now we don't know that she was involved—it wouldn't be the first time she's acted out."

"Something like this?"

"Well, not exactly." Emma shook her head. "Let me give you an example. When the girls were twelve, Daphne planned a sleepover party. She invited a bunch of girls over, but purposely excluded Shae. Shae was devastated. She cried for three straight days before she finally broke down and told me what happened."

As we descended the bridge, the sidewalk slanted steeply. Another pair of walkers, also women, approached us, climbing upward. Emma and I moved to the side so they could pass.

"Thank you!" one of the ladies said.

"No problem." Emma smiled at them. Once they'd passed, she said, "Where was I?"

"Shae was upset about not being invited to Daphne's slumber party."

"Right. Well, at the time, the girls were taking dance classes together. Shae loved them, and she was a good dancer. In fact, she was the best in her class. That doesn't happen very often for Shae. She's rarely the best at anything. But she was at dancing. She was better than Daphne. Better than all the other girls. When it came time for the instructor to cast the spring recital, she picked Shae to be the lead. And Daphne was so angry, she cut Shae dead. She wouldn't speak to Shae, and then she got the other girls to snub her too. I think Daphne planned the sleepover just so she could exclude Shae."

"That's terrible," I said. "What did you do?"

"I told Genevieve what was going on, and she spoke to Daphne. She made her apologize to Shae and invite her to the sleepover. Shae went, and she had a ball. But . . ." Emma stopped and shook her head.

"What?"

"Shae quit dance classes that same week. She absolutely refused to go back."

"She wasn't the lead at the recital?"

"Nope. And even though Shae denied it, and I certainly can't prove it, I always thought that Daphne somehow made her do that. As in, if you give up dancing, I'll be your friend again. I tried to get Shae to go back to the dance school, but she flat-out refused. I even tried to talk her into making other friends so that Daphne wouldn't have quite so much power over her. But Shae wouldn't listen to me."

We walked in silence for a few moments while I absorbed Emma's story. It wasn't the first time I'd heard of girls that age being cruel. I had personally experienced it back when I was in middle school. But there was an extra layer of manipulation to this that somehow made it worse. If twelve-year-old Daphne could force her best friend to give up the dance classes she loved, what was seventeen-year-old Daphne capable of?

"Why would she want to hurt Alex? She barely knows her," I finally said.

Emma shrugged helplessly. I could tell that my pressing was making her uncomfortable, so I tried to explain.

"I don't mean to put you on the spot," I said. "But the last year has been traumatic for Alex. For both of us. I moved her across the country, hoping it would give her a fresh start. For this to happen now, here . . . it's awful. I need to find out who's responsible."

"I get where you're coming from, but, Kate—" Emma stopped abruptly and put her hand on my arm. "Please be careful."

I frowned. "What do you mean?"

"If Daphne was behind this, confronting her about it might make things worse for Alex."

"How can it get worse?"

When Emma looked at me, her eyes were unreadable behind the mirrored sunglasses. "That's just it. Things can always get worse."

CHAPTER SEVENTEEN

VIDEO DIARY OF ALEX TURNER

SEPTEMBER 21

Alex sat on her bed, her arms wrapped around her bare legs. She wore an oversize gray T-shirt with a black Nike Swoosh on the front.

I think I screwed up. Badly. In a way I can't fix.

Alex pressed her hands against her face, momentarily blocking it from the camera.

And I'm recording this on my tablet. I'll get to the reason why in a minute.

But school has pretty much sucked ever since everyone found out about my dad. It's just like it was back in Buffalo after the accident. People giving me weird looks, whispering to their friends when I pass by. I know it sounds paranoid, but that doesn't mean it's not happening. I'm the girl whose dad died all over again.

Alex shook her head.

No one will talk to me, not even at tennis team practice. Actually, especially not at practice, because Daphne's there. She's made it clear that I'm an undesirable, and no one wants to risk making her mad.

It was really hot out today. Coach made us run wind sprints and then do side-to-side ground stroke drills. It was so intense, one girl even threw up.

I was watching Daphne and Coach, like I do every day, to see if they were looking at one another or standing too close. But it's so weird—they barely interact. It's Callie who's always hanging around Coach. Chatting with him, joking with him. At one point, she even stole his whistle and was wearing it around her neck. I wondered if it bothered Daphne that Callie was flirting with him, but it didn't look like she even noticed.

Finally, Coach—who'd gotten his whistle back from Callie—blew three short blasts to let us know practice was over. Most of the team was more than ready to leave. I took a basket of balls to one of the courts to practice my serve. I needed to work on it, but I also wanted to avoid being in the locker room while the rest of the team was in there.

I spent about a half hour serving and then picked up the balls. I figured it was enough time for everyone else to have cleared out, so I went to the locker room to get my stuff. But as soon as I walked in, my heart sank. Daphne, Shae, and Callie were all still there, sitting on the wooden benches next to the lockers. They were waiting for me. I could tell by the way they were looking at one another and from the way they smiled when they saw me.

Callie said, "Hi, Alex. We saw you out there practicing your serve. You seemed very *intense*."

I ignored her and made a beeline to my locker. I just wanted to get out of there and away from them, as quickly as possible. I opened my locker door, and before I could stop myself, I screamed.

There was a naked Ken doll with a loop of yarn around his neck hanging from the hook inside my locker. His eyes had been x-ed out with a black marker, and he was swinging back and forth, his legs split apart. I know it was just a stupid doll, but it scared me. I jumped back and tripped over one of the wooden benches and almost fell over.

Daphne, Callie, and Shae started laughing. Like, scream laughing. It was so loud, it echoed around the locker room.

Callie was like, "Did you see her face?"

And Daphne said, "Oh, my God, that was priceless."

And then Shae joined in, because of course she did, and said, "She looks like she's seen a ghost."

She meant a ghost as in my dad. As though that was somehow hysterically funny.

Alex shook her head in disgust.

And then Callie said, "Maybe Ken reminds her of her dad."

And Daphne said, "Do you think he had plastic hair and no dick?"

That's who the Ken doll was supposed to be. My dad. My dead father. They thought it was funny to make fun of his death. I turned around slowly and stared at them.

And Daphne said, "What's wrong, freak? Do you want to film us again? Maybe you can get a good angle of my ass in my tennis skirt."

She turned and lifted her skirt, exposing her tennis shorties. The other two started screech laughing again, as though it was the funniest thing they'd ever seen.

And I just snapped. I didn't mean to. It just happened. The words came out of my mouth before I could stop them.

"Oh, I already have a video of you."

My heart was racing. And I knew that I shouldn't say it. That I should have swallowed the words back.

But then Daphne sneered at me and said, "I know. I was there, freak. I was the one who caught you."

I said, "No. I filmed you another time. Here, in fact."

And she said, "What? You took a video of me at school? What was I doing? Answering a question about the commerce clause? Whatever it was, I'm sure it was riveting."

I probably should have stopped there. Just turned around and walked away. I only have to make it through one year at this school, and then I'll never have to deal with those horrible girls again. Antagonizing them further wouldn't help.

But I didn't stop there. I couldn't. Not after the dead dad doll hanging in my locker.

"No," I said. "Here in this building. In Coach's office."

Maybe I imagined it, but I thought Daphne's expression changed. Like, she knew something bad was coming.

She was right.

I took out my phone, found the video of Daphne and Coach having sex, and hit the play button. And then I held it up so the three of them could see it.

They all stared at my phone, at the video of Coach and Daphne having sex on his desk. The sounds they made, the grunts and groans, filled the locker room. Shae gasped. Callie put her hand over her mouth. But I kept looking at Daphne, who was staring at my phone like she was mesmerized by the vision of herself.

"You are a fucking pervert," Daphne finally said. But she didn't sound quite so sure of herself as she had before.

"You had sex with Coach?" Shae asked.

"Shut up, Shae!" Daphne hissed at her.

I looked at Callie. She'd gone silent and so pale, it was as though all of the color had drained from her face, her lips, even the tips of her ears. She was staring at the video, which had reached the end and then started over again. Daphne and Coach having sex on an endless loop.

Callie finally asked, "When?"

"It's none of your business," Daphne said. She looked around at all of us, almost defiantly.

"When did it happen?" Callie crossed her arms, and she looked like she was about to cry.

Daphne didn't seem to care that her friend was upset. She actually laughed and said, "Oh, Cee. You didn't seriously think he was interested in you, did you?"

And then suddenly, Callie was furious. Her eyes narrowed, and she clenched her hands into fists. She took a step toward Daphne, and for a moment, I thought she was going to punch her. But instead, Callie said, "You don't know him at all. You just think you do. But to him, you're just a stupid girl he can use and then discard when he gets tired of you."

Which was a weird thing to say, right? But while I was trying to process what Callie meant by that, Daphne suddenly turned toward me and swatted my phone out of my hands. It skidded across the tiles, spinning across the floor until it came to a stop near Shae's sneakered feet. The screen had cracked, but the video of Daphne and Coach was still playing through the fragmented glass.

Daphne took a step forward, and before I could stop her, before I could say a word, she lifted her foot up and stomped it onto my phone, breaking it.

The video stopped playing.

But Daphne wasn't done.

She stomped on my phone again, and again, and again, until pieces of plastic and glass lay strewn across the cold tile floor. Finally, when she was done, Daphne looked up at me. Her eyes were weirdly bright, and her lips were twisted.

Daphne said, "Oops. Looks like you broke your phone."

And then the three of them turned and left, without saying another word.

Alex shook her head and pressed her hands against her face.

I don't know what's going to happen now. But I'm pretty sure Daphne will be out for blood.

CHAPTER EIGHTEEN

Kate

"Kate!"

I was standing in my driveway, unloading groceries from the back of my SUV, and turned at the sound of my name. Lita Gruen, my next-door neighbor, was picking her way across the lawn toward me, wearing a faded oversize T-shirt over black leggings. She tried—and failed—to skirt around the automatic sprinklers watering my grass.

"Hi, Lita," I said. "Your pants are getting soaked."

Lita waved a dismissive hand. "I'll dry. Besides, it's so hot out the water feels good."

"I know what you mean. I think this is the hottest day we've had since we moved here." I glanced at my groceries, which included ice cream that was probably already melting. It was late afternoon, and the sun was intense and the air thick with humidity. I hoped Lita wasn't planning on an extended conversation.

"I've been meaning to talk to you. Ever since I saw you leaving the yoga studio the other day with Genevieve."

"Oh?" I tensed, bracing myself for whatever Lita was about to say.

I already knew Lita hated Genevieve, and I really didn't want to get into another discussion about it with her. It all seemed so silly and juvenile, as though high school never really ended and no one ever really grew up. Sure, there were some things I'd learned about Genevieve that concerned me, but I also didn't trust Lita's motives.

"I guess you didn't heed my warning," Lita said.

I blinked, wondering at her ominous choice of words. *Heed her warning?*

"Look, Lita." I sighed. "Genevieve is a friend. I know the two of you don't get along, but that doesn't make her a bad person."

"No, it doesn't," Lita agreed. "The fact that she's an evil bitch makes her a bad person."

I started pulling grocery bags out of my car and then reached up to slam the tailgate shut. Joe's words came back to me, warning me about Genevieve's history of getting into conflict with people.

"I feel really uncomfortable talking about this further. Like I said, Genevieve is a friend. I don't want to get in the middle of whatever disagreement you have with her."

Lita glowered and crossed her arms in front of her chest. She suddenly looked almost menacing and even a little crazy. Her hair was sticking up, as if she hadn't bothered to brush it, and there was a smear of toothpaste on her T-shirt.

"You don't know the whole story. How could you? You're new here."

"Which is why I really don't want to be mixed up in drama that has nothing to do with me."

Lita let out a barking laugh. "You think I'm the one causing drama?"

"No, I'm not saying that," I said, trying to pacify her. The last thing I needed was to have my next-door neighbor hate me as much as she hated my friends. It would make block parties awkward. "I just don't want to get involved."

"I'm trying to help you," she insisted.

"And I do appreciate that," I said firmly. "I should get my groceries inside before the ice cream melts."

I was starting to turn away, but Lita followed me, walking with me toward my house. I wondered if she was going to try to push her way inside with me. She suddenly grabbed my wrist so tightly, I yelped in pain.

"Ouch!" I pulled my arm back. "That hurts!"

Lita held up both hands, as though surrendering. "I'm sorry. But there's something you really need to know. And if you won't listen to me, maybe you'll listen to Taylor."

I rubbed my wrist. "Who's Taylor?"

"Taylor Taunton. A friend of mine. Someone who used to live here. She's the one you need to talk to. Will you do that?"

I looked at Lita, at her agitated expression, her eyes so wide open, they looked almost bugged out. She took a step closer to me, and I instinctively stepped back.

"Please," she said.

"How would I meet her? You just said she doesn't live here anymore."

"She moved to West Palm Beach last year, so she's only about forty-five minutes away. I know she'd drive up to talk to you about this."

I hesitated. I'd meant what I'd said—I really didn't want to get involved in whatever was going on between Genevieve and Lita. Also, Lita was starting to scare me. I wanted to get away from her, to go inside my house and lock the door behind me. But I had to admit, I was curious about what this Taylor Taunton had to say.

"Fine. I'll meet her."

Lita nodded and looked relieved. "Good. You won't be sorry."

I was putting away the groceries when Alex wandered into the kitchen.

"Hi there. Did you get your new phone set up?" I asked.

Alex nodded. She selected a banana from the fruit bowl.

"Will you put this in the freezer?" I handed her a carton of ice cream. "How did you break your phone again?"

"I told you, I dropped it."

"Your phone was in pieces. That doesn't happen just by dropping it," I pointed out.

Alex looked at me with an expression I couldn't read. "What if I told you that Daphne Hudson stomped on it? Would you believe me?"

I felt a lurch in my stomach. "Is that what happened?"

"Answer my question first."

"Of course I'd believe you."

"And then what would you do?"

"We'd go to the Hudsons' and talk to Genevieve and Daphne about it. That phone cost six hundred dollars. If Daphne broke it, she should be responsible for paying for the replacement. And if she's bullying you, that needs to end immediately."

It was a perfectly reasonable response to Alex's hypothetical—or perhaps not-so-hypothetical—question. And yet, even as I spoke, I felt the same queasy feeling in my stomach. I did not relish the idea of confronting Genevieve about her daughter's behavior. I had a feeling it might just create even more conflict. Perhaps it was Emma's warning the morning we walked the bridge. *Things can always get worse.* Alex shook her head. "Forget it. I dropped my phone. It was just an accident."

I hesitated. "Alex, I'm always here if you want to talk. Or tell me something. I'm always on your side."

Alex turned away, peeling her banana and taking a bite. I thought it was her way of ending the conversation, but then she surprised me by replying. "Actually, I do have something to tell you. I've challenged Daphne for her singles spot on the tennis team lineup."

"Oh," I said, confused. "Is that how they do things here?"

"Apparently. Unless you're able to get Coach's attention another way."

This seemed like a cryptic remark. "What do you mean?"

"Never mind. But I thought I'd warn you."

"Warn me about what?"

Alex finished her banana and tossed the peel in the garbage. She looked at me with something almost approaching pity.

"Your new friends aren't going to like it," she said. "You should be ready for the fallout."

"I'm sure no one's going to get upset about teenagers playing for a spot on a high school tennis team."

Alex snorted. "Yeah, right. I'm sure Genevieve Hudson is going to be thrilled when I knock her daughter out of her first-place spot."

I wondered whether Alex was right. Genevieve was overly invested in her children's athletic prowess. But there was something more going on here. Alex hadn't randomly picked Daphne to challenge.

"Is something going on between you and Daphne?" I rested my hands on the kitchen counter, suddenly feeling like I needed the support. "Something I should know about?"

"Nothing I can't handle on my own." Alex moved away, ready to decamp to the isolation of her room, where she spent every minute she wasn't at school or playing tennis.

I was planning to go to Joe's house for dinner that night. He was cooking for me, but I wondered whether I should cancel.

"I'm supposed to go out for dinner tonight," I said. "But I don't have to go. We could have a movie-and-popcorn night. We haven't done that in a while."

Alex stopped and looked back at me. "Where are you going?"

"I was going to have dinner at a friend's house."

"Which friend is that?" Alex folded her arms over her chest.

"Joe Miller. You met him at the Thackers' house. The night we went there for barbecue."

"It's a date." Alex's voice was flat.

"No. Well. Sort of." I sighed. "Honey. I know that there's been a lot of change over the last year. And I know you've struggled with it. I don't want to upset you."

"No," Alex said. "Go to your dinner. I have a ton of homework to do, so I can't watch a movie anyway."

I hesitated. "Are you sure?"

"Yeah, Mom. I'm not five years old. I won't burn the house down while you're gone." Alex turned and left, her feet thumping up the stairs.

I stood rooted in the kitchen, still torn about whether to go or stay. I wasn't worried that Alex would burn down the house. But I was very concerned that my daughter wasn't telling me the full story about how her phone had ended up in pieces. And I was certain that she had lied when she said Daphne Hudson hadn't been involved.

CHAPTER NINETEEN

KATE

I sat perched on a stool in Joe's kitchen, a glass of cold white wine in hand, watching him cook dinner. He stood at the stove, his shirtsleeves rolled up, his attention on the frying pan, where he was sautéing garlic, shallots, and herbs in a froth of hot butter.

"I'll just get the sauce done, and then we can sit outside and talk for a bit before dinner. Sound good?" Joe looked up and smiled at me.

"Sounds great."

Joe's condo was small, but it was bright and open and looked out on a well-manicured golf course. His style veered toward male bachelor—black rectangular leather couches, glass-topped tables with steel bases, an enormous television on the wall. But there was an interesting series of framed urban landscapes hanging on the wall behind the kitchen table. I hopped off my stool to take a closer look.

"I took those in Miami," Joe said.

"You took them? They're very good."

"The one on the top is the restaurant where I got my first head-chef position." Joe pointed with his spatula, and I looked closer at the art deco building flanked by palm trees.

"Do you miss Miami?"

"God, no." Joe shook his head. "The crime, the traffic. I occasionally miss the restaurant scene, but it's only two hours away. We should go down sometime."

I felt a now-familiar swoosh in my stomach every time Joe suggested another date. And this one would be out of town.

"That sounds like fun."

Joe tapped his spatula against the pan and turned the heat down. "I'll let the sauce simmer. Do you want to sit on the patio?"

—

We sat on Joe's screened-in porch, looking out at the fairway. The sky was low and gray, and thunder rumbled off in the distance.

"Is it safe to be out here?" I asked nervously.

"We've got some time before the storm reaches us." Joe reached over and took my hand, threading my fingers in his. "This is nice. Having you here. Getting to cook for you."

"Dinner smells delicious."

"I hope it will be." Joe squeezed my hand. "How's your week going?"

"Actually, a little strange," I admitted. "And it all has to do with Genevieve, at least tangentially." I told him about how Daphne and her friends had filled Alex's locker with copies of the article about Ed's death and that I suspected Daphne was involved in whatever happened to Alex's phone. And then I detailed my run-in with Lita.

"I don't know Lita," Joe said. "Or at least, I don't think I do. I don't recognize the name."

"She seems a little off," I admitted. I didn't want to engage in the unkind characterizations Genevieve and the others had used to describe my neighbor. "I'd like to say she's well intentioned, but I'm not even sure about that. I feel like she's trying to drag me into whatever conflict she has with Genevieve."

"You're not obligated to talk to her friend," Joe pointed out.

I nodded. "I know. But I think I should. I need to figure out what's going on. With Alex, with Daphne, even with Genevieve."

"Speaking of Genevieve. Do you remember what I told you the other night about the conflict she had with my ex-wife?"

I nodded. "Of course."

"Well, I didn't tell you the whole story. It's a little awkward."

"I don't want you to tell me anything you don't want to," I said quickly.

"No, it's fine. And with the way the gossip mill works around here, you'll probably hear about it eventually. Maybe you already have heard part of it. About the anonymous text I received that confirmed my ex was cheating on me?"

I blushed. "Genevieve did mention something about that."

"The part she probably didn't tell you, and that I don't know if it's true or not, is that Kim has always thought that Genevieve was the one who sent the text."

I sat there, stunned, absorbing this. "But you have Genevieve's number, don't you? You said she called you."

Joe nodded. "I do, back from when we were neighbors. And the photos came from a different number. But that wouldn't be hard to pull off. She could have used a burner phone or texted it from an online account. You can register for one of those anonymously."

Would Genevieve do that? I wondered. Would she break up someone else's marriage out of revenge? And revenge for what? Joe's ex-wife not being fun at a party? It seemed implausible. And yet . . . somehow not impossible.

"What do you think?" I asked. "Do you think Genevieve sent it to you?"

"I'm not sure how to answer that," Joe said carefully. "I don't have any proof that it was Genevieve. But I don't think it would surprise me to learn that she did."

I shook my head and took a sip of my wine. Was Genevieve capable of doing something so manipulative, so underhanded?

"If she did, that's terrible. She interfered in your marriage."

"No one made Kim cheat on me. That was her decision. I didn't love finding out via an anonymous text, but it's better than not finding out. I don't regret getting divorced."

"Do you regret getting married?" I blurted the words out before I had the chance to think them through. "I'm sorry, ignore that. It's none of my business."

"It's okay, Kate. That's kind of the point of dating, right? To get to know one another. And the answer is no, I don't regret it. If I hadn't married Kim, we wouldn't have had Sean, and I can never wish him away. But looking back, Kim and I were never particularly well suited for one another."

"How so?"

Joe spread his hands out in front of him. "The life of a chef isn't always the easiest. I work long hours, including most nights. I thought owning my own restaurant would make things easier, but suddenly, I was running a business on top of the crazy hours. And that took a lot of my time and attention away from my family. I think Kim wants what she has now. A husband who's home every night by six and who can go on out-of-town trips on the weekends."

"You don't sound bitter."

"What's the point? Our marriage didn't work out, but I wish her the best."

I nodded and took a sip of my wine. "I hope that's how I would have felt. I hate to think that I would have wasted time being angry about the past."

"Are you angry now?"

I considered this. Ed and I had grown so far apart, we couldn't find a way to bridge the space between us. And by the time he died, I knew I couldn't fix what was wrong between us. I doubted there was anything I could have done. Ed had had serious problems, and he certainly hadn't had any interest in seeking help for himself.

"No," I said. "I'm making my peace with the past."

There was a sudden boom of thunder, and lightning lashed through the sky, so bright I had to blink. I could see a dark wall of rain moving in our direction.

"Maybe we should go inside," Joe suggested.

I smiled. "I'm starving. I haven't eaten all day."

"We should remedy that immediately."

Joe stood and held his hand out to me. I took it, and suddenly we were standing very close to one another. His hand touched my cheek, and I tipped my head back to look up at him. He was definitely an attractive man, I thought. And he had kind eyes. Joe leaned forward and gently pressed his lips lightly against mine.

And for the first time in a long time, I didn't worry about anything at all.

CHAPTER TWENTY

Video Diary of Alex Turner

September 26

Alex sat outside, leaning back against a tree. Her face was red and beaded with sweat, and her hair was pulled back in a low ponytail.

Something seriously weird just happened.

Alex glanced around to make sure no one was close enough to overhear her.

We just had practice, and afterward, I asked Coach if I could speak to him alone. I mean, that was hard enough. I can barely look at him after seeing him and Daphne . . . well, whatever. He didn't seem like he wanted to talk to me either. He said he was busy going over the stats for the next team we're playing. But I told him I only needed a few minutes, so he finally agreed and told me to stop by his office. Which I just did.

I took a deep breath, braced myself, and told him, "I want to challenge Daphne for her spot on the tennis team."

And Coach said, "I already put the lineup out for the next match."

I said, "I know. But I want to challenge to be on the lineup for the match after that."

And the whole time I was talking to him, Coach wouldn't make eye contact with me. Instead, he was staring at the screen of his computer and just sort of occasionally glancing at me from the corner of his eye.

And the whole time we were speaking, his leg was jiggling up and down, like he was nervous. I wonder . . .

Alex gasped, and her eyes widened.

Oh, my *God.* I wonder if Daphne told him I saw them together. That I have a video of them. Because Coach said he'd just put me in the next lineup and that I didn't have to do the challenge. And then he told me he needed to get back to work, so I didn't have a chance to ask any questions. I just left and came out here.

I mean . . . that's weird, right? He didn't even say that he'd watch me in practice or see how I was doing against the other girls. Just that I'll play the next match. After weeks of ignoring me, he's going to put me on the lineup just because I asked.

I bet Daphne did tell him that I saw them together. I wonder if she also told him she got rid of the video I took of the two of them. Which actually she didn't.

Alex smiled.

She might have smashed my phone, but I back up all my photos and videos to the cloud. So I still have it. Not that I'd use it to blackmail Coach into giving me a spot. But maybe he thought I would? Well, I guess if it got me what I want, then that's good, but . . . it's all seriously weird.

Alex suddenly looked up. Her eyes narrowed, and her lips thinned.

Oh, shit. Callie's headed this way. What the hell does she want?

Alex tapped the screen of her phone, which reversed the camera angle. Callie Nord approached. She was dressed in a tank top and running shorts and had her tennis bag slung over one shoulder.

"Can I talk to you for a minute?" Callie asked.

"What do you want?" Alex asked.

"Look, I'm sorry about the whole Ken-doll thing," Callie said. "It was Daphne's idea."

"Which you seemed to find hilarious," Alex replied.

Callie tilted her head to one side and looked at Alex for a long beat.

"Have you ever had a friend like that?" Callie finally asked. "Who makes you do things you don't want to do?"

"No. I've had friends who were troublemakers. But no one ever made me bully anyone. Or talked me into hanging a doll in someone's locker to make fun of their dead father."

Callie sat down on the grass, crossing her legs in front of her. Her face was slightly off frame. She tucked a strand of her fine strawberry-blonde hair behind one ear.

"You're right. That was fucked up," Callie said.

"It was seriously fucked up," Alex said.

Callie sighed and looked down, running her hands lightly over the top of the grass.

"When we were in second grade, we were all over at Shae's house one day, swimming in the pool. Her mom told us she'd get us Popsicles but that we had to get out of the water first and that we couldn't go back in until she'd returned. As soon as Shae's mom was inside, Daphne dared me to jump into the pool. I said no, because obvs, I didn't want to get in trouble. Get this . . . Daphne pushed me in." Callie shook her head. "And when Shae's mom came out and saw me back in the pool, she freaked out. It wasn't like I was in danger, not really, I knew how to swim at that point. But it was one of our childhood rules. One we weren't allowed to break. And I instantly knew I was in big trouble. Like, as big trouble as you can get into at that age. Shae's mom called my mom, and my mom had to leave work to come pick me up early, and there was all this drama.

"And I could have told my mom what Daphne did. That I didn't jump in, that she pushed me. I don't know if Shae would have backed me up. She isn't exactly known for having a backbone where Daphne is concerned. Although"—Callie shrugged—"you probably don't think I'm one to talk. But for whatever reason, I didn't tell. Daphne looked at me, and I knew. If I had told, there would have been repercussions.

Worse than whatever I was going to face from my mom. I never told on her."

"Why are you telling me this?" Alex asked.

"Just to give you some perspective. What it's like to have a friend like Daphne."

Callie said the word as though it tasted sour in her mouth.

"You're the one who chose not to say anything," Alex said.

"I was just a kid. We were in the second grade."

"And now you're a senior in high school. And you're still going along with whatever Daphne wants?"

Callie's head bowed, and her long hair fell forward, sweeping against her freckled cheeks.

"I know, you're right. I'm not exactly proud of it. Of what we did to you."

"You could have fooled me," Alex said. "You were cackling like it was the funniest thing you've ever seen."

Callie shrugged one shoulder. "That's the thing you don't get. The Daphne Thing. She makes you do things you don't want to do. And you can't say no. It's, like, her superpower."

"Whatever," Alex said. "We don't have to relive it."

"No, I want you to understand," Callie said.

"Why? So you'll feel better about yourself?"

"No. Well . . . okay, yes. That's part of it. I've felt like shit ever since that happened," Callie said.

"Okay. What's the other part?"

"I want you to give me a copy of the video. The one of Daphne and Coach."

"Why do you want that?"

Callie shook her head. "It doesn't matter. I just do."

"I don't have it anymore. You saw what Daphne did to my phone."

Callie looked at Alex. "Bullshit. You saved a copy."

"Why do you think that?"

"Because if it were me, I would have saved it."

"If I did still have it, why would I give it to you?" Alex asked. "We're not friends. In fact, you've treated me like shit ever since I got here."

"I said I was sorry about that. And I am. It won't happen again."

"Why should I believe that?"

"Because Daphne and I aren't friends anymore. And I'm probably not friends with Shae anymore, too, because she's, like, Daphne's minion. But I need that video."

"I'll think about it," Alex said. "My mom's here. I have to go."

Alex fumbled with her phone and then abruptly stopped the recording.

CHAPTER TWENTY-ONE

Kate

When I arrived at the Roasted Bean, the same coffee shop where I'd met Joe, Lita Gruen was already there. She was sitting at a café table with a striking Black woman in her early forties. Taylor Taunton, I presumed. She had a slim, lanky build and wore an orange wrap dress and gold sandals, and her hair was twisted up and secured with a tortoiseshell clip.

Lita waved at me, and I waved back and headed over toward their table. Lita had an iced coffee in front of her, and her companion was drinking an espresso.

"Hi," I said when I reached their table.

"Kate!" Lita stood and gave me an awkward hug. I fought the impulse to push her away. There was still a faint bruise on my wrist from where she had grabbed it. "This is Taylor. Taylor, meet Kate."

"Hello, Kate," Taylor said.

"It's nice to meet you. Let me just order a coffee, and I'll join you."

I stood in line at the counter behind a few other customers before putting in my order for a latte. The baristas were more interested in chatting loudly with one another over the sound of the hissing espresso machine than in taking orders, so the line moved slowly. I watched Lita and Taylor surreptitiously while I waited. The two women were talking intently, their heads bent toward one another. Lita occasionally glanced up in my direction.

Once I had my coffee, I made my way through the crowded shop, back to the table. I took a seat in the open chair.

"I heard you just moved to Shoreham," Taylor said.

I nodded. "My daughter and I moved here from Buffalo just before the school year began."

"How are you liking it so far?"

"It seems like a lovely place to live," I said.

"Yes, I always thought so too. Although sometimes it almost seemed a little too perfect." Taylor lifted the white espresso cup and took a small sip. "All those beautiful people in their beautiful homes, living their beautiful lives." She set down her cup and smiled. "I always wondered if I was up to that level of perfection."

I smiled faintly. "I've wondered the same thing."

"No one's perfect," Lita interjected. "Everyone has their problems. Look at Genevieve. On the outside, she seems perfect, when really, she's rotten to the core."

We were going to get right to the subject. That was fine with me. I looked at Taylor. "Lita mentioned that you have a bad history with Genevieve."

"And Emma and Ingrid too," Lita cut in.

"But here's the thing," I said, still addressing Taylor. "All three of them have been kind to me. I feel uncomfortable talking about them like this."

Taylor nodded. "I completely understand. A few years ago, I would have said the exact same thing. And I'm not here to convince you of anything. Lita asked me to share my story with you, so I will, if you want to hear it. Believe me, I'd rather be doing just about anything other than dredging up that history. It's not exactly a pleasant memory for me."

Taylor's reluctance disarmed me.

"Do you have children?" I asked her.

Taylor smiled, her face softening. "Yes, two. A son and daughter."

"That's how I met Taylor," Lita said. "Her son, Isaac, is friends with Aiden."

"And my daughter, Jasmine, is a senior in high school," Taylor added.

"My daughter is the same age," I said.

"It's a tough one." Taylor laughed. "There are days when my daughter seems like a perfectly normal person and then other days when she freaks out about the way I chew my toast."

"Life with a teenager," I said wryly.

"Anyway, Jazzy became friends with Daphne, Shae, and Callie. That's how I got to know their moms."

"Is she a tennis player?"

"No." Taylor took another sip of her espresso. She was wearing a set of thin gold bangles that clinked together when she moved her arm. "Jazzy's a gymnast. She met the girls in French club their freshman year. The club met once a week and held fundraisers to take a trip to Paris during the summer before their junior year. Jazzy was so excited about going. And by her new friendship with Daphne and the other two girls. Although I had concerns from the beginning."

"Concerns about her being friends with them?" I asked.

"About why they befriended Jazzy. I don't mean to sound like I'm bragging, but Jazzy is very pretty."

"She's *gorgeous*," Lita said. "She could model."

"You think that's why Daphne and the others wanted to be her friend? Because she's pretty?" I asked.

Taylor shrugged. "I think that was part of why they first noticed her. They were queen bees at that school, even as freshmen. They were the prettiest, the most popular, the most everything." She frowned, two lines appearing between her brows. "But there was something about them that made me uneasy. Something sharp and unkind."

I nodded. I knew exactly what she was referring to. I almost told Taylor about my suspicions that Daphne had destroyed Alex's phone but stopped myself. I didn't trust Lita not to spread the story around to anyone who would listen to her.

"But I didn't say anything to Jazzy. How could I? They hadn't done anything at that point. It was just a feeling I had. Jazzy started spending a lot of time with those girls. And through that friendship, I got to know their mothers."

"I tried to warn you about them," Lita told her. "Just like I've tried to warn Kate." She looked at me, eyebrows raised in two meaningful arcs. I felt a sharp spike of dislike for the woman.

"You did," Taylor agreed. "But at first, they were just so nice. The moms, I mean. They'd invite me out to lunch, and to parties, and in time, I came to consider them friends. Even as I continued to have concerns about Jazzy being close with their daughters."

My unease stirred. "What were your concerns?"

Taylor sighed and took a tiny sip of her espresso before answering. "It's not like they were running wild or staying out all night partying. But they weren't nice girls. They'd make mean comments about the kids who weren't as pretty or popular as they were. But isn't that how a clique basically functions? You're either in or you're out."

"But Jazzy was in," I said.

"And that's when I really started to get concerned. Jazzy has always been a kind girl. She'll see a kid eating lunch alone in the school cafeteria, and she'll go sit with him to keep him company. And then all of a sudden, almost overnight, she changed. She started making mean comments about other kids who were overweight or nerdy. It was deeply concerning. She and I had several talks about it, and she'd seem contrite. But it didn't stop. You know how kids are at that age. They just want to fit in with their friends."

I thought about Alex and her lack of interest in making friends since we'd moved, but I nodded.

"But it was my fault too. I was friends with the moms, and if I'd voiced my concerns about the girls' behavior, it would have caused waves," Taylor continued.

Guilt pricked at me. Hadn't I also worried about causing waves?

"Are you sure Genevieve, Emma, and Ingrid wouldn't have listened to you if you'd gone to them with your concerns?" I asked.

Taylor looked at me, her expression neutral. "I know for a fact that they wouldn't have. Because of what happened later."

I wasn't sure I wanted to hear whatever she was about to tell me. My fingers began twisting the gold heart pendant I always wore on a thin chain. It was a nervous habit. I made myself stop, instead folded my hands together and rested them on the table.

"It all started with a French-club party that Daphne hosted at the end of their freshman year. All of the kids in the club were invited, but Jazzy told me later that Daphne had made it clear that only certain kids, the ones she deemed cool enough, were really invited. The rest were basically told to stay home."

Taylor moved her espresso to the side and leaned forward, her forearms resting on the edge of the table.

"Later, it came out that the kids had been drinking at the party. And even though it didn't happen on school property, it was a school-related activity, so there were consequences. A few of the boys on the lacrosse team had to sit out for a few games, and there was talk of suspending all the students who'd attended the party. The parents managed to convince the principal not to do that. Instead, the kids had detention and spent one Saturday picking up garbage on the high school campus."

"I remember that," Lita interjected. She leaned forward too. "Half the town thought it was all overblown, and the other half thought that the kids got off too lightly because they all came from wealthy homes. And that less advantaged kids would have been given suspensions."

Lita's bangles clinked against one another as she rubbed her hand against her arm as if she were cold.

"I assume one of the kids either confessed to his or her parents or the parents figured it out when the kid came home drunk," Taylor continued. "And then that parent notified the principal. But no one knew which student ratted out the others.

"But Daphne started telling everyone that it was Jazzy who tattled. And you know what?" Taylor let out a sound that was somewhere between a laugh and a huff. "I wish she *had* told me. But I only found out when I got called into the school with the other parents."

"Why did Daphne think it was Jazzy?" I asked.

"Honestly?" Taylor asked. "I don't think she really did. There was a boy Daphne liked who was paying attention to Jazzy at that party. She told me about it later. Aiden Green. He had a crush on Jazzy, and Daphne wasn't happy about it. She always had to be the center of attention," Taylor said. She took another sip of her espresso and then looked up, her expression serious. "And the idea that a boy she liked would prefer someone else? That wasn't tolerable."

"Jazzy became a threat," I said.

Taylor nodded. "We could have weathered that. But it didn't end there."

Lita took a startlingly loud slurp of her coffee. Taylor and I both turned toward her.

"Sorry," Lita said. She looked over at the bakery case, where there were rows of cookies, slices of cake, and scones. "You know, I'm kind of hungry. I could get a couple of pastries for us to share."

Food was the last thing I wanted. My stomach felt acidic. I shook my head.

"No, thank you," Taylor said.

"Are you sure?" Lita looked disappointed. She glanced at the pastry case again.

"Please feel free to get something," I said.

"No, I don't want to miss a word," Lita said. When she looked from Taylor to me, her eyes bright and expression alert, she reminded me of a bird.

I turned back to Taylor. "What happened after that?"

"Several things happened at once. Jazzy was targeted at school. And by that, I don't mean casual unkindness. The kind that Jazzy had been guilty of herself. First, Daphne, Shae, and Callie iced her out. They told her she wasn't welcome to eat lunch with them, and whenever she ran into them, they'd either pretend she wasn't there or just laugh at her if she tried to speak to them. And then it got even worse."

"The bullying escalated?"

Taylor nodded. She pursed her lips together, and I could tell from the flash in her eyes that it still made her furious to remember how her daughter had been treated. "One of them, or maybe all three girls, started a rumor that Jazzy had spent the night of the party giving blow jobs to a number of boys in the closet."

"Oh, my God." I could only imagine how devastating that would be to a fourteen-year-old girl.

"The boys didn't deny it, which of course meant the other kids believed it. Then someone left a dildo on Jazzy's desk, so it was waiting for her when she walked into English class."

I sucked in my breath. Blow job rumors and dildos? That wasn't just bullying. It was psychological warfare.

"That was the day Jazzy finally broke down," Taylor said. "She called me from school, where she'd locked herself in a bathroom stall, because she was half-hysterical. She finally told me what was going on. All of it. I went to the school to pick her up, and while I was there, we spoke to the principal. And then I decided to do what seemed like the normal thing any mother would do in that kind of a situation."

"You talked to their moms," I said.

Taylor nodded. Her large brown eyes were solemn.

"And that's when things got crazy," Lita said. "Go on. Tell her."

Taylor glanced at Lita, who was sitting on the edge of her seat, her face flushed with excitement. I thought I saw a flicker of distaste pass over Taylor's face.

"I sent out a group text and asked Genevieve, Ingrid, and Emma to meet me for lunch. None of them replied. I tried calling each of them. They wouldn't pick up. By this point, I knew something was going on. We always took a hot yoga class together on Tuesday mornings and then had coffee after, so I thought I'd catch them there. But when I walked into the studio, the three of them completely ignored me. They were sitting on their mats, chatting to one another. They wouldn't speak or even look up at me.

"I finally stood right in front of them and said, 'Hey, you guys. What's going on?' And then Genevieve finally did look up at me." Taylor seemed lost in the memory for a moment. She finally shook her head. "And she said, 'I saw you on the website cheaters.com.' I literally had no idea what she was talking about. But Genevieve went on to tell me that it was a website where people whose spouses have cheated can post about them. Outing the cheater. I guess it's a form of revenge?"

I hesitated, not quite sure what to say. It was certainly none of my business whether Taylor had had an extramarital affair.

Taylor sensed my hesitation, and she smiled for the first time. "No, I didn't cheat on my husband. And he certainly didn't post the story about me on cheaters.com. But someone did."

"Did you ever find out who?" I asked.

"It was Genevieve, obviously," Lita interjected.

I stared at her as I tried to absorb this. It reminded me, of course, of Joe's story and the anonymous photo he'd received over text that proved his wife was having an affair. It wasn't exactly the same, but it was similar enough.

"That was my guess, although we weren't ever able to prove it. I even had to hire an attorney to get the story taken down. Although by that point the damage was done," Taylor said.

"Why do you think Genevieve was behind it?" I asked.

"Because that day in hot yoga after she told me about the website, she smiled up at me. This big, wide grin. And she said, 'Maybe you should teach your daughter not to be a tattletale.' And I knew it was her."

I could feel my pulse start to thrum and my stomach churn. Who were these women that I thought of as friends? I already knew their daughters were bullies, but if Taylor was right, the mothers were bullies too. Two generations of mean-girl cliques.

"I know what you're thinking," Taylor said. "It sounds too crazy to be true."

That wasn't what I was thinking. I shook my head. "I didn't say that. And, no, I don't think it sounds crazy."

"Well, I would, if I hadn't lived through it," Taylor said.

"What happened with Jazzy? Did the girls ever leave her alone?" I asked, hoping desperately that they had. I knew they'd already targeted Alex, but I didn't know whether the bullying would continue to escalate.

"No," Taylor said. "Dildos became a theme. I think the girls must have bought them in bulk. They left them in her locker, stuck them in her backpack, even slid them on her lunch tray, all without ever getting caught by a teacher. We complained to the principal again. She was sympathetic but said the girls denied the bullying so it was their word against Jazzy's. We even consulted our attorney about taking legal action against the girls and their parents, although that never went anywhere."

"Their parents?" I repeated. "You mean because of the cheating website?"

"No," Taylor said. "Because Genevieve, Ingrid, and Emma raised their daughters to be bullies. Intentionally. Purposefully."

"What? What do you mean?" I asked. But even as I spoke, I remembered my conversation with Emma on the bridge that day. When she told me that the three women had made a pact to raise their daughters to be strong young women.

"Ingrid wrote her graduate school thesis paper on the subject. She argued it was time to stop viewing bullies as antisocial creatures. That assertive adults are more successful, and so it only made sense to train children to be dominant over their peers."

I stared at Taylor, thinking that she had to have misunderstood. "But no parent would intentionally raise their child to be a bully," I protested. "That's crazy. Strong and independent, maybe. But not a bully. No one would want their child to bully others."

"Are you so sure? Those girls were so vicious to my daughter, we had to sell our house and move out of town to get her away from them." Taylor set down her empty espresso cup. "Fine. You don't have to believe me. But for the sake of your daughter, I hope you do whatever you can to keep her away from those girls. If they keep this up, they're not going to stop until someone gets seriously hurt."

And with that, Taylor stood.

"It was nice meeting you, Kate, but I need to go. I don't want to spend one more minute in this town. It gives me the creeps just being here."

Taylor nodded at me, gave Lita a tight smile, then turned and strode away. And even though it was yet another warm day, I felt chilled.

CHAPTER TWENTY-TWO

Video Diary of Alex Turner

October 4

Alex sat in her bedroom, cross-legged on her bed. She was wearing a tank top and pajama shorts, and the room was dark, other than the glow of the phone lighting her face.

I've been thinking about the law of unintended consequences. My econ teacher was talking about it the other day. It's when a policy is put into place to achieve a specific result, and instead something completely unexpected happens. Like back during Prohibition, when they banned alcohol sales and it led to a rise in organized crime. But it happens on a smaller scale too.

Oh, but wait, before I get to all of that . . . I played my first tennis match for Shoreham High today. And I *won*.

Alex smiled and raised a fist in the air.

I sort of had to, after all of the drama that happened after Coach put me on the lineup. Because guess whose spot I took? *Daphne's*. And Coach didn't tell her ahead of time that she wouldn't be playing singles. Daphne ended up flipping out in front of the whole team.

Alex leaned closer to the camera, wrapping her arms around her body. She looked animated, and her eyes were bright.

Coach had already told me I'd be on the lineup. But then Daphne lost her match against County High School. County took four courts that day, which knocked our team into second place. Coach announced at practice yesterday that he was shaking things up. He put me on first-court singles and kept Callie in second-court singles, because she was the only one who won last week. And then he completely changed up the three doubles courts. He originally had Daphne on number one doubles with Bella.

But when Daphne saw the lineup, she stood up in the middle of the team meeting and said, "Are you fucking kidding me? I'm not playing doubles."

And everyone on the team froze. Like, no one made a noise. It was just Coach staring at Daphne and her glaring back at him. She had her arms crossed in front of her. She looked like she wanted to kill him.

Daphne said, "I either play first-court singles, or I don't play."

Coach just shrugged and crossed Daphne's name off the lineup he'd written on his whiteboard.

And then Daphne said, "Fine. Whatever. I quit."

And then she turned and walked out of the meeting. And she didn't show up to the match today, even though we're all supposed to go and support the team, even if we're not on the lineup. No one knows if she's still on the team, or if she really did quit.

I'm just glad I won. If I hadn't, Coach might have never given me another chance. But I *did* win. And Coach has already told me I'll be playing the next match too. That's the good news. I mean, I'm sure Daphne will try to punish me in some way for taking her spot. Although maybe not. Because I did something. Something that I probably shouldn't have done but did anyway.

Alex stilled, and her expression became somber.

In econ class today, I gave Callie a thumb drive with the video of Coach and Daphne on it. I slipped it into her hand, and she winked at me. Like it was all just a joke, when really . . . there's absolutely nothing funny about it. I don't even know why I gave it to her. I don't trust

Callie at all. Maybe I'm tired of being passive. Or maybe I'm just a bad person and I don't care what happens . . . as long as something happens.

That's what got me thinking about unintended consequences. Because I'm not sure what Callie's going to do with that video. But I have a feeling everything is about to blow up.

Alex held up her hands and spread her fingers out, mimicking fireworks.

Boom.

CHAPTER TWENTY-THREE

KATE

The homecoming meeting at Emma's house was strained from the beginning. Genevieve hadn't shown up. No one knew why. She hadn't called or even texted to let us know she'd be late. And I could tell that something was going on between Ingrid and Emma. They sat across from one another at Emma's long kitchen table but were avoiding eye contact.

Ingrid was on her laptop, placing an order for party decorations.

"I think we should get a Mylar balloon display." She typed as she spoke, her fingers clicking quickly against the keyboard. "The kids can get their photos taken in front of it."

"Sounds good," Emma said, not looking up from the piles of tickets she was organizing.

"Is everything okay with you two?" I finally asked, looking up from the to-do list I'd somehow been put in charge of.

"Fine," Ingrid said tersely.

Emma glanced at her and then smiled apologetically at me. "Our girls are in a fight. We're not sure what's going on exactly, because none of them will tell us."

And when their daughters don't get along, the mothers have to fight too? I wondered. But maybe it wasn't that strange. Conflict was inevitable, and parents tended to stick up for their kids.

"Speaking of which." Ingrid looked up from her laptop. "Genevieve is pissed off at you."

"Me?" I asked, surprised. I had been trying to figure out what to say to Genevieve about Daphne bullying Alex, or whether I even should, after both Alex and Emma had insisted that would only make things worse. But what could I have done to anger her? I hadn't seen or spoken to Genevieve in days. "Why would Genevieve be angry at me?"

"Why do you think?" Ingrid asked. "Alex took Daphne's spot on the tennis lineup."

I smiled, thinking that she must be joking. But Ingrid and Emma stared back at me, neither one smiling.

"It's a school sports team," I said. "All the kids should get a chance to play."

"But it's Daphne's spot," Emma explained. She snapped a rubber band around a stack of tickets and set them to one side. "She earned it."

"That's the first time Alex has been on the lineup all year." I tried to keep my tone calm and measured. "And she won, so doesn't that prove she deserves a chance to play?"

"It's just not how things are done here," Emma said.

"The girls are supposed to challenge for spots on the lineup. Alex just skipped ahead," Ingrid added. "And really, if Coach was going to make changes to the lineup, he should have moved Callie to first court and put Alex on second. It's not fair that Alex got the top spot the first time she played."

"But she won," I said again.

Anger pressed in my chest. Alex had been through a tough past year. When she won her first match for Shoreham High, it was the happiest I'd seen her look since before Ed died. Her face had been bright and her smile genuine as she waited at the net to shake hands with her opponent. As I watched her, the usual clenching in my shoulders and stomach had softened. And these women, my supposed friends, didn't think she deserved that sliver of joy, that one moment of victory?

"I mean, we get it. You're new," Emma continued with a tight smile. "You don't know how things work yet. But you'll figure it out."

"I don't want to figure it out." I could feel my cheeks flushing hot. My anger made me bolder than I would normally be. I stood, setting the list on the table. "I think I'm done."

"I don't know how much we're going to accomplish without Genevieve here anyway," Ingrid said.

"I can't believe she just blew off the meeting. She's the one who scheduled it." Emma checked her phone. "She hasn't responded to my texts, which isn't normal for Gen."

Emma and Ingrid didn't seem to notice that I was upset. Or maybe they just didn't care. I picked up my leather tote bag and stood, suddenly wanting to put as much distance as possible between us. Neither Emma nor Ingrid said a word to me as I headed toward Emma's front door.

"I'm sure she's fine," Ingrid said. "I talked to her yesterday."

"It's just not like Gen to ignore texts," Emma said.

"True."

I opened the front door. Genevieve was standing there on the front porch, about to ring the doorbell. She looked flawless, as always. Her hair was blown out in a sleek blonde bob, and she wore a ribbed white tank dress. A chunky gold bracelet encircled her narrow wrist. She also looked furious. Her eyes were flashing dangerously, and her lips were drawn tightly together. I took a step back.

"You." Genevieve spat the word out at me. "I can't believe you'd show your face here after what your daughter did."

"Excuse me?" I asked, stunned at the strength of her vitriol.

"You know exactly what I'm talking about."

"It's just a game. The whole point is for the kids to learn teamwork and get some exercise and have fun," I said, my anger quickly returning. "I don't know why everyone's so upset that my daughter finally got a chance to play."

"I'm not talking about tennis. Although, yes, it's ridiculous that Coach took Daphne off the lineup. He'll be hearing from me about that."

"Then why are you upset?"

Genevieve raised one eyebrow. "You don't know what your daughter has been up to?"

I could sense Ingrid and Emma behind me, even before Emma spoke. "What's going on, Genevieve? No one's heard from you all day. Where have you been?"

"I've been at the school, reporting this woman's daughter for bullying," Genevieve said, pointing at me.

"What?" It didn't make any sense. Alex had never bullied anyone.

"Your daughter has been sending anonymous texts to Daphne. Calling her a whore and a slut. Accusing her of sleeping around. Disgusting, mean texts."

"If thc texts are anonymous, why do you think Alex is the one who sent them?" I asked.

"Because it's not the first time she's targeted Daphne. Last week, your daughter falsely accused Daphne of breaking her phone."

"Why would she do that?" I asked, remembering Alex's supposedly hypothetical question when I asked her what had happened to her phone. *What if I told you that Daphne Hudson stomped on it? Would you believe me?*

But of course it hadn't been hypothetical. I had known that at the time, but I hadn't made Alex tell me every detail. I hadn't wanted to push her. Maybe I should have.

"I have no idea. Probably because she's emotionally unstable," Genevieve said.

I stared at her, feeling my cheeks growing hot and my nails digging into the soft flesh of my palms. "What exactly are you insinuating?" I asked, my voice cold but steady.

"I'm not insinuating anything. Everyone knows there's something wrong with that girl."

"There is nothing wrong with my daughter," I said, the words thick in my throat.

"Save it, Kate. I read the news article about your husband's death. I know Alex was driving the car that day. That she killed her father. Your daughter is clearly disturbed, and now she's targeting Daphne."

Every word, every single word that fell out of Genevieve's mouth, felt like a razor blade cutting into my skin. I couldn't stand there for one minute longer, listening to her poison.

"I'm leaving." I stepped out the door. Genevieve didn't move, so my arm brushed ever so slightly against hers as I passed by.

"Don't push me!" she said.

I turned to look at her standing there on the doorstep, her body rigid with righteous indignation. And behind her, Ingrid and Emma stood in the doorway, neither of them offering up a single word of defense for me. Instead, the three of them were closing ranks. Just as they'd done to Taylor. Just as they probably always did.

I turned and strode toward my car, willing myself not to cry. I didn't want to give them the satisfaction.

"What's going on with Daphne?" I heard Emma ask Genevieve. "Did you say she's getting anonymous texts?"

"Kate's daughter sent them," Genevieve said loud enough for me to hear. I paused, then opened my car door, but before I could slide inside, close the door, and silence her voice, Genevieve continued, her voice loud and carrying. "There's something seriously wrong with that girl. I think she might be a sociopath. But she's not going to get away with it. I'm going to put a stop to it."

CHAPTER TWENTY-FOUR

KATE

I drove straight to the high school to pick up Alex from tennis team practice. At the traffic light, I noticed that my hands were shaking. I flexed them and then gripped the steering wheel, trying to calm myself.

Genevieve was targeting Alex. My sad, fragile daughter who had already been through so much. And she was going to use Ed's death as her weapon. Rage flooded through me.

How dare she, I thought. And in that moment, another thought came. One that I couldn't stop. An image of Genevieve suffering a terrible pain. Something so awful, her life would tip upside down, never to be righted. And not just Genevieve. Ingrid and Emma too. Their lives were so easy, so blessed. It was why they could afford to be so casual in their cruelness. It never washed back on them.

I wanted all of them to suffer like Alex had suffered.

"Stop it," I said, looking at myself in the rearview mirror. "Just stop it."

Hadn't I learned my lesson? This was why I went through life in such a lonely state. I thought terrible things. And then those terrible things came true.

And just like that, I was flooded yet again with memories of the last time it had happened.

It had been a beautiful, crisp autumn day. I'd closed up the store at six, and after turning the key in the lock, I stopped to tip my face up to enjoy the cool snap in the air. I returned home, surprised to find the house was empty. Ed had taken Alex to the courts to practice, but I thought they'd be finished by then. I started chopping vegetables to make soup and wondered whether Ed and I would finally tell Alex about the divorce over dinner. I had told him that morning that I'd hired an attorney. He'd been angrier than I thought he would be, and I was starting to realize that my original plan—that we would continue to live in the same house together until one of us found somewhere else to live—might not work after all.

I later found out that while the soup simmered, Alex and Ed had finished practicing and left the tennis courts to head home. Alex had been driving and ran the red light at a four-way intersection. A pickup truck hit the passenger side of their car, killing Ed instantly. Alex escaped with a concussion and no memory of what had happened.

But I didn't know all of that until much later, after the soup had overcooked, the vegetables turned to mush, and a police officer showed up at our front door to tell me that my husband was dead and my daughter was in the hospital.

Most of the rest of that day existed in only fragments of memories. The smell of the fast-food french fries in the police cruiser that took me to the hospital. A woman standing alone in the waiting area of the emergency room crying loudly, sobbing into her hands. Alex sitting on the edge of the hospital bed, holding her head in her hands. When she looked up and saw me, she started to sob.

I shook off the memory as I turned in to the high school parking lot. Practice was just ending, and the girls were packing up their belongings. I sat and waited, my hands still gripping the wheel, while I watched Alex walk off the courts, her shoulders straight and her chin held high. She was so beautiful, my girl. No, she didn't have Daphne's lacquered polish or Callie's sophistication or Shae's unsettling sensuality. Alex was an athlete. She was strong and fierce and ready for whatever life was going to throw at her.

Or that's what I'd always thought.

"Hi, Mom," Alex said as she climbed into the car. She sounded more upbeat than usual, her mood sparking with her recent success on the court. I wanted her happy, and yet I had to tell her what had happened. She needed to be prepared for whatever Genevieve was planning.

"Hi, honey," I said.

Alex glanced at me. "What's wrong? You sound weird."

I exhaled. "I spoke to Daphne's mom earlier. She said someone's been sending Daphne anonymous texts. Mean texts. Saying awful things about her."

"I'm shocked," Alex said sarcastically.

My heart skittered. "What do you mean? Have you heard something about it?"

"No, but Daphne's a terrible person. I bet there's a lot of people who'd want to send her mean texts."

"Alex, this is serious. Genevieve saw the principal today to make a formal complaint. They take bullying seriously these days. This could escalate quickly."

"Okay." Alex shrugged and turned to look out the window. "Whatever."

I realized I'd left out the most important fact. "Honey, Genevieve thinks you're the one who's been sending the texts."

"What?" Alex's head snapped back around. "Why would she think that?"

"Daphne told her mother that you falsely accused her of breaking your phone and that you sent the texts. I guess in revenge?" I sighed. "Although I don't really get that part. Either she broke your phone or she didn't."

"That's absolute bullshit!" Alex exclaimed. "I didn't send her texts."

Relief flooded through me. "Good."

"You think I would do that?"

"No, of course not. I told Genevieve that you would never do anything like that. But the problem is, how do we prove it?"

"Why do we have to prove anything?" Alex asked. "You can look at my phone if you want. I've never texted Daphne. I don't even know her number. We're not exactly friends."

"I don't need to look at your phone," I said. "I believe you."

"Good." Alex crossed her arms and turned to stare out the window.

"The problem is, Genevieve isn't going to let this go. I don't know how far she's going to push it, but at the very least, the principal will probably want to talk to you. Hear your side of whatever happened."

Alex didn't reply, so I tried again.

"What really happened to your phone?"

She sighed heavily. "Daphne broke it. She knocked it out of my hands and then stomped on it until it was in pieces."

"Why would she do that?"

"I told you. She's evil. You didn't believe me."

"Evil's a strong word."

"She, Shae, and Callie hung a Ken doll in my locker. It was supposed to be Dad. They'd made *x*'s over his eyes with a black Sharpie marker."

I nearly swerved into a car parked on the side of the street. "Are you serious?"

"Yep."

"When did this happen?"

"Last week. The same day Daphne broke my phone."

"Why didn't you tell me?"

"How would that have helped? You would have talked to Daphne's mom. But that would have just made it worse. Daphne and her friends would never have left me alone." Alex sounded tired, resigned to a world where being bullied was inevitable. "Although I guess that's going to happen now anyway."

"Is this all because you took over Daphne's spot on the tennis team lineup?" I asked.

Alex shrugged again. "It started before then, but it's probably why Daphne's claiming I sent her those texts. She might have sent them to herself."

I hadn't considered that possibility. "Do you think she'd do that?"

"I told you, she's evil. I wouldn't put anything past her."

"But why would she send ugly texts to herself? What would be the point?"

"I don't know. Maybe she thought that if everyone felt sorry for her and that I was made out to be the bad guy, that she'd get her spot back on the lineup. That's what manipulative girls do, right? They manipulate people."

I exhaled. "I had no idea things were this bad."

Alex glanced at me and then looked back out her window again.

"It's only going to get worse," she said. "You do know that, right?"

CHAPTER TWENTY-FIVE

Video Diary of Alex Turner

October 12

I'm totally freaking out.

Alex sat cross-legged on her bed. Her hair was piled on her head, secured by an elastic, and she was wearing a T-shirt with a yellow cartoon Minion on it.

Yesterday, my mom told me that Daphne's been getting mean texts from someone. And Daphne thinks I'm the one who's been sending them to her, or at least that's what she told her mom. Which is bad enough on its own.

But now on top of that, Callie texted the video I took of Coach and Daphne having sex to dozens of people! It was sent from an anonymous number, but I know it was Callie. Obviously, it was her, she's the only other person who had a copy of the video.

And the people Callie sent it to sent it to everyone they know, and then those people forwarded it. It went all over the school. I eventually even got it on a group text for my calculus study group, which I haven't even ever been to. So basically just about everyone at Shoreham High has seen the video and knows that Daphne and Coach Townsend were sleeping together.

I don't know if Daphne came to school and left or if she just stayed home, but she wasn't in econ class. Not that I blame her. I wouldn't have wanted to go to school either with a video like that circulating.

Alex paused and stared blankly at the camera for a few beats.

I thought making Daphne miserable would make me happy. But I'm not. I just feel incredibly guilty. I'm the one who took the video. And I'm the one who gave it to Callie. I didn't know she was going to text it to, like, everyone in the school. But I think I knew it wasn't going to stay a secret.

And that's another thing. I know Callie isn't hanging out with Daphne or Shae anymore, but they've all been friends forever. It's pretty screwed up that Callie would revenge porn Daphne just because they're in a fight. She's basically ruined her life.

So, yeah, I can't stand Daphne, but . . . now I almost feel bad for her. Coach is an adult, and he shouldn't have had sex with her. And her best friend shouldn't have spread the video of it around the school. I really wish I hadn't been a part of any of it.

Alex blinked and slowly shook her head from side to side.

Daphne's going to be out for revenge. I don't know what she's going to do, but it's going to be bad. Like . . . end-of-the-world-level bad.

CHAPTER TWENTY-SIX

KATE

I stood in the empty commercial space and slowly circled around. It was dusty and in need of sprucing up. The walls were an oppressive dark green, and the cheap plywood shelves left behind by the previous tenant were crooked and needed to be pulled down. But the space definitely had possibility. It was large and airy and had a fantastic black-and-white checkerboard-tiled floor. With the shelves removed, a coat of paint—eggshell, or perhaps a pale gray—and more advantageous lighting, it would be transformed. I could picture it filled with high-end consignment furniture, carefully staged so that customers would want to buy not just a couch but also the vintage sideboard and sculptural lamps nearby.

"What do you think?" Joe asked. "As soon as I saw this place, I thought of you and your consignment store."

"I think it might be perfect. With a little work. The green walls have to go."

"I'm handy with a paintbrush." Joe waggled his eyebrows at me, and I laughed.

"I'll keep that in mind," I said. "The main challenge is that it's one open space."

"That's bad?"

"My old store was a warren of rooms. It made it easier to set each one up as a particular living space. But that doesn't mean this couldn't work too." I looked around again, trying to picture it. It would be a challenge to transform the large space into a coherent retail shop. Then again, it would be a relief to have something to think about other than my constant worry over Alex being bullied or Genevieve's misplaced anger.

"You sound like you're seriously considering it," Joe said.

I turned and smiled. "I'm considering it. I don't know how serious I am yet."

"I like it. And the vegetarian restaurant next door gets a big lunch crowd, so you'd have a lot of foot traffic going by."

"It's not this particular space or even the work of setting up the shop that's making me hesitate," I said. "It's Alex."

"She doesn't want you to open a store here?"

"No, no. It's not that. She's just going through a lot. The bullying, and now Genevieve's accusations. Opening up a new store will take a lot of time and energy, and I want to make sure I'm around for her."

Joe put his hands in his pockets and looked around at the space. The sun was shining through the front windows, highlighting the dust motes floating in the air. The light was nice, if a little intense.

"I guess you didn't follow my advice of not getting on Genevieve's bad side," he said.

"I guess I didn't. But I know my daughter. She's not a bully."

"Of course she's not. And the idea of Alex bullying Daphne is ridiculous." Joe shook his head. "No one could bully Daphne Hudson. Quite the opposite, from what Sean tells me. One of his friends asked Daphne out, and she practically ran over him and then backed up over his dead body. That kid probably won't ask out another girl this decade. And I get it, freshman boys should know better than to approach senior girls, but Daphne didn't have to absolutely destroy him."

"That's just it," I exclaimed. "Daphne has been bullying Alex, not the other way around. And it wasn't just normal kid stuff. Daphne and her friends made hundreds of copies of a newspaper article about Alex's father's death and left them all over the school. And they hung a Ken doll in Alex's locker that was supposed to be Ed's dead body."

"No." Joe exhaled. "That's pretty serious. At what point does it qualify as criminal harassment?"

I shrugged helplessly. "I have no idea. But this isn't the first time Daphne has bullied another girl at the high school. Another girl left the district to get away from that clique of girls. She has a history of this behavior."

"Have you reported the bullying to the principal?"

"No. Alex asked me not to, and I want her to feel like she can trust me to talk about what's going on in her life. But I'm not sure that's the right call."

"More anonymous texts," Joe said. "Just like the one I got about my now ex-wife."

"I thought about that too. How common are anonymous texts? I've gotten texts from strangers trying to sell me things, but I've never gotten an anonymous text from someone who knows who I am."

"I looked into it. It's not that hard. There are websites that you can log into anonymously and then message through that platform. If you want to target someone, all you need is their phone number. The recipient can't really do anything about it."

"They can block the texts."

"Yes, but if the sender was really determined, he or she could just create another anonymous account and send a text from a different anonymous number."

"Who would go to that trouble to harass someone?" I asked, bewildered.

Joe shrugged. "I don't know. It seems like the more advanced our technology gets, the more people figure out a way to weaponize it against one another."

"Genevieve said the texts were abusive. They called Daphne a whore and a slut."

"There are some sick people out there," Joe commented.

I nodded, although I remembered Alex's speculation that Daphne had sent the texts to herself. I didn't know which scenario was worse.

"Hey." Joe reached out and gently took my hand in his. "It's going to be okay. Don't worry about Genevieve. She'll get over it and move on."

"I don't think she will. I think she's the sort of person who holds a grudge."

"She'll be too busy with her plot to take over the world. Or to be cast in one of those reality shows where the housewives are at one another's throats. I think she'd be happy with either option."

I laughed. "I could actually totally see her on one of those shows."

Joe leaned over then to kiss me. The touch of his lips against mine caused a swirl of warmth to flood through me. Joe rested one hand on my waist, and the other cupped the back of my neck. I relaxed into him, trying to push aside my worries and stay in the moment.

And then my phone rang.

"I think that's your phone," Joe murmured, his lips millimeters from mine.

"I'm ignoring it."

"It's okay." Joe straightened. "I'm not going anywhere."

I looked at my phone. It was the school. My stomach dropped.

I hit the accept button. "Hello."

"This is Evelyn Montrose calling from Shoreham High School. I'm calling for the parent or guardian of Alex Turner."

My heart began to race as though I'd been spiked with a shot of amphetamines.

"This is Kate Turner. I'm Alex's mom. Is everything all right?"

There was a maddening pause. "Principal Hopkins has scheduled an emergency meeting for the parents of players on the girls' tennis team for four o'clock this afternoon. Attendance is mandatory."

"Why? Has something happened?" I asked.

Joe looked at me, his expression concerned. I shrugged to signal I had no idea what was going on.

"There's a situation Principal Hopkins wants you to know about," Ms. Montrose said delicately. "She'll explain it all at the meeting."

The meeting was held in a classroom that smelled like sneakers, body spray cologne, and hormone-infused sweat. Lines of desks faced the teacher's desk and whiteboard. There were already twenty parents there, all of whom looked worried. I spotted Emma and Ingrid sitting together in the back, but they didn't look up when I entered. They either didn't see me or were studiously ignoring me. Genevieve was not there, which was a relief. I certainly wasn't looking forward to our next confrontation. I took a seat in the front of the classroom.

"Thank you all for coming," Principal Hopkins said as she strode into the room, shutting the door firmly behind her. She was wearing a conservative bottle-green suit paired with stylish booties. "I know it was short notice, but there's a situation that you all need to know about.

"Seth Townsend, the coach for the girls' tennis team, has been arrested for allegedly having an inappropriate sexual relationship with one of the girls on the team. The . . ." She paused, her composure slipping for the first time. ". . . sexual act in question was filmed. Someone, I don't know who, texted the video to a number of our students, and some of them forwarded it to others. I believe that quite a few students at the school have seen it."

I stared at her, her words slowly sinking in. A sexual relationship? Caught on video? With which girl? And then, panic set in. Had he targeted *my* daughter?

Apparently, every other parent was wondering the same thing. There was an outburst of noise as nearly every parent in the room started to talk at once.

"Who filmed it? And what's on the video?"

"Which girl was it?"

"The kids have all seen it?"

The principal raised her hand.

"Please, let me finish," she said, raising her voice to be heard above the din of parental outrage. "I'll tell you as much as I can. But I can't disclose who the victim is. Please be assured her parents have already been notified."

The noise level went down a notch or two at this, although a low-level buzz of whispering remained. From what I could pick up from the snippets of conversation around me, everyone was wondering which girl was involved.

"The girl in question is a minor, and Coach Townsend is both an adult and an employee of the school district. The case seems rather open and shut. However, this remains an open investigation, so the police may be in contact with some of you," Principal Hopkins continued. "We have obviously terminated Coach Townsend's employment."

One of the fathers raised his hand. When the principal nodded at him, he asked, "What about the team? They're in the middle of the season."

"Practice has been canceled for the rest of the week. We're going to look for a replacement who will hopefully be able to step in quickly," Principal Hopkins said. "We'll send out an email as soon as we have a new coach in place. Any other questions?"

Once the meeting was adjourned, I stood, hoping to get away quickly. I didn't know whether Emma and Ingrid would snub me, the way they had snubbed Taylor, but I decided not to give them the opportunity.

But before I could leave, Principal Hopkins said, "Is Mrs. Turner here? Alex's mother?"

I raised my hand. "Yes, I'm here."

"Will you stay a moment?" she asked.

I waited by the bulletin board, which was decorated with a history theme—a laminated poster of the Constitution, pictures of famous United States monuments—while the other parents filed out. Emma and Ingrid were either in deep conversation or pretending to be as they swept by without even glancing in my direction. A number of parents were eagerly waiting to speak to the principal. From what I could hear, all of them wanted to make sure their daughter wasn't involved, while also digging for additional information.

Finally, Principal Hopkins held up a hand. "I know you all have questions, but I've told you all I can for now. I'll be in contact when we've hired a new coach."

Her tone was firm and final enough that the lingering parents gave up and filed out. Principal Hopkins glanced at me.

"Mrs. Taylor?" the principal asked.

"Please, call me Kate." I held out my hand, and she shook it. "What did you want to talk to me about?"

"Why don't we go to my office so we can speak in private."

I followed Principal Hopkins out into an exterior corridor that skirted around a courtyard. We passed by loose knots of teenagers who stood or sat at the outdoor picnic tables, chatting and laughing together.

"Just in here." The principal opened the exterior door to a suite of administrative offices. She breezed in, greeting the staff sitting at the desks.

"I have some paperwork for you," a young man who looked to be in his late twenties said. He held up a sheaf of papers.

"Give me five minutes to talk to this parent, and then I'll give it my full attention," Principal Hopkins told him. She waved me into her office, which was small, with an enormous desk that took up most of the space. There was a narrow bookshelf against one wall, filled with books and framed family photographs.

"Please take a seat." She gestured toward two leather-upholstered chairs and then sat behind her desk, which was covered with orderly stacks of paper.

"I'm afraid that there's been a serious allegation made. About Alex," Ms. Hopkins began.

"Let me guess." My voice sounded too thin and too sharp. "Bullying?"

If the principal was startled, she hid it well. She inclined her head. "You're aware of the situation?"

"I know some of the details. The girl who accused Alex is Daphne Hudson, correct?" The principal didn't deny or confirm this statement, so I plowed on. "Well, actually, it's Daphne who's been bullying Alex. Not the other way around. And I know this isn't the first time Daphne's bullied another student. She has a history of targeting girls in this school."

"Obviously, I can't discuss other students with you."

My hands, sitting on my lap, were clenched. "You can if you're accusing my daughter of being a bully. I spoke to Taylor Taunton. Her daughter used to attend this school. She told me that Daphne and her two friends, Callie Nord and Shae Thacker, bullied her daughter so badly, Taylor had to move her family out of the district to get away from them. And the thing I don't understand is, How is it that this one group of mean girls is allowed to get away with this, not once but multiple times? Has any action been taken against them?"

Ms. Hopkins seemed surprised by my anger. She spread her hands in front of her.

"At the moment, the allegation is that someone sent Daphne Hudson a series of disturbing texts. She believes that your daughter is behind them."

The principal turned to the file cabinet behind her. She opened one drawer, pulled out a manila file, and then retrieved a sheet of paper, which she handed to me. I looked down at it. It contained a printout of a series of texts.

You are such a skanky whore.

Coach only fucked you because you're a slut.

If I were a whore bag like you, I'd kill myself.

The list of texts went on, but I stopped reading them at that point and set down the paper on the edge of the principal's desk. I'd gotten the point. If anything, they were worse than Genevieve had said. I felt shaky just reading them.

"That's terrible," I said quietly.

"Yes, they're quite disturbing."

"I assume you tried calling the number the texts were sent from?"

The principal nodded. "Several times. There's an automated message that says the customer is unavailable."

"I'm very sorry that Daphne received those texts. They're awful. But I can assure you Alex didn't send them. And there's absolutely no proof that she did."

"No, there's not," Principal Hopkins conceded. "But when I asked Daphne if she'd had a conflict with another student, Alex was the only person she named. Apparently, the two have had some conflict about the tennis team."

"It seems like there are quite a few problems with that tennis team."

The principal took off her glasses and pinched the bridge of her nose. It was the first sign I'd seen of the stress she must have been under. I knew there wasn't any point in asking, because she wasn't going to confirm or deny it, but it wasn't that hard to connect the dots. The coach had been fired for having a sexual relationship with a player. The anonymous texts accused Daphne of having sex with the coach. And Genevieve hadn't shown up at the parents' meeting.

Now I just needed to find out how Alex figured into this mess.

"There's also the issue of the video that went around the school. I'm going to ask you to keep this information to yourself, but the girl on it is Daphne."

"After reading those texts, I thought it might be her. I'm so sorry that she's going through this."

"Yes. I can't help but wonder if the video and the texts are somehow related. Whoever sent the texts already knew about the video. And both were texted anonymously. It would seem an odd coincidence."

I stared at her. "I hope you're not suggesting that Alex was the one who sent that video to her classmates. She barely even knows anyone here."

Principal Hopkins held up a hand to stay me. "I'm not accusing Alex of anything. I'm letting you know my concerns."

I shook my head, overwhelmed by how terrible the situation was. Alex had been upset before. Now she was being dragged into a scandal involving abusive texts and an underage sex video. It was hard to imagine it could get any worse.

"I know Alex. She didn't have anything to do with any of this." I stood, bringing the meeting to an end. "I'm very sorry about what's happened to Daphne. If I can be of any help, please let me know."

"I appreciate that, Mrs. Turner. Thank you for your time."

CHAPTER TWENTY-SEVEN

VIDEO DIARY OF ALEX TURNER

OCTOBER 13

Alex frowned down at her tablet. She reversed the camera image so that the deserted school courtyard suddenly appeared on screen. Alex propped up the tablet so that the camera angle was pointed at the empty seat kitty-corner to her.

"Okay, I'm here. What do you want?"

Callie appeared and sat down at the table, in full view of the camera. Her long red-blonde hair was loose around her face.

"Thanks for meeting me," Alex said.

Callie snorted. "Like you gave me much of a choice. Although I don't know how you think you'd prove that I was the one who texted everyone that video. You're the one who filmed it."

"Why did you do it?" Alex asked.

"Because the two of them having sex is wrong." Callie tossed her hair back over her shoulders. "They shouldn't get away with it."

"You know Coach is probably going to go to jail, right? My mom and I watched it on the news last night. They said that if he's convicted, he could get a twenty-year prison sentence."

"He shouldn't have slept with a student."

"You're right. But . . ." Alex hesitated. "From what I saw, Daphne didn't seem unhappy about the situation."

"Oh, I'm sure Daphne planned the whole thing. But it's Coach's fault if he let her ruin his life. He should have exercised some of that self-discipline he's always telling us we need."

"Isn't that victim blaming?" Alex asked. "Or is it slut shaming? Either way, I don't think you should say that."

"But Daphne *is* a slut." Callie laughed. It was a hard, mean sound. "And now she's going to pay for it."

"Nothing's going to happen to Daphne."

"Are you sure about that? This is a small town. From now on, Daphne will be known as the girl who slept with her tennis coach. The video's already been posted online. Even if it gets taken down, someone will just put it up again. It's going to follow her forever. No matter where she goes or what she does, whenever someone googles her, they'll find that video. The internet is forever."

"Why do you hate her so much?" Alex asked. "She was your best friend, like, five minutes ago."

"Daphne isn't capable of being a real friend. The only person she's ever cared about is herself. I think I've known that for a long time."

"Because of Coach?"

Callie shrugged. "Let's just say this whole situation opened my eyes. Daphne's not a good person. And she deserves everything that's coming her way."

"I wonder if they'll cancel the rest of the tennis season. My mom said they're trying to find a replacement coach, but we've already missed one match."

"No idea. I don't really care either way. I'm just focusing on getting my college applications finished so I can get away from this toxic town and all of the toxic people that live in it."

"I don't get you," Alex said. "I can't wait to go to college, too, but everyone here hates me. You don't have that problem. Everyone likes you."

Callie frowned, the corners of her pink lip-glossed mouth curving down. "Do they? I don't think that's true. I think they suck up to me because they're afraid of Daphne. Or they were afraid before this happened. Where are you applying to?"

"NYU, Boston University, Tufts. You?"

"You're lucky you can go out of state. I have to go to a state school, so hopefully UF or FSU. As far away from here as I can get."

"That's definitely the goal," Alex agreed.

"There will be life after Shoreham High. Thank God." Callie stood, shouldering her floral print backpack. "I'm going to head home. I have a ton of homework to get through, and Daphne wants me to meet her later."

"Wait, what? I thought you just said you weren't going to hang out with her anymore."

"Oh, I'm not. But she texted me this morning and asked me to meet her tonight. She probably wants to find out what I know about the video."

"I'm sure she thinks I was the one who sent it to everyone," Alex said.

"Yeah, Daph's going to freak out when she finds out it was me. I can't wait to see the expression on her face." Callie grinned. "Why are you making that face? You should be glad I'm going to tell her the truth. Who knows, she might even leave you alone once she finds out. I know she thinks you're the one who sent her those texts."

"Did you send those to her?"

"No, that wasn't me. I don't know who sent them. A lot of people hate Daphne. It could be literally anyone."

"Is it weird I kind of feel sorry for her?" Alex asked.

"Yep. Because she wouldn't hesitate to make your life miserable, and she wouldn't feel the least bit sorry about it. She'd enjoy it because she's a terrible person. Anyway, I'm going to get it over with tonight."

"Get what over with?"

"The breakup." Callie smiled thinly. "That's what it is, isn't it? We're not going to make up, so we'll break up. And we've been best friends since we were babies."

"You don't have to stop being friends with her," Alex said.

"That's exactly what I have to do."

Callie turned to leave.

"Wait," Alex said.

"What?"

"Where are you meeting her?"

"At Isle Beach tonight at midnight. I'm going to have to sneak out, but hopefully my mom won't notice. She's usually asleep by ten, so I should be okay."

"I think it's a bad idea."

Callie tipped her head to one side. "Why? We go there all the time."

"When you were friends," Alex pointed out. "Not after you sent a video of her having sex with Coach to everyone in the school."

"You worry too much," Callie said. She shook her hair back and used an elastic to secure it in a ponytail. "What do you think she's going to do? Attack me?"

Alex hesitated. "Do you want me to go with you?"

"I don't need a babysitter." Callie laughed. "I'll be fine. Trust me, I know how to handle Daphne."

Callie turned and walked away, her step confident, her ponytail bobbing.

CHAPTER TWENTY-EIGHT

Kate

Ingrid's counseling practice was located on the first floor of a nondescript office building near downtown Shoreham. The tiny waiting room had a few chairs, a magazine rack, and a philodendron on a plant stand. There wasn't a receptionist, so I sat down and waited. I knew Ingrid was at work that day. Her car was parked in the small lot adjacent to the building.

After I'd been sitting there for a few minutes, the door to the outer hallway opened, and a man came in. He was older than me and had a slight limp. He sat down in one of the other empty chairs, crossed his arms, and stared at the framed poster of a mountain range that hung on the opposite wall.

At precisely two o'clock, the door to the inner office opened, and Ingrid stood in the doorway. She was wearing a crisp white button-down shirt tucked into navy-blue linen trousers. She blinked at the sight of me.

"Kate?" She glanced from me to the man sitting silently in the other chair. "This isn't a good time. I have an appointment."

"I just need a few minutes," I said.

Ingrid looked at her patient again and then said, "Okay. Just give me five minutes, Roger."

"Thank you," I said.

I followed Ingrid back to her office. It was a calm space, with pale walls, a dark-gray sofa, and a Danish modern armchair. Abstract paintings in muted colors hung on the walls. There was a desk tucked discreetly away in one corner, where I could imagine Ingrid sitting, writing notes on her patients while she sipped green tea.

Ingrid motioned for me to sit on the couch, which was too low to be comfortable. She perched on the edge of the Danish modern chair. She practically vibrated with impatience, and I realized it was the first time I had ever seen her anything less than composed.

"I really don't have time—" Ingrid began.

I cut her off. "Is it true that you wrote a thesis advocating that parents raise their daughters to become bullies?"

Ingrid stared at me for a long moment. "That's a gross mischaracterization of my work."

"Then explain it to me."

"You've barged in on me, into my office, to demand that I defend my graduate school thesis to you?" Her thin pale eyebrows arched.

"I have a right to know if you trained your daughter and her friends to bully my daughter."

Ingrid regarded me. "My understanding is that your daughter is the one who's been accused of bullying."

"By Daphne. Who has a track record of bullying other kids," I said. "Including Alex. And Jazzy Taunton."

There was a small table next to Ingrid's chair, which held a water carafe, a glass, and a gold pen. Ingrid picked up the pen and rotated it slowly as she considered this.

"I never advocated that parents should raise their children to be bullies," Ingrid finally said. "What I argued for was that we should stop raising our daughters to be people pleasers. To stop making them feel like they have to smile and get along with everyone. Little girls are praised for being kind or good at sharing. Little boys are praised for being assertive. It's no wonder men are more successful in the workplace."

"I don't disagree with you."

"There was a famous study that videotaped children interacting with one another. When it was two girls, or a boy and a girl, the girl would point out similarities. 'You like biking? I like biking, too!' or 'Let's play LEGO together.'

"But when it was two boys, or a boy and a girl, the boy would try to win. 'I'll build a rocket that will go higher than that skyscraper.' 'Oh yeah? I'll build a rocket that will go to the moon!' 'Well, I'll build a rocket that will go to Mars!'

"It doesn't matter what the subject was. The little girls looked for common ground, the little boys wanted to outdo one another. I thought if we could stop telling our daughters to always get along and encourage them to be the ones to build rocket ships to Mars, that would be a good thing."

"There's a big difference between teaching girls to be more assertive and training them to be bullies," I said.

"Yes, there's a distinct difference. That's not what I was advocating for. Although—" Ingrid paused. She looked at me for a long moment, as though deliberating how much to say. "I will admit that Genevieve might have taken the idea a bit too far."

And there it was. It was the one thing I could count on with this toxic trio of women—they might pretend to be the closest of friends, but they were always so quick to turn on one another.

"How so?" I asked.

Ingrid lifted a hand almost wearily, her pale palm facing the ceiling. "I told Gen and Emma about my thesis back when we were pregnant with the girls. We joked that we should train them to become the next generation of alpha females. Or, at least, Emma and I thought it was a joke. But almost from the moment Daphne started crawling, Genevieve would reward her whenever she was aggressive. Even if it was naughty. Especially if it was naughty."

I frowned. "How would you do that with a young child?"

"Think about everything that happens on a playground at that age. For example, the kids are told they must take turns on the swings. If Daphne refused to give up her swing, Gen would praise her. If Daphne gave up her swing to another child, Gen would frown."

"And Daphne would somehow discern that she needed to be unkind to other kids to get her mom's approval?" I remembered the playground days well. Alex would run around wildly, joyfully moving from the climbing structure to the slide to the swings, delighted to play with other children and never paying much attention to me.

"Once, a little boy brought his toy truck to the playground, and Daphne took it away from him. She didn't even like playing with toy trucks. She only took it to upset him. The boy ended up in tears, and Gen took Daphne out for an ice cream. Trust me, Daphne caught on quickly. She's always been a smart girl."

"But that's insane. Why would anyone want their child to be a bully?"

"I didn't say that Genevieve wanted Daphne to be a bully. I said she rewarded her for being assertive."

"And that turned her into a bully."

Ingrid spread her hands. "I suppose it's better to be the bully than the victim. Genevieve was bullied when she was young, and she didn't want that to happen to Daphne."

"Why would you allow Callie to be friends with Daphne?" I asked.

"What do you mean? The girls grew up together. They've been friends since they were all babies."

"At some point you must have known that Genevieve was raising Daphne to be a bully. Why would you want your daughter to be friends with someone like that?"

Ingrid's stare grew icy. "I don't have to explain myself to you."

"Daphne knocked my daughter's iPhone out of her hand and stomped on it until it was in pieces."

"She did?" Ingrid paused and then shook her head. "I don't always approve of Daphne's behavior. And I can't say I've always been thrilled about the influence she's had on Callie. But people aren't all good or all bad. Daphne can be controlling and selfish, but she can also be funny and sweet."

"I'll have to take your word on that," I said.

"When the girls were in middle school, Daphne started a project where the kids created bags full of necessities for homeless people. Bottled water, granola bars, hygiene items. The whole class got into it. They held fundraisers to buy the supplies and assembled the bags after school. Daphne was the one who spearheaded the whole effort."

"And that excuses her bad behavior now?"

"Of course not," Ingrid said. "But you seem to have this idea that Daphne is like the evil witch in a fairy tale. She's a teenage girl. You know what they're like. Sometimes they're great, sometimes they're difficult."

"I have a teenage daughter. And I know that she wouldn't hang a doll in another girl's locker to mock the death of that girl's father. Or paper the school with copies of a newspaper article about her father's death. Or spread around a story about a fellow classmate being promiscuous and then leave sexual toys on her desk to humiliate her in front of her classmates. That's what your daughter and her friends did."

Two spots of red appeared on Ingrid's face. "Callie wasn't involved with any of that."

"You can keep telling yourself that, Ingrid, but that won't make it true. It's gotten out of hand. The texts, that video. This isn't simple schoolyard bullying. It's harassment."

"And Daphne insists that your daughter is behind the bullying."

I shook my head. "My daughter isn't a bully. She wouldn't have done any of that."

"The truth of the matter is, we don't know what our children are really capable of. They all keep secrets from us. Now, I have an appointment." Ingrid set down her pen. "I'd like you to leave."

"Fine," I said. "But I hope you know there will be consequences. I'm not going to let this go."

Ingrid's eyebrows arched. "Are you threatening me?"

"Take it however you'd like," I said.

CHAPTER TWENTY-NINE

Video Diary of Alex Turner

October 13

Alex sat outside on a wicker patio chair. It was dusk, and the sky behind her was streaked with pink and orange. There were children's voices from a neighboring backyard, laughing and play screaming. Alex wore an Adidas tee and black running shorts, and her long hair was pulled back in a ponytail.

I've decided I'm going to major in journalism in college. Making these videos has made me realize that's what I want to do with my future. I want to uncover facts and find out the truth behind every story.

Take tonight, for example. Callie's planning on meeting Daphne at the beach. I think it's a stupid thing for her to do. Why meet in the middle of the night? And why somewhere so remote? I mean, she just sent a revenge porn video of Daphne to the entire school.

I texted Callie and told her I don't think she should go. And she just texted me back a crying laughing emoji and then a pile of shit emoji. She's obviously not taking me seriously.

Alex shook her head.

And I get it. They've all known each other forever. Why would she listen to me? But I really think something could happen tonight. So I need to be there. And I need to get it on video. Whatever happens, I want to record it. Just in case.

There's going to be a full moon tonight, which will reflect off the water and hopefully make it light enough so that I can film them. I found a video on YouTube about how to make videos at night with an iPhone. There's a setting I can put my phone on that will make the picture easier to see.

I just need to make sure Daphne and Callie don't see me. There are dunes back behind the beach, so my plan is to hide there, in the beach grass. That should be enough cover. As long as I make sure the light on my camera isn't on, no one should be able to see me.

Of course my mom would never let me go, especially if I told her where I was going and why. She's already freaked out about the allegations against Coach and the anonymous texts that Daphne got and the sex video. She wants me to stay as far away from Daphne, Callie, and Shae as possible. She even suggested that I drop off the tennis team, if we actually have a team going forward. If I'm going to be there, I'll have to sneak out. I've never done that before, but I think it'll be okay. My mom goes to bed early and sleeps pretty soundly. She won't even know I'm gone.

A voice called out from off camera. "Alex! Dinner is ready!"

Shit, I have to go. Hopefully, I won't get caught sneaking out tonight. Because if my mom finds out what I'm about to do . . . she'll absolutely kill me.

CHAPTER THIRTY

Kate

"Is it too late to call?" Joe's voice was warm and low. "I just got off work."

"Not at all." I was lying in my bed, reading a novel that was barely keeping my attention. Joe's phone call was a welcome distraction. "How was the restaurant?"

"Crazy busy. We were backed up most of the night. But I'm not complaining. I'd rather be busy than sitting around, waiting for customers to show up."

"I know exactly what you mean. I hated slow days at the store. It happened every time a snowstorm was about to blow through."

"Luckily, we don't have many snowstorms around here." I could hear the smile in Joe's voice.

"True enough." It was the first night since we'd moved to Shoreham that was cool enough to open the windows. The breeze blew softly into the house, ruffling the drapes and chasing away the stale air.

"Have you made a decision about that commercial space we looked at?" Joe asked.

"Not yet." I hadn't told Joe that I was worried I'd made a terrible mistake moving to Shoreham. My daughter was miserable; I'd been ostracized by the first friends I'd had in years. There was nothing to keep us here, other than the house, which I could always sell. Did I really want to sign a lease on a commercial space when I wasn't sure that we should stay here? Instead, I said, "I'm still thinking about it."

"Hey, I had an idea I wanted to run by you."

"What's that?"

"I'm taking Sean to the Universal Studios theme park next weekend. Do you and Alex want to come with us?"

"That's your time with Sean. He won't want us tagging along, will he?"

"He won't care. He's pretty laid back, and besides, he'll be too distracted by the roller coasters. There's one that goes straight up in a ninety-degree angle and then plunges straight back down again. You'll love it."

"I should probably tell you about my strict no–roller coasters policy. I'll stay safely on the ground while you all ride it."

"So you'll come." Joe sounded so delighted, I felt warmth curl through me. The idea of getting away from Shoreham, and all of the conflict and strife, sounded really nice, even if there were roller coasters involved.

Would Alex agree to go? I wondered. I didn't want to force her, but I thought we could both use a weekend away.

"I'll check with Alex tomorrow."

"Would you mind asking her now? I'd like to make the hotel reservations when I get home."

"Sure, I can do that." I threw back the duvet and swung my legs out of bed. Still holding the phone to my ear, I padded down the hallway and knocked on Alex's door.

"Alex?" I waited a few beats, but she didn't respond. I guessed that she had on her headphones, so I rapped my knuckles against the door harder. When she still didn't answer, I opened the door slowly. "Honey?"

Alex's room was empty.

"Hold on," I said into the phone. "I can't find her."

"She's not home?" Joe asked, sounding concerned.

"I'm sure she's around somewhere. She's probably just downstairs."

But Alex wasn't in the kitchen. Or the living room. Or on the back patio. Or in the garage, or anywhere else I looked.

"Alex!" I called out. But my voice just echoed through the emptiness. I put the phone back to my ear. "She's not here. She's . . . gone. But where would she go?"

"I'll be right over," Joe said.

"Any word?" Joe asked ten minutes later, when I let him in the front door.

I'd searched the house again, looking everywhere, calling her name. But I already knew she wasn't there. The house felt too empty.

"I've tried calling her, but she won't pick up. I texted her to call me immediately. And that phone is permanently attached to her hand."

I felt tears welling and wondered whether I was overreacting. Alex was seventeen, not seven. But Alex didn't have any friends in Shoreham. At least, none that I knew of. Where would she be at eleven o'clock on a school night? And why wouldn't she have told me she was going out?

"I'm probably overreacting," I said.

Joe shook his head. "I'm sure she's fine. Do you have a way to track her phone?"

"No. I know those apps exist, but I never got around to getting one. And besides, Alex never goes anywhere. She's always either here or at school or at tennis. Occasionally she goes for a run, but that's about it."

"Does she run at night?"

"Never. Should I call the police? But what would I say, my teenager isn't home at curfew? They'll just think I'm a crazy helicopter mom."

"We could go look for her," Joe suggested.

"But we don't know where she is. Are we going to just drive around hoping we spot her on the street?"

"It's better than nothing. Come on. I'll drive."

Joe's SUV was almost freakishly neat. There wasn't any of the clutter I always had rattling around in the back of my car—Alex's tennis bag, library books, the odd travel coffee mug. It even smelled good, like sandalwood and pine.

We drove slowly up and down the streets near my house. I peered out the window, looking for my daughter and not seeing her. This seemed like a pointless exercise. I had no idea where Alex was. What were the chances we'd spot her out on the street?

"Has she ever done anything like this before?" Joe asked as he signaled and turned right onto another dark, quiet street.

"No, never. But Alex went through a traumatic experience last year."

"When your husband died," Joe said. "It was a car accident, right?"

"Yes. And Alex . . . she was with him. She was in the accident too."

"Oh, no." Joe exhaled and shook his head. "That must have been awful for her."

"She doesn't remember what happened. Any of it."

"She was with her father when he died, and she doesn't remember it?"

"It's worse than that." I turned to look at Joe. "Alex was the one driving the car when the accident happened. She ran a red light. I know she blames herself for the accident."

And then I had to say the part I didn't want to admit but that was getting harder to ignore. "Alex hasn't been the same ever since it happened. It's like she's a different girl altogether."

"She doesn't remember running the light?"

"Not just that. She doesn't remember any of it. The last thing she remembers that day is leaving the tennis courts. She and Ed had been practicing, and . . ." I stopped and rested my head against my hands. "I don't know exactly what happened, but I think they argued. Ed texted me about it."

I swallowed. It had been the last communication I'd had from my husband.

Alex told me she wants to quit tennis. Fine with me. I'm done with both of you.

It had been an ugly final message. And even though I had my issues with Ed, I was sad that the last moments he spent with Alex were so unhappy. Although, perhaps, not surprised. Ed hadn't been a happy man.

"Ed was obsessed with Alex becoming the next Serena Williams," I explained. "He read an article about how Serena's father turned her into a superstar and decided he was going to do the same with Alex. It was all he thought about, all he talked about. It wasn't healthy."

We passed by a streetlight, and Joe's face was momentarily lit in profile. He looked tired. It was late, and he'd been working. I felt a wrench of guilt that I was keeping him up, driving around, but I was also grateful for his company. He reached over to gently take my hand.

"That's a lot of pressure to put on a kid," Joe said.

"Yes, it was. I think Ed was clinically depressed. He'd go through periods where he'd withdraw. He'd lock himself in our home office and would spend hours watching old tennis matches online. I tried to get him to go see a doctor, but he refused. And then, eventually, he'd sort of snap out of it, and then it was like he'd become almost manic. Which, in a way, was even worse than the depression. Because that's when his obsession with Alex becoming a tennis star would take over."

"He sounds intense," Joe observed.

I nodded. "He had a daily training regimen for Alex. He'd schedule her practices, her time in the gym, her daily runs. I kept trying to intervene and convince him that he was pushing her too hard. That it was all too much. But part of the problem is that Alex wanted it too. She wanted to be a professional tennis player. Or . . ." I stopped and shook my head. "She used to. When she was younger, she went along with it. But as she started to get older, she started pushing back."

"She didn't want to play tennis anymore?"

"No, she loved playing tennis. She still does. But she started having other interests. And Alex is good, but she's not Serena Williams. And I think Alex knew that. She started to talk about going to college and possibly graduate school after that. And I thought at the time, great, this will finally be the end of it. But instead, Ed just pushed harder. He went too far. He started waking her up to train before school, and he'd interrupt her homework in the evenings to make her watch videos of her matches. He even tried to stop me from buying her a birthday cake, because he wanted to cut sugar out of her diet. It was too much. He was too controlling. And I . . ."

I stopped and inhaled deeply. I remembered Alex accusing me of not crying for her father. She had been wrong. I cried plenty. For the mental illness that had taken over and that he'd refused to get treatment for. For the end of our marriage. For the future our family wouldn't have together. It's just that I had run out of tears by the time Ed died.

"I told him we needed to separate," I said. "And that I was going to request to be the custodial parent, at least until he got his mental health under control." I pressed my hands to my temples. "I know that must sound harsh."

"It doesn't sound harsh at all. You were trying to protect your daughter."

"It was like throwing gasoline on a fire. Ed was furious. And that day, the day of the accident, I told him I'd hired a divorce attorney." I closed my eyes. "I should never have let Alex go with him to the courts that day. And she didn't want to go. But Ed wanted her to work on her serve, and he talked her into it. If I was home, I might have stopped him, but I was at work. And by that point, I was so tired of fighting."

I looked up to see Joe pulling over at a deserted playground. Light pooled on the outdoor basketball court. I could see a fenced yard with swings and a slide just beyond it.

"What are we doing here?" I asked.

"Sometimes kids hang out here. But it looks pretty deserted tonight," Joe said.

Two teenage boys walked by, their shoulders hunched forward, their hands in their pockets. Both wore hoodies, and one had his hood pulled up over his head. I glanced at the clock on the dashboard. It was 11:32. What were these two boys, who looked like they were only fourteen or fifteen years old, doing out walking around in the dark on a school night? And what was Alex doing out this late?

Joe rolled down his car window and called to the boys. "Have either of you seen a girl around? Tall, thin, long dark hair?"

The boys looked spooked. They glanced at one another, and then the taller of the two said, "Nah. We haven't seen no one."

"Thanks." Joe rolled up his window and looked over at me. "Where do you think we should go next?"

"Home," I said. "I should be there in case Alex comes back. Maybe she's already there."

Joe nodded, and we drove back to my house in silence. But when we got there, the house was still empty. There was no sign of Alex. And she still hadn't replied to my calls or texts. I dialed her number again, but it just rang and rang and eventually went to voice mail.

I sat heavily on the living room sofa. Joe went to the kitchen and poured us each a glass of water. He brought one to me and then sat down. "She'll be okay," he said.

I shook my head numbly. "I don't know if that's true. She's changed so much."

"Since the accident?"

I nodded. "Something happened between the two of them out there on the tennis court that day. I'll probably never know what exactly because Alex doesn't remember any of it. But I do know they left the tennis courts earlier than planned, and Alex was driving Ed's car. She'd gotten her license that summer. On the way home, she ran a red light just as a young man in a pickup truck was crossing the intersection. He hit the passenger side of Ed's car. Ed died on impact."

"That's terrible." Joe squeezed my hand.

"Alex briefly lost consciousness, but in the end, she only had a mild concussion, thank God. But now she has all the guilt of having caused the accident and none of the resolution of knowing what happened. And after the accident, she changed. She withdrew. She stopped spending time with her friends or participating in any of the activities she enjoyed before the accident. Except for tennis. And I've always wondered if that's because she feels like she owes it to her father to keep playing. But honestly, she's not the same on the court either. She just seems so . . . joyless. And now she's disappeared in the middle of the night. Which she's never done before."

"She'll be back," Joe said. "She's only been gone for a few hours."

I nodded mutely, remembering the chilly dinner we'd shared. I'd made pasta carbonara, and Alex had picked at it, twirling the spaghetti around her fork without eating much. Then she'd told me she had calculus homework and gone up to her room. I hadn't seen her since. I couldn't even remember having heard her. When had she sneaked out? While I was doing the dishes? When I was in the shower? Or had she become adept at moving silently through the house?

"Sometimes it feels like I don't know her anymore," I admitted. "Not really."

Tears began sliding down my cheeks. I wiped at them with the back of my hand, but now that I had finally begun to cry, I couldn't seem to stop.

PART TWO

After She Died

CHAPTER THIRTY-ONE

KATE

The house was dark and silent. Joe had fallen asleep on the couch, his head tilted back, his mouth slightly agape, his arms crossed over his chest. He was snoring softly. I wondered whether I should wake him and send him home, or at least let him lie down in a more comfortable position. But I couldn't bring myself to disturb him. And, selfishly, I didn't want him to leave. Joe's presence helped, even if he was asleep. It calmed and steadied me, even as I watched the clock tick forward. The moments strung together, one after another after another. And in each one, I still didn't know where Alex was, or whether she was safe.

I checked my phone for the umpteenth time that night. In the past forty-three seconds, Alex still hadn't called or responded to any of the many texts I'd sent her.

Where are you? I asked silently.

"What time is it?" Joe asked, stirring next to me.

"Just after one."

He shifted, stretching his back. "You shouldn't have let me fall asleep."

I lifted one shoulder. "I should have made you go home so you could get a proper night's sleep."

"I'll stay until Alex gets back."

A sob caught at the back of my throat. "If she comes back."

"Don't say that. I'm sure she's fine. She's just being a teenager. Pushing the boundaries. She probably sneaked out to a friend's and ended up crashing there."

I would normally have agreed with him. It was typical rebellious teen behavior. Except that Alex didn't have any friends here. At least not any that I knew about. I thought of all the true-crime television shows I'd watched over the years. Stories about pretty young girls who vanished, never to be seen again. Every single one of those stories started like this. With a girl who didn't come home.

Joe and I looked at one another, me wild eyed, and his dark-brown eyes clouded with fatigue.

"Maybe you should call the police," Joe said.

I nodded. It was now late enough that the police would have to take me seriously. "I think you're right."

And then we heard a sound. A scraping sound coming from outside, followed by a metallic clatter. Joe and I both leaped up. I made it to the front door first and threw it open.

It was Alex. She was struggling to pick up her bike, which had fallen on the front path. It hadn't occurred to me to check to see whether her bike was in the garage. She never rode it.

"Where have you been?" I asked, my voice shrill with fear and relief.

Alex straightened slowly and then turned to look at me. Lit by the outdoor wall sconce, her face looked sickly white, and her clothes were filthy. Her knees, bare in her running shorts, were blackened, as if she'd been kneeling in dirt. She stared at me mutely. I wasn't even sure she'd heard my question.

"Alex, where have you been?" I demanded. "It's the middle of the night!"

Alex's gaze flickered toward Joe and then down to the ground. She shook her head but remained silent.

"I should probably go," Joe said.

I turned toward him, relief and gratitude flooding through me. "Thank you. For everything."

"Anytime." Joe leaned forward and kissed me on the cheek. "Get some sleep. Bye, Alex."

I opened the front door and ushered Alex inside, lit by the headlights on Joe's car as he reversed out of our driveway. Alex was shivering.

"You're freezing!" I exclaimed. I could see goose bumps on her arms. "It isn't even cold out."

Alex shook her head and wrapped her arms around herself. She still hadn't spoken, and I wondered whether it was possible she was in shock. I gently rested my hands on her shoulders.

"Alex, you need to tell me. Are you hurt? Did someone hurt you?"

"N-no," Alex finally said.

"Where have you been?"

"I just went for a bike ride."

"In the middle of the night? Why on earth would you do that? You've been gone for hours."

Alex just shook her head again, staring down at the ground.

I sighed. "Go take a shower and get to bed. We'll talk about it in the morning."

Alex nodded stiffly and turned away from me.

"Alex?"

She glanced back at me. Her expression was haunted. "Yes?"

"Are you okay?"

Alex stared at me for a long moment. Her dark-brown eyes were wide. For a moment, I thought she was going to tell me what had happened. Where she'd been. But in the end, she just said, "I'm fine."

I let Alex sleep in late the next morning. It was a school day, but I figured the conversation she and I were going to have was more important than school, so I called the attendance office and told them she wasn't feeling well. I spent the morning taking care of paperwork, the sort of mindless tasks that I could accomplish while my eyes were scratchy with fatigue and my thoughts skittered between fear of what could have happened and anger at what Alex had done.

In the midst of the paperwork, I found the flyer for the commercial rental space I'd looked at with Joe. Where I'd stood in the middle of the empty space and imagined a newer, better version of my shop springing up around me. A foothold in my new life here in Shoreham. I crumpled up the advertisement and threw it in the garbage.

Joe was the only good thing that had happened since we'd moved to Shoreham. But I couldn't stay in a town where my daughter and I had both become pariahs for the sake of a relationship with a man I'd only just met. Although I had to admit, to myself if no one else, that the idea of not seeing Joe again, not hearing his laugh or the warmth in his voice, hollowed me out. I shook my head and pushed the paperwork aside. I needed more caffeine.

I started a pot of coffee, and once it had brewed, I poured myself a mug and went outside to sit on our back patio. When we'd first bought the house, I'd envisioned having an in-ground pool put in back here, maybe with a hot tub on one end or with a soothing waterfall feature. Now I doubted we'd stay long enough to do that. I didn't want to uproot Alex yet again, but I wasn't sure keeping her at Shoreham High School was a better prospect. Maybe at this point, it would be better to take her back to Buffalo, to where it was familiar.

Although I hadn't told Joe the whole story. I hadn't told him why we'd left Buffalo in the first place.

After Ed died, the immediate response from our community had been kind and sympathetic. I was so overwhelmed with flowers and casseroles, I ran out of vases and refrigerator space. I privately vowed that the next time I had a bereaved friend, I'd give them a gift certificate for a massage or a nice bottle of whiskey.

But then, shortly after the funeral, something changed. The first time I noticed it, I was at the grocery store. I had just run in to buy a few things—the peach yogurt Alex liked, a head of romaine lettuce, a carton of eggs. I spotted Jamie Ryan pushing her cart down the pasta-and-canned-vegetable aisle. I knew Jamie from way back when our daughters were both in grade school and had attended the same gymnastics class. We used to chat on the sidelines while they tumbled around on cushioned mats. We'd always been friendly, even if we weren't exactly friends.

Jamie had come to Ed's funeral, I remembered, although I hadn't had a chance to speak with her. Impulsively, I turned my cart up the next aisle so that I could bump into her and thank her for attending the service. I'd realized, even at that point, that I needed to make more of an effort with people. I needed friends, not just acquaintances. And I thought Jamie seemed like good potential friend material. She always had a mischievous glint in her eye and a wicked sense of humor.

But then, just as I was passing the display of bagged coffee, I heard her, her voice carrying over from the next aisle.

"I know! Not only was she the one driving the car, but I've heard that family has a history of emotional problems. Mary Medvin told me the father was ejected from the grounds of a tennis tournament the kids were playing at because he yelled at a chair umpire."

Jamie's voice dipped into a whisper, so I couldn't hear what else she had to say about that. I remembered that weekend. We had been at a juniors tournament in Orlando. Ed asked the umpire whether he was blind and then called him an asshole when he refused to reverse his call. It had been mortifying, and Alex hadn't spoken to her father for the rest of the weekend. Suddenly, Jamie's voice rose again.

"I've talked to people who don't think it was an accident. I'm not saying it was intentional, not exactly, but maybe there were some serious underlying emotional issues. I mean, I would hate to think that was true, but just think about her being at school around our kids next year! That doesn't seem right."

I had turned around and left, abandoning my cart and its contents in the middle of the aisle.

It hadn't been the only time I heard ugly insinuations. A neighbor stopped me while I was pulling out the garbage cans one morning to ask me if I planned on letting Alex drive again. She was clearly worried that Alex might run her over. On Thanksgiving, a distant acquaintance cornered me before dinner so that he could lecture me on the likelihood of depression being genetic and symptoms I should watch for in Alex. He didn't relent even after I told him Ed had never been diagnosed with depression. Alex's guidance counselor called me in to discuss her concerns over how withdrawn Alex had become, and during the meeting, told me her pet theory that people never really overcome this sort of trauma and Alex might struggle for the rest of her life.

That was when I first got the idea that maybe we should just move.

And the more I thought about it, the more sense it made. We could go somewhere where no one knew Alex as the girl who had been driving the car at the time of the accident that killed her emotionally unstable father. She'd just be another teenage girl. And we'd at least be able to go to the grocery store without having to listen to school moms gossip about her.

It hadn't quite worked how I'd hoped.

I sipped my coffee and gazed up at the sky, which was a clear blue with white fluffy clouds. It was so absurdly pretty, it almost looked fake, like a painted movie set.

"Kate!"

I turned and saw Lita waving at me from her backyard. She didn't have a pool either. Instead there was a giant circular trampoline behind her house that I had never seen anyone jump on. Lita skirted it and headed straight toward our shared fence. I made a mental note that if I did stay here, I would have to install a privacy fence. Something so high, Lita wouldn't be able to peer over it.

"Kate!" she exclaimed. "Have you heard what happened? It's *terrible*."

Lita looked both horrified and delighted in her horror.

I assumed it had something to do with the video of Genevieve Hudson and Coach Townsend having sex. I had no interest in discussing it. As much as I disliked Daphne and was angry for how she'd bullied Alex, she was the victim in this situation. It was sordid and depressing, and I didn't want to hear Lita gloat about it. And besides, I was so tired, hungover from a lack of sleep and the aftershocks of the adrenaline that had coursed through me all night. I couldn't think of a single word to say, so I just shook my head mutely.

"A body was found at the beach this morning. A teenage girl," Lita said excitedly.

"A body? How horrible." It was horrible. I wondered whether someone walking the beach had suffered a heart attack, or whether it was possibly a drug overdose. I shivered.

"They haven't made an official announcement, but the news is already out. My son's best friend's uncle is a paramedic, and he was one of the first on the scene. They found her body on the beach, and get this . . . she was *naked*."

She? I thought numbly. And then, as my brain scrambled to catch up, Naked?

"What happened?"

"That's just it. No one knows yet. No one knows how she got there or what happened to her. It's a mystery!" Lita said excitedly.

"Lita!" I said, more sharply than I meant. "Whose body did they find on the beach? Who died?"

Lita suddenly looked somber, as though she finally realized how serious the situation was. This wasn't a particularly juicy piece of gossip. Someone had died. Lita sucked in a deep breath.

"It was Callie Nord. Ingrid Nord's daughter. Her body was found on Isle Beach this morning."

CHAPTER THIRTY-TWO

KATE

"That's . . . that's terrible," I said, trying to keep my voice steady, even as there was a roaring in my ears.

Callie was dead. Ingrid's Callie. And Alex had been out until late last night. Was it possible those two things were connected? But how? And why?

"It is terrible. I can't imagine what Ingrid is going through. I mean, you know I've never liked her." Lita raised a hand as if I'd accused her of hypocrisy. "But I wouldn't wish this on my worst enemy. Poor Ingrid. I don't think I'd be able to survive losing one of my boys."

I usually hated it when people made comments like that. I'd gotten them when Ed died. The truth was, you have no idea how you'll handle grief until it presents itself. But I knew what Lita meant. Being a bereaved parent must be a special kind of hell.

"How did she die?"

"From what I've heard, they think she drowned," Lita said. "Her body was found on the beach, and the tide was going out last night, so . . ." She raised her eyebrows meaningfully.

I stared back at her, not comprehending what she was trying to say. My mind was sluggish from lack of sleep followed by this terrible shock.

"If she was swimming alone and accidentally drowned, her body would probably have been washed out to sea," Lita explained. "If she did drown, which is what I think they presumed happened, someone must have moved her body back onto shore."

"That means she probably wasn't alone," I said.

Lita jumped in, eager to deliver the scandalous conclusion. "I heard the police are treating her death as a possible homicide."

Homicide. The word felt like a physical blow. I had to talk to Alex. Immediately.

"That's terrible." I nodded toward my house. "I'd better head back inside. I'm in the middle of a pile of paperwork. I was just taking a short break."

"That's okay, I'm going to call Karen Weaver and see if she's heard the news yet!"

Lita turned, and I headed back into the house, my legs stiff, my heart pounding. I wanted to call for Alex as soon as I was through the door, but I was afraid Lita might still be outside and hear my panicked shout.

Callie and Alex weren't friends, I reminded myself. Callie had bullied Alex. And yet Alex had disappeared for hours on the same night that Callie died. Was it possible Callie's death and Alex's unexplained absence were related?

And then there was the perhaps larger issue. Who would believe it *was* a coincidence?

Think about what needs to be done, I told myself as I strode into the kitchen and rinsed out my coffee cup. Make a list. Right now. Of everything that needs to be done to protect Alex.

I needed to wash the clothes Alex had been wearing the night before. I needed to think of a reason my daughter hadn't been to school that day, other than that she'd been out of the house the previous night. Although would that even work? Many of our neighbors had video doorbell systems. What were the chances that Alex had left and returned the night before without being caught on a camera somewhere along the way? Probably slim to none. And then there was Joe. He knew she'd been out late. Joe was a nice guy, but I could hardly expect him to lie to the police for us.

"This is bad," I said aloud.

"Mom?"

Alex appeared in the doorway, the sunshine streaming in behind her, her long hair loose around her shoulders. In that moment, she looked younger than her seventeen years. I saw the small girl she'd once been, all long limbs and endless energy.

"Get your clothes," I told her. "The ones you were wearing last night. Actually, get me all of the clothes in your hamper. I'm going to wash everything."

"What's going on?"

I slapped my hand against the kitchen counter so hard, Alex jumped.

"Just do it," I told her. "And then we're going to talk. I don't think we have a lot of time."

Fifteen minutes later, Alex and I were sitting in the living room. Alex was tucked into a corner of the leather sectional, her legs curled under her, and I was sitting on one of the cream-upholstered side chairs. It was hard to sit still while anxiety swirled through me, tightening my chest and making it difficult to breathe.

"Tell me what happened last night," I said.

Alex shrugged one shoulder and shook her head. "I already told you. I just went for a bike ride."

I realized my hands had started to shake, and I braced them against my knees.

"Callie is dead," I said. "Her body was found on the beach."

Alex just stared at me. She didn't gasp in surprise. She didn't cover her mouth with her hand in horror. She didn't even ask how Callie had died.

Maybe she already knows, I thought, and I had to push the horror of that realization away.

"Alex," I said, trying to keep my voice calm. "Lita told me that the police are already treating Callie's death as a possible homicide. They think someone was with her at the time she died."

Alex nodded solemnly. She began twisting a strand of her hair absentmindedly around one finger. I wanted to scream and forced myself to instead take a deep breath. She clearly wasn't understanding the significance of the situation.

"Were you there?" I asked. "Were you at the beach last night?"

Alex stilled. "Why would you ask me that?"

"Because you were out so late. And you didn't tell me where you'd been. And now one of the girls you were having conflict with is dead."

"Actually, Callie and I got along okay. Well." Alex shrugged again. "We sort of did. She apologized for her part in hanging the Ken doll in my locker."

I stared at my daughter. "You don't seem to understand how serious this is."

"Of course I do. Callie died." Alex shook her head solemnly. "That's awful."

"And now the police are going to find out that you weren't home last night, because there's a doorbell camera on practically every house on this street. And probably on all the streets around here. Someone, somewhere, has a picture of you out in the middle of the night. Then the police are going to learn that those girls have been bullying you for months. Don't you see how terrible this is going to look?"

"But I didn't do anything. I didn't kill Callie."

I released a breath I hadn't realized I'd been holding.

"We have to make a plan. I don't know how much time we have until the police will want to question you. We have to figure out what we're going to tell them about where you were last night and why you weren't in school today."

"I'll just tell them the truth. That I went for a bike ride and got home late."

I stared at her mutely, shaking my head. Was she really this naive?

"Where did you bike to?" I asked, hoping she'd come clean and tell me she'd been at a friend's house. Or even a boyfriend's house. It was against the rules for her to sneak out to see a boy, obviously, but it was by far the preferable alternative. "You were gone for hours."

"Just around. I don't really know. It was dark, and I didn't really know where I was going."

"Did anyone see you?" I asked.

Alex considered this and then shook her head. "I'm not sure. I mean, I saw a few cars go by, but I don't think anyone was paying attention to me."

"Did you talk to anyone?"

"No."

I exhaled. "I think we should say that you and I got into an argument and that's why you left. That you went out to blow off steam."

"Why do we have to lie?" Alex looked at me blankly.

"Because we need to explain why you were out of the house in the middle of the night. What *were* you doing, anyway?"

Alex's gaze skittered away. "Nothing. Just thinking about things."

"You've never done anything like that before. Just taken off, without telling me where you are. I was worried. I called you. I texted. You ignored me."

"Sorry," Alex muttered.

"But why did you go out?" I pressed. "Were you planning on meeting someone?"

Alex shook her head. "I don't know."

"That doesn't make any sense. How do you not know what you were doing?"

Alex stood suddenly, her hands balled at her sides. "God! Stop interrogating me!"

"I'm trying to help you." I spread my hands helplessly. "Maybe we should hire an attorney."

"For *what*?"

To keep you safe, I thought.

But then I realized it might already be too late for that.

CHAPTER THIRTY-THREE

Video Diary of Alex Turner

October 14

Alex sat in front of her window, the sky behind her a slice of brilliant blue. She held her phone up in front of her, and the picture was slightly shaky as a result. The rims of Alex's eyes were red, as if she'd been recently crying.

Last night was . . . well. It was horrible. I can't even talk about it. My mom has asked me, like, a thousand questions, but what can I tell her? If I tell her anything, even the smallest detail, she's going to want to know more. And there are things that happened last night that she can't know about. That she can never find out.

I told her I just went for a bike ride, but my mom isn't stupid. I knew she was hoping that I was out at a party with a bunch of drunk kids, like a real-life version of the graduation party at Jake's house in *Sixteen Candles*. She wants a normal daughter with normal wacky teenage problems.

And instead, she's stuck with me.

Alex glanced over her shoulder, out the window, and then looked back at her phone.

I don't know what I'm going to do. I don't think anyone saw me last night, but what if I'm wrong? If I am, I could be in serious trouble. I know my mom thinks I am. Which is actually pretty screwed up on its own. She didn't say it, but I know she was thinking about Dad.

About the accident. I don't think she's ever fully believed me that I don't remember what happened that day.

Tears welled in Alex's eyes, and she wiped at them with the back of her hand.

Maybe she's right. Maybe there *is* something wrong with me.

She thinks we might need to hire a criminal defense attorney. She thinks I need one. Maybe I do. And I'm pretty sure the first thing he'd tell me is to stop making videos about what happened. So that's exactly what I'm going to do.

Alex stared into the camera for a few beats and then abruptly ended the recording.

CHAPTER THIRTY-FOUR

KATE

I sat at the kitchen table, drinking a mug of tea while I read the local news coverage of Callie's death on my iPad. In the past twenty-four hours, I'd imagined endless terrifying scenarios that all ended the same—with Alex being accused of killing Callie. The imaginary scenes flipped through my mind. Alex being arrested. Alex being held in jail without bond awaiting trial. Alex sitting at the defendant's table during her trial, looking fragile and young, while prosecutors accused her of having committed a terrible crime.

Alex still hadn't told me where she'd been the night Callie died. In fact, she wasn't speaking to me at all. When I finally gave up trying to get answers out of her, Alex had stomped up to her room and hadn't come out for the rest of the day. She hadn't even come down for dinner. I left her a plate on the counter, covered in plastic wrap. The next morning, the plate was in the sink, washed clean. She must have crept downstairs to eat after I went to bed.

I tried to focus on the newspaper article. The news of Callie's death was the lead story.

TEEN REMEMBERED AS BRIGHT LIGHT OF THE COMMUNITY

The body of Callie Nord, seventeen, was found

> yesterday morning on Isle Beach. The cause of death has not been released by the Calusa County medical examiner.
>
> Callie is being remembered as a lively and creative young woman, who was well liked by friends and teachers alike.
>
> "She was such a bright light," Alison Spencer, a guidance counselor at Shoreham High School, said. "Everyone is shocked and saddened by her loss."
>
> Callie was a member of the Shoreham women's tennis team, which was recently rocked by the allegations that the coach, Seth Townsend, had been having an inappropriate relationship with one of the players on the team. Townsend has been charged on multiple counts of unlawful sexual activity with a minor. He's been released from custody on bond and is awaiting trial.

I frowned at my tablet, wondering why the newspaper had brought up Seth Townsend. The implication was that his arrest was somehow linked to Callie's death. But Coach Townsend had been involved with Daphne, not Callie. Or, at least, that's what I thought. Was it possible that the coach had victimized other girls on the team?

The doorbell rang, and I dropped the iPad. It fell on the table with a loud clatter. I pushed my chair back and stood, hoping it was only Lita, wishing for a reality where the worst thing that could happen was an annoying neighbor stopping by without warning.

But it wasn't Lita. Instead, two men stood on the doorstep.

"Good morning." The older of the two men smiled genially. "I'm Detective Mike Monroe. This is my partner, Gavin Reddick. We're with the Calusa County Sheriff's Office."

I stared at them. Mike Monroe looked a bit older than me, probably in his midfifties. He was a barrel-chested man with a pleasant face and thick hair. I guessed his partner, Gavin Reddick, was in his late thirties. Reddick was tall and gaunt. He had a sharply angled face and dark narrow eyes.

"I'm Kate Turner," I said.

"We're here to talk to you about Callie Nord, the teenage girl who died yesterday," Detective Monroe said. "May we come in?"

I wanted to say no, to step back inside my house and shut the door firmly in their faces. But I knew that if I did that, it would look like I was hiding something. A young girl had died, the daughter of a former friend and the teammate of my daughter. Only someone who was guilty would refuse to help the investigation into her death. And right now, I needed them to focus their attention elsewhere.

"Sure, come in." I held the door open for them. I glanced at the stairs and wondered whether Alex had heard the detectives arrive. She was still in her room, and I hoped she'd stay there. I led the two men into the living room. They took seats on the matching cream-upholstered chairs, while I sat opposite, perched on the edge of the sofa.

"Can I get you anything? I just made some coffee," I offered.

"No, thank you," Detective Monroe said. His smile was open and friendly. "Your name came up in connection with our investigation. Were you acquainted with Callie Nord?"

"Sort of," I said. "I met her a few times, but I don't think we ever spoke." I wondered whether my talking to Callie and her two friends while they floated around in the Thackers' pool, staring blankly at me, counted as having spoken. None of the girls had said a word to me.

"Callie played on the Shoreham High tennis team with my daughter, Alex. Mostly, I know Callie's mother, Ingrid."

"Ingrid Nord said that you showed up at her office the day Callie died," Detective Reddick said. He stared at me intently. "She said that you became quite aggressive. That you made accusations that her daughter was bullying your daughter. That you claimed Callie hung a doll in your daughter's locker."

I stared at him, momentarily stunned into silence. Somehow, between my fear when Alex disappeared that night and my horror at the news of Callie's death, I had completely forgotten about my conversation with Ingrid. I knew the police would hear about the bullying, but for some reason, I'd assumed that information would come from Principal Hopkins. The fact that the source had been Ingrid made it sound worse.

"Ingrid and I did speak," I finally said. "Although I take issue with the characterization that I was aggressive. But, yes, I had learned that Callie and her two best friends, Daphne Hudson and Shae Thacker, had been bullying my daughter. I wanted to talk to Ingrid about the situation."

"What were you hoping to accomplish by confronting her?" Detective Reddick asked.

"I didn't confront her. I was hoping she could give me some information on the dynamic between the girls. Both as Callie's mother and in her professional capacity," I explained. "I'd been told that she wrote a doctoral thesis advocating parents raise their daughters to be bullies."

"Come again?" Detective Monroe said. His thick dark eyebrows rose in disbelief.

"Another mother whose daughter had been bullied by the same group of girls told me about it. That the mothers—Ingrid Nord and her two friends, Genevieve Hudson and Emma Thacker—trained their daughters to be bullies. They rewarded their daughters when they were unkind to other kids. I know it sounds ridiculous. I didn't believe it at first either. But the bullying my daughter endured was extreme, so I wanted to discuss it with Ingrid."

"And what did she tell you?"

"She admitted she wrote her doctoral thesis on the subject." I shook my head, still not quite able to believe it was true. "I never heard of anything like it before. Most parents would hate for their kids to become bullies. And Ingrid phrased it differently. She said that she advocated for girls to be raised to be more assertive. But she also admitted that Daphne's mother, Genevieve Hudson, took the theory too far. That when Daphne was growing up, Genevieve rewarded her when she was aggressive toward other kids."

"I'm a parent," Detective Monroe commented. "My kids are grown now, but I remember what it was like when they were younger. If they got picked on, it would make my blood boil."

I felt another surge of shock. I'd been so focused on keeping Alex safe, it hadn't occurred to me that the police might also consider me as a possible suspect.

"I am angry at how my daughter has been treated." I fought to keep my voice level. "But I would never hurt anyone. And I certainly didn't hurt Callie."

"Where were you on Thursday evening?" Detective Reddick asked.

"I was here. At home," I said. And then I remembered that I hadn't been home the whole night. Joe and I had driven around the neighborhood, looking for Alex. Would anyone have seen us? I had to assume it was possible.

"All night?" he pushed.

"Well," I hedged. "I might have left to run an errand."

"Is there anyone that can verify where you were that night?" Detective Monroe chipped in.

"Actually, yes. I had a friend over. Joe Miller. He owns the Surfside Grill, and he's the chef there. He stopped by after work."

Detective Reddick made a note of this. "And your daughter?"

"What about her?" I hesitated. This was the moment I'd been dreading. If I lied, would I be protecting Alex or putting her in greater danger? If they found out I hadn't told the truth, it might heighten the police focus on her.

"Was she home all evening?" he asked.

"No," Alex said from the doorway. We all looked up in surprise. I hadn't heard her come down the stairs. "I wasn't here that night. I went out."

"Alex, these two men are police detectives," I said, trying to warn her before she said anything more.

Detective Monroe stood and held out his hand. "I'm Detective Monroe, and this is my partner, Detective Reddick. It's nice to meet you."

Alex shook each of the men's hands in turn, and then sat down next to me on the couch. My heart was racing. I wasn't sure what to do. Should I stop Alex from talking to the two detectives? Or, at the very least, have an attorney present while they interviewed her? But if I did, that might raise their suspicions. Then I realized that was probably inevitable, now that Alex was telling them she wasn't home the night Callie died.

"You said you weren't at home on Thursday night?" Detective Monroe asked.

"I went out for a bike ride after I finished my homework," Alex said.

"Is that something you normally do?" Detective Reddick asked.

"No," Alex said. "But I wanted to clear my head and get some exercise. Our tennis team hasn't had practice since Coach Townsend was arrested."

"Where'd you bike to?"

"Nowhere in particular. I don't know the area that well. I just rode around."

"How late were you out?" Detective Monroe asked.

"It was late." Alex glanced at me. "Like, around one?"

The two detectives exchanged a look, and my heart began to thump rapidly. I should never have let them in the house, I thought.

"You were out riding your bike until one in the morning?" Detective Monroe repeated. "That seems late to be out exercising."

Alex nodded. "I got a little turned around. Like I said, I don't know my way around that well yet. We just moved here a few months ago."

"You weren't worried that your daughter was out in the middle of the night?" Detective Reddick asked me.

"I was worried. I tried calling her," I said. "And I went to look for her. Drove around for a bit, in case she was lost."

This last part wasn't entirely true. It had never occurred to me that Alex had gotten lost, and I didn't believe that part of her story. She'd always had an excellent sense of direction. But I thought it sounded better than the alternative—which was that I'd been worried about Alex's state of mind. Her mental health. What she was capable of.

"But I'd turned my ringer off, so I didn't hear my phone ring," Alex said.

I was struck by her composure. I was a nervous wreck, while Alex seemed almost serene. She sat very still, had her hands folded in her lap, and was answering every question the detectives posed to her in a calm, measured tone.

"Did you meet anyone while you were out biking until one in the morning?" Detective Reddick asked. I wondered if he always sounded so skeptical.

"No," Alex shook her head. "I wasn't meeting anyone."

"Did you know Callie Nord?" Detective Monroe asked.

"Yes, we were in the same class at school. And we were on the tennis team together," Alex said.

"Your mom told us that she and a few of her friends had bullied you," Reddick said.

Alex nodded. “They hung a Ken doll with *x*’s over his eyes in my locker.”

“Why a Ken doll?” Detective Monroe asked.

“He was supposed to represent my dad. He died last year,” Alex said flatly.

“And you’re sure it was”—Detective Reddick consulted his notepad—“Callie Nord, Daphne Hudson, and Shae Thacker who put the doll in your locker?”

“I’m sure. They waited in the locker room to see how I’d react when I saw it. They thought it was hilarious. I’m also pretty sure they’re the ones who printed out hundreds of copies of an article about how my dad died and pretty much papered the school with them.”

“Why would they do that?” Detective Monroe asked.

“I really think maybe it would be better—” I began, not even sure what I was going to say.

“It’s okay, Mom.” Alex looked down at her hands. “My dad died in a car accident. I was driving, and I ran a light at an intersection. It was my fault he died.”

“It was an accident,” I said reflexively.

“And they used his death to bully you?” Detective Reddick looked appraisingly at my daughter. “That must have really pissed you off.”

Alex nodded. “Yeah, of course. It was really mean. I don’t even know why they were going after me. I never did anything to any of them.”

“Did it piss you off enough that you decided to do something about it?” Reddick asked. “Enough that you wanted to kill Callie Nord?”

“All right, that’s enough,” I said, standing.

Alex ignored me. “No,” she said calmly. “I wasn’t mad at Callie. She apologized to me for her part in all of it. I think she really was sorry. After that, she stopped hanging out with Daphne and Shae.”

"And you forgave her, just like that?"

"Well, I don't think we were ever going to be best friends, but yeah." Alex shrugged. "We were fine. If you want to find out what happened to Callie, you should really talk to Daphne Hudson and Shae Thacker. If anyone would know what happened to her, they would."

"Why's that?" Detective Monroe asked.

"They were all really close. But I think Callie started to see what kind of a person Daphne really is. And it bothered her. Callie once told me that Daphne made her do things. Things she didn't want to do."

"It sounds like you have a lot of insight into Callie's life," Detective Monroe said. "Any idea why she would have gone to the beach that night?"

Alex hesitated and for the first time looked flustered.

"How would I know that?" she asked.

I knew it was time to step in. "This interview is over. If you want to speak to Alex in the future, I want her to be represented by an attorney."

The detectives looked at one another, and then Detective Monroe nodded.

"Would you be willing to give us your mobile phone?" Detective Reddick asked Alex.

"My phone? Why?"

"We can download the GPS data. It would show us where you were on Thursday night."

"I don't think—" I began, but before I could continue, Alex cut me off.

"No," she said. "You can't have my phone."

Detective Reddick gave her a long, measured look. "We can get a warrant for it."

Alex shook her head. "I'm not giving it to you."

"I'd like you to leave now," I said.

I walked to the door and held it open for the detectives. The two men stood reluctantly. But as they filed out of the living room, Detective Reddick turned to give a last lingering look in Alex's direction that chilled me to the core.

"Thank you for your time," Detective Monroe said with a nod. "We'll be in touch."

CHAPTER THIRTY-FIVE

KATE

I wasn't able to take a deep breath until the two detectives were safely out of the house. I closed the door behind them and then locked it. I stood there for a moment, waiting for the blind panic that had engulfed me to pass.

We'll be in touch, Mike Monroe had said. What did that mean? Would they be back with a warrant?

Alex wandered out of the living room. She seemed to be reading my thoughts. "Can they really get a warrant to come back and take my phone?"

I shrugged helplessly. "I have no idea. I know they need probable cause to arrest someone, but I don't know what the standard is for getting a warrant."

"My phone is private," Alex said. She seemed to be missing the larger, existential threat that the police posed.

"I don't think that matters to them," I said numbly. "They're viewing you as a possible suspect in Callie's death."

"They can't be. I didn't do anything. They're probably just talking to everyone who knew Callie."

"But Callie just died yesterday, and the police were at our house today. That means you must be high on their priority list. I'm going to start looking for a criminal defense attorney. I think we're going to need one."

Alex stared at me for a long moment. I wondered whether, finally, she was starting to appreciate the danger she was in. But then she shrugged, turned, and headed upstairs to her room again.

Joe stopped by in the late afternoon before his work shift. I'd called him after the police left, and he'd immediately volunteered to bring Alex and me supper. His arms were full of reusable grocery bags. He set them down on the kitchen island and then reached into one bag and pulled out a bouquet of perfect white roses.

"For you," he said, presenting the flowers to me.

"Thank you," I exclaimed. "They're beautiful! Let me put them in water."

I arranged the roses in a fluted vase while Joe unpacked the bags. He pulled out a large pan of lasagna and a loaf of garlic bread ready for the oven. These were followed by a platter of sliced tomatoes and mozzarella, a large tossed salad, and a plate stacked high with brownies. I stared at the sheer quantity of food as he unpacked it onto the kitchen island.

"You didn't say what Alex likes to eat, so I brought crowd favorites," he explained.

"Are we expecting a crowd? You've brought enough to feed one."

"I'm a feeder. I probably should have warned you about that. At the first sign of stress, I start cooking."

"Do I need to do anything?"

"Not really. The lasagna needs to cook for an hour at three hundred fifty degrees. Then stick the garlic bread in when there's about twenty minutes left on the lasagna. Toss the salad with the dressing at the last minute, and that's it. Do you need me to write any of that down?"

"No, I'll remember. This was incredibly nice of you."

"It's my pleasure." Joe glanced at me. "The police came by my condo today after we spoke. They wanted me to confirm what you and Alex told them. That I was here on Thursday night with you, and that Alex was out until one."

My stomach plummeted. I had meant what I told Alex—it was a bad sign that the police had shown up on our doorstep so quickly. Now they had already verified my alibi. That meant they were focusing on us. Or, more specifically, on Alex.

"The problem is that Alex says she was alone that night. Which isn't surprising. She hasn't made any friends here, or at least none that I know of. But that means she doesn't have an alibi for when Callie was killed. And apparently that, combined with the fact that Callie and her friends bullied Alex, is enough for the police to treat her as a suspect."

"Why didn't you tell the police that she was here, home with you?" Joe turned to look at me. "I would have backed you up."

"I couldn't have asked you to lie," I said. "You might have gotten in trouble."

Joe kissed me on the forehead. "I can handle it. Trouble's my middle name."

"I think that saying means that you cause trouble," I said, smiling for the first time in what felt like forever.

"Maybe you're right." When Joe smiled at me, the edges of his eyes creased. "I would have backed you up, though."

"I appreciate that. I did actually consider lying and telling the detectives that Alex was home. Just to keep her safe. But Alex told them the truth. She said she had nothing to hide."

"That's admirable, but maybe a bit naive."

"Or maybe not. She had her cell phone with her that night, and the police said they can use the GPS data on the phone to track her movements that night. They asked her to voluntarily give it to them, but Alex refused. The detective said that they could get a warrant for it. Maybe it's smarter that she told the truth rather than say something that can later be proven to be a lie." I shrugged. "I know I should probably be proud of her for her honesty."

"It does speak well of her character."

"I just wish she'd be more forthcoming with me," I admitted. "At least that way, I'd be able to protect her."

"She's a teenager. They're sort of known for being secretive and not telling their parents stuff," Joe pointed out. "My parents never knew what I was up to when I was that age."

"Did you ever sneak out of the house in the middle of the night?"

"I don't think I had to sneak. It was the eighties. Our parents didn't pay enough attention to us to notice when we weren't home. I don't think mine knew where I was most of the time." Joe rubbed my shoulder. "Alex will be okay. It sounds like she's handling the scrutiny well."

"She seems to be. I'm just worried. And I'm second-guessing my decision to cooperate with the police this morning."

"Maybe you should talk to a criminal defense attorney," Joe suggested.

"I was thinking the same thing. I spent part of the day looking for an attorney online, but it's impossible to know who's the best. Do you know a good one?"

"I'll ask around and try to find a referral," he promised.

"Thank you. I'm overwhelmed."

Joe leaned forward and kissed me. I touched his cheek.

"Are you still going to Orlando this weekend? To go to the theme park? In all the chaos, I forgot about it."

Joe laughed softly. "I forgot about it too. I never did make reservations."

"It's probably for the best. Roller coasters scare the hell out of me."

Alex walked into the kitchen and surveyed the food spread across the island.

"Is that lasagna?" she asked.

"Yes. Are you a fan?" Joe said.

"As long as it's not all vegetables. I had mushroom lasagna once, and it was gross."

Joe clutched his chest in mock horror. "I can't believe you'd accuse me of bringing vegetable lasagna! What kind of a monster do you think I am?"

Alex regarded him coolly. "I don't know. I don't know you."

"For starters, I make the best lasagna you've ever had. Zero vegetables, if you don't count tomatoes, onions and garlic, and four kinds of cheese. And just wait until you try my garlic bread," Joe bragged.

"You're modest too." Alex took a tomato off the platter and popped it into her mouth. "What roller coaster were you talking about?"

"Oh." I glanced at my oddly composed daughter to Joe and back again. "Joe invited us to join him and his son, Sean, at the Universal Studios theme park in Orlando this weekend."

"That sounds fun," Alex said.

"With everything that's been going on, I don't think going away this weekend is a good idea."

"No," Joe said. "But we can go another time."

"Cool. Nice flowers." Alex nodded at the roses before turning and disappearing back to her room.

I stared after her. Alex seemed . . . off. She was far too composed for someone who was under police suspicion in a homicide investigation. Why was she so calm when I felt like the entire world had spun out of control over the past two days?

"Do you have time for a glass of wine before you go?" I asked. "Because after the day I've had, I could use one. It's medicinal at this point."

"Sounds great."

I poured us each a glass of wine and handed one to Joe.

"Let's go sit on the patio," I suggested.

We went outside and sat on the wicker chairs. For the first time since we'd moved here, the intense heat had finally relented. The tropical surroundings were still a novelty, the stately palm trees and brightly colored plants and flowers, which were still blooming in October. Back home, the trees would be losing their leaves, and it would be a long winter before the bulb flowers would push up toward the sun. Sweet alyssum scented the air, and I breathed it in. It was so beautiful, I could almost forget that there had been two police detectives at my house that day. Almost.

Then I thought of Ingrid. However difficult the situation was for me, it didn't match the hell that Ingrid must be in. Lita was right—I wouldn't wish this on anyone.

"Have you heard how Ingrid is doing?" I asked Joe, careful to keep my voice quiet, just in case Lita was eavesdropping. I hadn't seen her in her backyard, but I wouldn't put it past her to sneak out and try to listen in on our conversation from her side of the fence. "I can't even imagine what she must be going through."

"I heard she collapsed when the police went to her house to notify her," Joe said sadly.

It was hard to picture that. Ingrid was always so cool, so unruffled by life. But, of course, any parent would be knocked sideways by such terrible news.

"I would reach out to her, but I'm sure I'm the last person she wants to hear from." I shook my head. "I can't imagine how awful it would be to lose a child. Maybe it's even worse if it's the result of a crime."

"Oh, I'd be surprised if this was a crime."

"Really? Why do you say that?"

"My guess is that it was probably an accidental drowning. It happens more often than it should. Kids drink and go swimming when they shouldn't. The riptides in the ocean can be brutal. Even experienced swimmers can get caught in one and find themselves in serious trouble. It's probably even more dangerous at night, when there's no one around to help."

"I wonder what she was doing out there in the middle of the night," I said. Had Ingrid, like me, checked her daughter's room to find her gone? But unlike Alex, Callie hadn't returned.

"I have no idea. But unfortunately, until the medical examiner comes out and officially states that it was an accident, people are going to assume the worst. The way some people talk . . ." Joe shook his head and exhaled deeply. "I think they almost hope she did get murdered, because it would make for a better story."

"What is it about Shoreham and gossip?" I asked, shaking my head in disgust. "It's like the official pastime in this town."

"I don't think it's any worse here than anywhere else," Joe said mildly. "It's just what people do. I suppose it's easier to focus on other people's problems than deal with your own."

"I'm just really worried," I admitted. "I know Alex wouldn't hurt anyone, but it looks bad for her that she was out that night and her whereabouts are unaccounted for. How do you prove a negative? That she didn't do something she was accused of?"

"Don't get ahead of yourself. She hasn't been accused yet."

"Someone gave Alex's name to the police. They didn't just happen to show up on our doorstep the day after Callie's body was found. From what I heard, Daphne bullied a lot of kids. Why did they focus on Alex so quickly?" I shook my head in disgust. "And I know exactly who told them she was involved."

"You're going to say Genevieve."

I nodded grimly. "I'm sure of it. I don't know why she has this vendetta against Alex. Maybe it started with Alex taking Daphne's spot on the tennis team lineup. But it's gone way beyond that. I don't think she'll be happy until Alex's life is ruined."

"I know Genevieve can be high drama, but I don't think she's evil."

"I'm not so sure about that."

And then I remembered sitting in my car, wishing that something terrible would happen to Genevieve, to Emma . . . to Ingrid. I had wished for it. And now it had come true. Shock coursed through me.

"It's my fault," I said out loud, before I could stop myself.

Joe shifted in his seat so that he was looking right at me, ready to listen attentively. I realized how rare that was in my life. For someone to set everything aside just for me.

"How could it possibly be your fault?" he asked.

"Because I wished for this. They were all so awful to Alex, the girls and their mothers, and I was so angry. I wanted something bad to happen to them. And now it has."

"Your hands are shaking."

Joe plucked the wineglass from my hand and set it on the table. Then he folded my hands in his. His touch calmed me, but that made me feel even worse. I didn't deserve to be comforted.

"Everyone has bad thoughts," Joe said. "I certainly do. It's part of the human condition."

"My bad thoughts have a way of coming true. I know that sounds crazy, but it's true."

"Kate." Joe shook my hand gently. "I don't think you're crazy. I think you're under a tremendous amount of stress. Go easy on yourself. You're a good person and a good mom."

I looked up at him, meeting his steady gaze.

And I knew I didn't deserve his kindness.

CHAPTER THIRTY-SIX

Kate

When my phone rang on Sunday afternoon and I saw my mother's picture pop up on the caller ID, I thought about rejecting her call. My mother was incapable of empathy or kindness. She had never been someone I could lean on for support. But I thought talking to her might distract me from the worries playing on a loop in my head, so I picked up.

"Hi, Mom."

"Kate. Do you have your calendar?"

"I use the calendar on my phone."

"No, I mean your *real calendar*," my mother said, enunciating the words very slowly as if I were very stupid.

"What do you need, Mom?" Thirty seconds in, and I was already regretting answering her call.

"Your father and I are going to come visit," she announced, as if this were the best treat anyone could possibly hope for.

My mind immediately went back to my loop of worries. Alex's odd refusal to say where she'd been the night Callie died, and the fact that the police were focusing their investigation on her, and whether she would be charged with a crime. I didn't know how I was supposed to deal with any of that, much less with the unwanted diversion of my parents showing up. My mother would insist on being treated like a very important guest in a high-end hotel, with her every need met the moment she had it. She would pretend that she wanted to help with dinner or spend time with Alex, but she wouldn't do either. Instead, she'd expect everyone—Alex, me, my dad—to revolve around her and her changing whims. My father was a little easier. He spent his days watching professional golf on the television and reading military history books. But he'd also expect all of his meals cooked, and since he was philosophically opposed to renting a car, I'd become the on-call chauffer.

"I don't know if this is a good time," I said, trying—and failing—to think of a reason why we couldn't have guests. Telling my mother that Alex was a person of interest in a possible homicide was out of the question. Instead, I went for a lie. "I'm having some work done on the house. The laundry room needs remodeling."

"Oh, good, then it should be done when we come in February," my mother said brightly.

"February?"

"Yes, after the holidays, we'll be in the mood to go somewhere sunny. Somewhere warm. And I'll be able to help you with the house."

"I don't need help," I said quickly.

"I meant with decorating. You've never had the best sense about putting together a cohesive room. You're always mixing up different styles. It's jarring."

I stood there, blinking, as her words penetrated into the fog of stress and worry I'd been living in. I'd run a consignment furniture store. My *job* had been putting together cohesive rooms. And mixing up different styles was one of the things I was best at.

"Also, Dad will be able to golf. You're near Boca Raton, right?" she continued.

"Not really. I haven't been that far south, but I think it's about ninety minutes away."

"That's not too bad. He'll want to golf with his friend Alan Dreyer, who has a vacation home there. I told him you'd drive him down."

"This really isn't the best—" I began, again wildly thinking of something I could be doing on a Sunday afternoon that would give me an excuse to get off the phone with her. Then the doorbell rang.

My relief at having a ready excuse was quickly followed by a sickly dread. The last time the doorbell had rung, there were two police detectives standing at my front door. Were they back? With a warrant this time?

"I have to go," I said. "Someone's at the door."

She completely ignored me. "The second weekend in February, I think. The Lansings and the Browns will be down at about the same time, and I said we'd have them all over for dinner one night."

The last of my patience ebbed away. "You're coming to Florida to socialize with your friends from Buffalo who you see all the time, not to see Alex and me?"

"You don't have to put it like that."

The doorbell rang again. I headed toward the front door. "I have to go."

"I need to know if those dates work for you first."

"If you need an answer right now, then no. They don't. Goodbye."

I ended the call abruptly. Then I drew in a deep breath and tried to steel myself for whatever was on the other side of the door. What if it was the police? What if they were here to arrest Alex?

I exhaled and opened the door.

It wasn't the police.

"Hi, Kate," Emma said. "Can I come in? I think we need to talk."

Emma and I sat at the kitchen table. I had opened a bottle of chilled chardonnay, and we each had a glass in front of us. Emma looked haunted. Her face was bare of makeup, and dark circles were smudged under her eyes. Even though it was a warm day, she had her light-gray cardigan wrapped tightly around her, as if she were freezing.

"How's Ingrid?" I asked.

Emma shook her head. "She's a mess. I don't know how she's going to get through this. Or if she's going to get through it."

"I can't even imagine."

"She's been sedated, just enough so she can do what needs to be done right now. Making decisions, funeral arrangements. But once that's over, I don't know how she's going to cope. Gen and I are doing what we can. Making sure she's never alone. Trying to get her to eat and sleep."

I wondered whether I should offer to help, but I knew it was pointless. Any offer would be rebuffed. Whatever friendship I had shared with these women was over. There was no point in pretending otherwise.

"I'm glad she has your support." I took a sip of my wine and waited. Emma had a reason for showing up on my doorstep. I wondered how long it would take for her to get around to telling me.

Emma picked up her wineglass and rotated it slowly. "You must hate us," she finally said. "I can't really blame you."

"I don't hate you," I said, even though I wasn't sure that was true. "But I don't understand why you all turned on me."

"No, I know. The thing is . . ." Emma stopped and sighed. "I like to think that I'm an independent woman with my own thoughts and opinions. And I am, for the most part. But sometimes, I think I let my friends have too much influence over me."

"You mean Genevieve," I said flatly.

Emma nodded. "Yes, but Ingrid too. I've just known them for so long that sometimes they feel like an extension of me. If they're angry at someone, I get angry too. Even when I have no reason to be. It's like a hive mentality, and I just let myself get swept along in it." She looked at me. "I'm not making excuses. I know it's not a great trait. But I am sorry."

I nodded, accepting her apology. It didn't really change anything. It's not like I could ever trust her, or any of them, ever again.

"But that's not the only reason why I came here today," Emma said. "Although I did owe you an apology, there's something else I wanted to talk to you about."

Something in her tone made me brace for whatever it was she planned to say.

"What's that?" I asked cautiously.

"I know the police believe Alex has knowledge about what happened to Callie on the night she died. And that they spoke to her yesterday."

"How do you know that?" I asked sharply.

Emma shook her head. "It doesn't matter how I know. I just do. And I came here today to ask you, as a friend, to urge Alex to do the right thing. If she knows what happened to Callie, she needs to tell the police. Ingrid is devastated. She deserves to bury her daughter with the peace of knowing what happened that night."

I blinked. "You came to me as a friend?" I repeated.

Emma nodded and reached out to place her hand on mine. "I am your friend, Kate. I hope you believe that."

I couldn't quite believe what I was hearing. Emma's daughter and her friends had bullied Alex. Emma and her friends had bullied me. It was one thing to accept her belated apology. It was an entirely different matter to agree to expose my daughter to possible harm for their benefit. I pulled my hand free.

"Alex doesn't have any information that would help the police investigation," I said.

"If she knows something, anything at all, she should come forward. And not only for Ingrid's sake. But for Alex's sake too. It can't be good for her to bottle this up. She'll feel better once she comes clean."

I drained the last of the wine from my glass, set it down, and stared at Emma, who was looking so earnest, I could almost believe that her motives were pure. That she really did have Alex's best interests at heart.

Except that I knew it was absolute bullshit.

I stood abruptly, and Emma looked up at me, blinking with surprise.

"There's somewhere I have to be," I said.

"Oh. Okay." Emma stood too. She looked uncertain. "Please pass on to Alex what I said."

"No." I shook my head decisively. "I won't. I already told you Alex doesn't have any information. In fact, when the police questioned her, she told them they should speak to Daphne and Shae. She thought they might know something about what happened to Callie."

Emma's face hardened. "Shae would have told me if she knew anything. And, unlike Alex, Shae was home that night."

"Then I guess neither one of our girls has any useful information," I said.

I stood and waited while Emma picked up her handbag. She gave me one last searching look and then turned and walked to the front door. I followed behind her.

Emma glanced back at me. "Think about what I said. The best thing for everyone would be for the truth to come out now, before things get ugly."

CHAPTER THIRTY-SEVEN

Kate

Three days after Callie's body was found, the police returned.

It was Monday morning. Alex had gone to school. I was home, cleaning out the refrigerator. We'd only moved in a few months earlier, and we were already awash in expired dairy products. I pulled everything off the glass shelves and put on yellow rubber gloves to scrub them clean. I knew it was busywork, but I couldn't settle my mind to do anything more productive. It was swirling with thoughts of Callie and Alex and the police investigation. It was almost a relief when the doorbell rang at nine thirty.

Almost.

This time, the two detectives standing on my front porch both looked stern. I don't think the younger detective, Gavin Reddick, had cracked a smile during our first conversation. But now, his more genial partner, Mike Monroe, had dropped the pretense that they were just here for a friendly chat. The point was punctuated by the six additional uniformed police officers that accompanied them.

"We have a search warrant," Detective Monroe said, holding a paper out to me.

I was still wearing the yellow rubber gloves when I took the warrant from him. I sensed some movement to my left and looked over to see Lita standing on her paved driveway. She was staring open mouthed at the scene unfolding at my house—the squad cars parked in the driveway, the officers spilling down the front walkway. Lita lifted her phone and snapped a picture of the chaos. I looked down at the warrant. The words on the paper swam in front of me.

"Please step aside, ma'am," Detective Reddick said. And then he and the other policemen walked right into my house without waiting for an invitation.

I called Joe immediately and explained what was happening, my voice choked with tears.

"I don't know if you've had a chance to look, but you said you'd try to find a referral for a criminal defense attorney. I called several over the past few days, just names I found online, but no one's gotten back to me yet. Probably because it was the weekend and their offices were closed. But now I need to find one immediately."

"I'll take care of it," he promised. "And I'll be there as soon as I can."

The police were everywhere, searching through drawers, cabinets, closets. I didn't know where to stand. I moved restlessly from the living room to the kitchen to the home office, and everywhere I went, there they were, invading my privacy and the privacy of my daughter. They bagged and took away seemingly random items. A bottle of strawberry-scented body lotion. A stack of notebooks taken from Alex's desk. My laptop. Things that couldn't possibly be related to whatever case they were making. And I couldn't do anything to stop them.

They even took my phone.

"Why do you need my phone?" I asked, clutching it to my chest when the young sheriff's officer asked for it. It was my lifeline to the outer world. I didn't even know anyone's phone number by heart anymore. They were all stored on my phone.

"All mobile phones belonging to members of the household are included in the warrant," he said.

I reluctantly handed it to him. He dropped the phone into a plastic evidence bag.

Joe showed up forty-five minutes later. We sat side by side on the sofa.

"I called an attorney I know. Scott Jones. Our kids were on the same soccer team in middle school. I don't know how good he is, but he said he'd come straight over and help out. He should be here shortly."

"Thank you so much," I said. "I've never even seen a search warrant before. I have no idea what I'm looking at."

"This must all be overwhelming." Joe took in the sight of the police officers tramping through my house, going through our things, invading our privacy, all in order to find evidence to prove my daughter committed a crime.

"That's an understatement," I said. I was determined not to cry in front of the police, but it wasn't easy. Fear pulsed through me. My breath was shallow, and my pulse was skittering. I looked at Joe, grateful for his presence. "I'm not taking you away from urgent restaurant business, am I?"

"No. And even if you were, I'd still be here." Joe squeezed my hand.

I smiled weakly. "Thank you."

Twenty minutes later, a man in his forties with a square chin and graying hair that was overdue for a cut walked in through the open front door. He was wearing a sports jacket and button-down shirt that was open at the throat. He stood in the front hall and looked around, as if he'd somehow wandered into the wrong house.

"Scott, over here. Thanks for coming over." Joe stood up to shake the man's hand.

"Joe, hi. I would have knocked, but the door was wide open."

"This is Kate Turner. Kate, Scott Jones is the attorney I told you about."

"Kate, it's nice to meet you." Scott smiled. It struck me that this was just normal business to him and to the police, while my world felt like it had been tipped upside down and shaken like a snow globe.

"I wish I could say the same," I said faintly.

"Don't worry, we'll get through it. But I have to say, they are putting on quite the show." Scott whistled. "Especially considering, as I understand it, that they haven't even established a crime has been committed."

I hadn't thought of that and felt the first glimmer of hope. If the police couldn't prove Callie's death had been a crime, it wouldn't matter what they took from the house. They wouldn't be able to charge Alex with anything.

I glanced around, wondering where my checkbook was. Had the police taken that off in a plastic bag too? Nothing would surprise me at this point.

"I have to pay you," I said.

"Don't worry, we can figure that out once things here settle down. Where's the warrant?" Scott took it and scanned through it. "It looks legit, although it's a little broad."

"They took my phone," I said. "Can they really do that?"

"Unfortunately, yes, they can. But they should be able to extract the data and get it back to you quickly. I'll see if they can expedite that," Scott said. "Where's your daughter? It looks like they want her phone and computers too."

"She's at school," I said.

"No, she's not." Gavin Reddick stood in the hallway, staring in at us. He seemed predatory, always looking for a vulnerability he could exploit. "We sent an officer over to the high school. Alex wasn't there."

"What are you talking about?" I asked. "I dropped her off this morning."

"Your daughter didn't show up to school today. The attendance office has her marked as an unexcused absence. Do you have any idea where she might be?"

"You don't have to answer that," Scott said to me at the same time as I said, "I have no idea where she is."

"We'd like to speak to her as soon as you find her," Detective Reddick said.

Scott Jones raised his hand, signaling that he would handle this question. "My client will not be answering questions at this time."

"Who's your client, her or her daughter?" Detective Reddick asked, jerking his chin toward me.

"They're both my clients," Scott said staunchly.

"Why do you want to talk to Alex?" I asked.

"She told us to speak to Daphne Hudson and Shae Thacker about where they were on Thursday night," Detective Reddick said. "I asked them. They each told me they were home, and their parents confirmed that."

"Okay," I said. "That doesn't answer my question, though."

"There's only one teenager, other than Callie Nord, whose presence was unaccounted for that night," the detective said. "And that's your daughter."

"Kate." Scott's tone was firm. "No more questions."

This time, I took my attorney's advice.

CHAPTER THIRTY-EIGHT

Kate

After the police left with our belongings in tagged plastic bags, and Joe left to do the predinner prep at his restaurant, and Scott left for wherever he went to when he wasn't in my living room, I surveyed the mess the police had left behind. They had not been neat when they picked apart our lives. It was like unpacking all over again, but this time with all my files scattered across the floor and our clothes spilling out of drawers.

I called Alex's school on the house phone. The attendance office confirmed that Alex had been marked absent all day. Apparently, in these digital days, attendance was taken in every class and sent electronically to the office so that they could monitor the students who ditched school midday. I tried calling Alex directly; it kept going straight to her voice mail.

I wasn't sure whether I should wait for Alex at home or go to the school car line to see whether she would be there, waiting for a ride. Ever since her tennis team practices had been canceled, I'd been picking her up directly after school. She hadn't driven since the day of the accident, and she refused to ride the bus. I'd been so eager to make the transition to Florida easy for her, I'd given in.

I was suddenly angry. Very angry. A white-hot fury pressed on my chest and caused my vision to swim. How dare she disappear again? And today of all days?

All I had ever wanted was to keep my daughter safe. And her response was to hide what happened the night Callie died from me. To give the police information they were already using against her. And now she'd skipped school just when the spotlight on her was at its brightest.

I knew teenagers made mistakes. They drank too much at parties or dated the wrong person. But the mistakes Alex was making were the kind that could ruin her life. Not just in the short term, but every day she had left on earth.

I picked up my car keys and headed out the door.

The school car line was always an ordeal. Dozens and dozens of cars snaked around the poorly laid out parking lot as parents waited to pick up their teenagers. The kids were almost never paying attention to which car had pulled up to the pickup point or were dillydallying inside instead of heading straight out after the last bell. The parents waited endlessly, growing increasingly irritated at how long it all took. I tapped my fingers against the wheel.

Suddenly, the SUV in front of mine stopped abruptly, and the driver's door was flung open. It was only when Genevieve stepped out of her vehicle that I realized I'd been behind her enormous white Cadillac Escalade ever since joining the car line. I'd been so distracted, I hadn't noticed. She strode toward my car, dressed in head-to-toe lavender Lululemon yoga wear. It was clear from her narrowed eyes and pinched lips that she wasn't coming to apologize for her last ugly outburst. I looked around wildly, wondering whether I could get out of the car line, but I was boxed in.

Unbelievable, I thought, stunned at her arrogance. I was pretty sure that she was the reason the police had ripped apart my house that morning, that she was the one who had told them to focus on Alex. And now she had the nerve to confront me in the car line?

Genevieve rapped on my window. I reluctantly rolled it down and then instantly wished I hadn't. Genevieve gripped the car door with both hands and bent forward, so that her angry face was just inches away from mine. She was so close I could smell the mint of mouthwash on her breath.

"Genevieve, this is not the time or the place," I said, leaning back away from her. "A young girl has died."

"I'm well aware of that. And I also know who the main suspect is. If you think your daughter is going to get away with what she's done, you are sorely mistaken. I've known Callie since the day she was born. I will do everything in my power to make sure she has justice."

"That's enough. Please move away from my car." It was disconcerting to have her so close.

"Oh, no. You are going to listen to me," she snapped back. "First, your daughter sent those disgusting texts to Daphne calling her a slut and a whore. Then she sent out that video of Daphne being sexually assaulted to everyone in the school."

"You have absolutely no proof that she did any of that," I pointed out.

But Genevieve didn't seem to hear me. "And now, after all of the damage she's caused, she went and told the police that they should focus their investigation on Daphne and Shae? Two innocent girls who just lost their best friend? I'm telling you right now, she will not get away with this. Richard and I intend to sue for defamation, harassment, and anything else our attorney can make stick."

Anger coursed through me again, hot and bitter. I had no idea what had prompted Genevieve's vendetta against Alex, but now she was blaming my daughter for things she obviously didn't do. And I'd had enough.

"Do not threaten my daughter," I warned her. "Or I will make you sorry you did."

"You still don't get it, do you? You are no one in this town. Your daughter is no one. You don't get to come in here and ruin other people's lives. She's going to have to pay. You both will."

"At least I'm not the world's shittiest mother." The words just popped out of my mouth, but I wasn't sorry. Genevieve was threatening Alex, confronting me. She deserved whatever I said to her.

"What did you say to me?"

"You wanted your daughter to become a bully. Congratulations. Mission accomplished. She's a monster. I hope you're proud."

Genevieve's face twisted, her fury reflecting mine. She leaned in even closer.

"You're calling my daughter a monster? After what your daughter did? I know the police were at your house today. They think she killed Callie. They're going to lock her up and never let her out!"

I hit the close-window button on my car door. As the window rose up with an electric whir, it forced Genevieve to take a step back. She said something else, but I couldn't hear through the glass. I ignored her, staring at a fixed point in front of me, until she finally gave up and returned to her Escalade. I wondered what the other parents thought about the commotion. Or maybe they already knew what was going on. If Genevieve had heard the police executed a search warrant at my house today, I had to imagine the story had spread all the way through this poisonous town.

We can't stay here, I thought. Then I realized that leaving might no longer be our choice. Not if the police arrested Alex.

When I finally reached the pickup spot and pulled in, Alex was standing by the curb, waiting for me. She had her backpack slung over one shoulder and looked coolly detached from the throngs of teenagers around her. She opened the door and climbed into the car.

"Hey," she said.

I didn't speak. I was so overwhelmed by the chaos of the day, it was taking all of my concentration to drive the car. I tried to focus on not hitting anything as I steered toward the exit from the school campus.

"Why are you being weird?" Alex asked.

My teeth were clenched so tightly, my jaw hurt. "I'd like to know where you were today. I know it wasn't at school."

"Oh." Alex shifted in her seat. "It's not a big deal. I'm a senior. It's not like this year counts."

"Actually, it is a big deal. The police were back at the house today," I said.

"So?"

My hands tightened on the steering wheel. Alex didn't seem to have any concept of how much danger she was in. She was the suspect in a possible homicide. It didn't get more serious than this.

"They were there to execute a search warrant," I said. "They spent all day at our house, searching through our things and taking away potential evidence. I've had to hire a criminal defense attorney."

That finally got Alex's attention. "Wait, *what*? Why were they searching our house?"

"They were too busy to stop and discuss the details of their case with me. But they clearly think you know something about what happened to Callie on the night she died. They're probably going to come back tonight and take your phone. And your tablet and school laptop. They were listed on the warrant."

"There's no way they're taking my phone! And how am I supposed to do my homework without my laptop?"

"We have bigger problems than homework to deal with at the moment."

We drove the rest of the way home in silence. When I turned on to our street, a placid block of stucco homes painted in pastel shades, I could see there was a sheriff's cruiser parked on the road outside our house. Detective Gavin Reddick was standing beside it, clearly waiting for us to return.

"Shit." I turned toward Alex. "Don't say a word to him. Do you understand? You don't talk to the police about anything without our attorney present."

Alex nodded. "Okay."

I pulled into our driveway, and we got out of the car. Detective Reddick was already walking up to us.

"Mrs. Turner. Alex." He nodded at us, his dark eyes serious. "Alex, I have a warrant for any personal electronic devices you have, such as a cell phone, tablet, or computer. Your mother and her attorney saw the warrant earlier."

Alex handed him her cell phone and then set down her backpack so she could pull out her tablet and school laptop.

"When will I get those back?" she asked.

"That depends on how cooperative you are. The faster we're able to close our investigation, the sooner you get them back," Detective Reddick said. "If you answer our questions truthfully, that will certainly speed things up."

Truthfully. The word sent a shiver through me. I knew he was doing his job and that it wasn't personal. But in that moment, I hated Detective Gavin Reddick more than I had ever hated anyone in my life.

"Alex, go inside," I said. For once, my daughter did as instructed. I turned back to the detective. "You do not have my permission to talk to my daughter when her attorney and I aren't both present."

"Sure that's the way you want to go?" Detective Reddick asked. "Because usually people who have nothing to hide are happy to help out the police."

"Goodbye, Detective." I turned and headed up the walkway toward my house.

Detective Reddick called out to me. "People always think they can hide what they've done. But the truth comes out eventually."

I went inside and shut the door firmly behind me.

CHAPTER THIRTY-NINE

KATE

Alex was waiting for me in the kitchen. She was leaning against the counter, her arms crossed in front of her. Her eyes were large, and she looked spooked.

It was almost a relief that she finally seemed aware of the danger she was in.

"Why weren't you in school today?" I asked.

Alex hesitated, twisting the end of her braid around her fingers. "I was in the courtyard, waiting for class to start, and everyone was staring at me. And whispering. I know that sounds paranoid, but they really were. They were looking at me like I was a bomb that was about to go off. And I just had to get away from everyone. So I left. I walked out the front doors and just kept walking."

And, somehow, despite my anger that she had disappeared once again, this time I at least understood why. The stress of the last few days had been unbearable. I would love to be able to walk away from it for a few hours. Of course this had all been overwhelming for Alex too. She'd just been hiding it better than I had.

"Where did you go?" I asked.

"Nowhere really. I sat in a Starbucks for a while. How did you find out? Did the school call you?"

"The police told me. I think they went there looking for you."

Alex stared at me, her eyes wide with fright. "I hate this place," she said quietly. "I wish we'd never moved here."

"I know. It didn't work out the way I'd hoped."

Alex nodded, and for a moment, I thought we were connecting again. That we could somehow go back to before the awful day of the car accident that killed her father and find the relationship we used to have. But then, her eyes shuttered, and she looked away.

"I'm going to go to my room," she said.

"Wait. What do you want to do about school?"

"What about it?"

"Do you want to transfer? Maybe to another one of the public high schools, or maybe we could look at private school options."

"Changing schools isn't going to fix this," she said flatly.

"It could give you a fresh start," I said, and then immediately regretted my choice of words. I'd told her repeatedly that moving to Shoreham was our fresh start, and look how that had turned out.

"Even if I transfer, the story is going to follow me. I'm not ever going to be able to escape from this."

"You can't just skip school. Maybe we should talk to your guidance counselor and see if you can switch to the virtual school?"

"Maybe. I doubt they'll let me in the middle of the semester. Anyway, I need a laptop to do that."

I was about to offer up mine, and then I remembered that the police had taken both my laptop and my iPad. They'd come in and upended our lives, and on what basis?

Because Alex had been gone that night, I reminded myself. That's why. She was gone for hours, and no one knew where she had been. And until she came up with a more plausible explanation for why she was gone and where she'd been, she was going to remain under suspicion.

"Why don't you plan on staying home tomorrow. We'll figure it out from there." I glanced around the mess in the kitchen. "I don't think

I'm going to be able to cook in here tonight. Let's order a pizza. What toppings do you want?"

Alex shook her head. "Get whatever you want. I'm not hungry."

The next morning, I stood in line at the bagel shop, waiting to pick up breakfast. It was early, but the store was already buzzing, crowded with commuters stopping to pick up breakfast on their way to work. While I waited, I grabbed a copy of the local newspaper since I couldn't read it online. The headline was again about Callie's death:

> IN WAKE OF TEENAGER'S DEATH, PARENTS FEAR KILLER COULD STRIKE AGAIN
>
> The body of Callie Nord, 17, was found at Isle Beach early on the morning of October 14. Calusa County Sheriff Alan Miller issued a statement that his office is treating the case as a potential homicide while they wait for the determination on cause of death from the medical examiner. The sheriff's office has not named anyone as a person of interest in connection to the case. But this has not allayed the fears of local parents.
>
> "Everyone knows who was involved," said one mother of a student at Shoreham High School, who asked to remain anonymous. "It's common knowledge the girl in question is troubled. She was involved in another death before she moved here. We're all terrified she'll target another one of our children before the police take action."

Shoreham High School has elected to cancel the homecoming dance planned for this Saturday.

"It didn't seem right to have a party while we're mourning one of our own," Principal Thelma Hopkins said.

The Shoreham High School homecoming football game against the Calusa County Knights will go ahead as scheduled on Friday night.

The quote had been attributed to an anonymous mother, but I could practically hear the words in Genevieve's voice. Of course it was her.

"That horrible woman," I muttered.

I glanced up, overwhelmed by the creepy feeling that someone was watching me. It was the young man at the cash register who was taking orders. His eyes widened, and he quickly looked away. Had he heard what I'd said? I glanced to my right and saw that a young couple with a baby in a stroller were also watching me avidly, the woman whispering in the man's ear.

I must be imagining this, I thought. These people can't possibly know who I am.

And yet when I reached the front of the line and it was my turn to place an order, the young man at the register wouldn't meet my eyes while he rang up my order.

"Could I have a dozen everything bagels and a one-pound container of cinnamon-raisin cream cheese?" I asked in a forced cheery tone.

"Sure." The cashier nervously grabbed a paper bag and then turned away to fill it with bagels.

I turned and saw a group of teenage girls, younger than Alex, get into line behind me. I smiled at them, but they were too busy chatting to one another to notice me. The bagel shop was just down the street from Shoreham High, and I assumed that the girls were students there.

"Ma'am, your order's ready," the cashier said.

I had paid for the bagels and was just leaving when I heard one of the girls say in a loud stage whisper, "I think that's that girl's mother."

"What girl?" her friend asked.

"You know. The one who . . ." She turned to look at me, and we locked gazes. She had long curly hair that had been dyed pink on the ends. Her eyes opened wide, startled at my attention. She quickly turned and whispered in a softer voice to her friends, who all immediately turned to look at me. "Stop, stop," the pink-haired girl hissed. "She'll see you."

I pushed open the door, which caused the bell hanging on it to ring cheerily.

I had no idea how any of those people recognized me. From social media? I wondered. I didn't spend much time on it, but I had posted pictures of Alex and me over the years.

Poor Alex, I thought. If this was anything like what she'd gone through at school, I didn't blame her for walking out of school and not going back.

This was followed by an even darker thought—if Alex was charged, how could she possibly get a fair trial in this town, where everyone had already decided that she was guilty?

CHAPTER FORTY

KATE

Alex was still in bed when I got home with the bagels. I went up to her room, stepping over the clothes and books that covered her floor, and opened the blinds. The room was instantly flooded with sunshine. Alex groaned in protest and pulled her duvet up over her head.

"I got bagels," I announced.

"What kind?" she asked, her voice muffled.

"Everything. And cinnamon-raisin cream cheese."

Alex threw off the duvet and peered up at me. "Fine, I'll have a bagel."

"As long as you're not going to school, I'd like you to help me clean this place up."

Alex sighed loudly but didn't protest.

After breakfast, Alex and I began clearing up the mess the police had made the day before. I organized the papers scattered across the floor of my home office, while Alex tackled the kitchen.

"Why did they take all of the food out of the pantry?" she asked, staring into the cupboard. "What did they think they'd find there?"

"I don't know." I had no idea whether the police really thought we were hiding evidence behind boxes of dried pasta and cans of tomatoes or whether this was all a stunt designed to put psychological pressure on Alex to confess. After all, if they had any evidence linking her to Callie's death, they would have arrested her.

I had just finished restoring the contents of my desk drawers when the house phone rang.

"Kate, it's Scott," the attorney said when I picked up. "The police want to formally interview Alex at the sheriff's office. I just got off the phone with them."

"No," I said reflexively. "You said not to let her talk to them."

"I know I did, but I think we need to look at this strategically. If Alex is viewed as not cooperating, that could be bad for her down the road. From a public relations perspective."

"Wait . . . are you talking about preparing for her to go on trial?"

"Not necessarily. But it would be good to have public opinion on our side. If she cooperates, it would take away oxygen from the perception that she was involved in a potential crime."

"I don't care about public opinion. I care about protecting my daughter."

"This is how we protect her," Scott said. "We don't want her to be turned into a pariah. She still has to live here, go to school here."

I thought about Alex walking out of the school the day before after everyone had been looking at her, whispering rumors to one another about her involvement in Callie's death. I hadn't even told Alex about the girls at the bagel shop. It was the last thing she needed to hear.

"Do we have a choice?" I asked.

"Yes, of course. Alex doesn't have to agree to the interview. But, like I said, I think as long as we prepare her ahead of time, it's better for her to cooperate. Once the police stop viewing Alex as a possible suspect, she can get on with her life. Get back to normal. And I'll be there, so I can always stop the interview if I think it's getting out of hand."

I had no idea whether his advice was sound. It was entirely possible that Scott might even have competing priorities. If Alex were to be prosecuted, the case would almost certainly get a lot of media attention and would generate publicity for her attorney. But what if he was right?

What if cooperating with the investigation was the most expedient way to clear Alex?

"I would feel better about this decision if I knew what Alex was actually going to say," I told him. "So far she still hasn't given a clear accounting of what she was doing that night."

"That's the main concern," Scott conceded. "Why don't I stop by this morning and talk to her? I'll assess what she has to say and what, if anything, we should share with the police."

"Okay," I reluctantly agreed.

Scott sat with Alex in the kitchen, going over her movements on the night Callie died. Alex had come up with a few more details. She believed she might have been near the beach at one point, because she could smell the salt air, but she couldn't tell for sure what time that was or which beach. It had been dark, and she'd been lost. She'd biked by a bar that had been playing loud country-and-western music. She'd passed a man out walking his dog. Alex couldn't remember what the man looked like, but she thought the dog had been a black-and-white Australian shepherd. Mostly, she had biked aimlessly around. She had been trying to clear her head, she explained, trying to process everything that had happened. The bullying she'd endured, Coach being arrested. Even her father's death.

"Should she bring up the bullying?" I asked. The police already knew about it, but I didn't think it was a great idea to highlight it. It didn't just give Alex a motive; it was practically a red arrow lit up and pointing at her.

"Yes," Scott said. "Absolutely. It will give her a chance to tell our side of the story. How the other girls were the aggressors and Alex was the innocent victim." Scott looked at Alex. "Just remember, the police are under no obligation to tell you the truth. They can, and will, lie about aspects of their investigation."

"Why would they do that?" Alex asked.

"To frighten you. To get you to tell them things you otherwise wouldn't say. Misinformation is an interrogation tool they use."

Alex nodded and nervously played with the end of her long braid. "Anything else?"

"Whatever they do or say, you have to remember, the police are not your friends. They're not there to help you, or protect you, or whatever else *Sesame Street* told you when you were a kid."

"So, what? The police don't care about the truth?" Alex asked.

Scott shook his head. "For our purposes, assume they're there to make a case against you. And to put you in prison for the rest of your life. Our goal is to persuade them you had nothing to do with Callie Nord's death. Got it? Good. Let's go over the timeline again."

I discovered that I had a low tolerance for listening to Alex repeat her story over and over until Scott was satisfied that the police wouldn't be able to trip her up. I left them to it and went outside to water the flowers I was growing in terra-cotta pots on the patio, until Scott announced that it was time to go.

CHAPTER FORTY-ONE

Kate

We were shown into an interview room, where we waited for the detectives to join us. The air-conditioning was set low, and it was far too cold for the lightweight jersey I'd worn. The room was small and windowless and just large enough to contain a long table surrounded by industrial molded plastic chairs. I'd expected a one-way mirror on the wall, like they have in detective shows, but there wasn't one. Then I noticed the red light of a camera mounted in the corner of the room. We were being watched electronically.

We sat there for a long time. Scott checked his emails and phone messages, but Alex and I didn't have our phones, which made the wait seem even longer.

"What's taking so long?" Alex muttered.

"It's another interrogation technique," Scott said. "They keep you waiting to make you nervous."

"Are they going to give back my phone and tablet?" Alex asked. "The laptop they took isn't even mine. It belongs to the school."

"I don't know," I said. I was also hoping to get my electronics back. If they weren't returned soon, I was going to have to buy backup phones for both of us and a computer for Alex to do her schoolwork on.

The door finally opened, and Detectives Monroe and Reddick entered. They were each holding a paper coffee cup.

"Can I get anyone anything to drink?" Detective Monroe asked cheerfully.

Scott had already advised against accepting beverages from the detectives. "They most likely have samples of your DNA from items they took from the house when they executed the search warrant. But just in case they didn't, let's not give them a chance to collect it off a disposable coffee cup," he'd instructed us on the car ride over.

"Why would they want our DNA?" I'd asked, but Scott hadn't explained. I wondered if it was just something he'd seen on a television police procedural drama.

Even so, Alex and I both declined the offer, so the detectives sat across the table from us. Detective Reddick was carrying a folder of papers, and he set it on the table in front of him.

"We have a few more questions for you, Alex. A few issues we're hoping to clear up," Detective Monroe said.

Alex nodded. She'd straightened in her seat when the policemen entered and was now sitting very still, her hands folded on the table in front of her.

"Why did you wipe all of the data off of your tablet and phone?" Detective Reddick asked.

I almost gasped but managed to stop myself. Scott had also instructed us not to react to any of their questions. Alex was supposed to give short, precise answers. And I was to stay quiet.

"It makes my tablet run faster if I periodically free up some memory," Alex said.

"It was wiped clean. There wasn't anything left on it. And your phone was reset to its factory settings," Reddick said.

"It's my phone. I don't have to keep data on it if I don't want to," Alex said.

I looked at my daughter. Why had she wiped her electronics? And when? She hadn't known about the search warrant until I told her in the car. The detective had taken her phone, laptop, and tablet right when we got home that day, before she would have had a chance to erase anything.

Which meant she must have wiped her electronics before she knew about the search warrant.

I remembered what Scott had said about the police being allowed to lie when they questioned a suspect. But I didn't think Detective Reddick was lying. And Alex hadn't denied that she'd wiped the data off her electronic devices. My pulse began to thrum.

"What were you trying to get rid of?" Detective Monroe asked. "Our tech guys are pretty good at finding what people think they've deleted, so we'll find it anyway. But you can save everyone some time and tell us what you were trying to erase."

Scott swiftly stepped in. "It's not a crime to reset your electronic devices."

"It is if she did it to destroy evidence," Reddick countered.

"My client denies any accusations that she knowingly destroyed evidence," Scott said crisply. "Do you have any other questions?"

Reddick ignored the lawyer, not taking his dark, probing eyes off Alex. "We have a witness who saw you entering the Isle Beach boardwalk on the night of October thirteenth at approximately eleven thirty p.m."

"Where is Isle Beach?" I asked, before remembering I wasn't supposed to speak. It sounded familiar, but I couldn't remember where I'd heard it before.

"It's on the island. It's the first public beach after you pass the Mariner Resort," Detective Monroe explained. Then, just as I was trying to remember where that was, he added, "It's where Callie Nord's body was found."

A cold dread spread through me. A witness could place Alex at the site of the possible crime scene? If so, then this interview had been a horrible mistake. Cooperating wasn't going to clear Alex. The police were actively building a case against her.

Scott seemed to realize this too.

"What witness?" he asked. "If you have a statement, I want to see it."

"You said that you weren't at the beach that night," Reddick continued, still speaking to Alex. "Do you want to revise your statement?"

Alex shook her head mutely.

"You want to explain why a witness saw you entering a beach that was a potential murder scene at the time the murder took place?" Reddick pressed.

Alex looked at Scott. "Don't answer that," he said.

"Why don't we go over your movements on the night of October thirteenth again, Alex," Detective Monroe suggested. "When you left from home that night, where did you go first?"

The police did not arrest Alex. After they'd interrogated her for two hours, their questions growing increasingly hostile, Scott finally ended the interview, and we left.

"That went well, I think," Scott said brightly as he drove us home.

"How can you say that?" I turned to look at him. "Alex is clearly the focus of their investigation. Nothing that happened today changed that. In fact, I think it made it worse."

"Alex didn't give them any information they don't already have," Scott said.

That was possibly true. But we had been given new information. The wiped electronics. The potential witness that saw Alex at the same beach where Callie was killed. And we already knew Alex didn't have an alibi for that night.

"I don't want her questioned again," I said.

"That's probably a good idea," Scott conceded.

The police had not yet given us back our computers and phones. The first thing I planned to do once I had access to the internet was to search for a more competent criminal defense attorney. Scott was charming and affable and, I was starting to realize, possibly not very bright. Alex needed an attorney who was as cunning as the detectives, who would be able to anticipate their next move, and who would keep her out of harm's way.

Unless it was already too late for that.

—

Scott dropped us off at our house and, thankfully, drove off without coming in. I saw Lita on her patio, watching us beadily while she pretended to be watering her container plants. I opened the front door for Alex and quickly followed her inside.

As soon as we were inside, Alex started to head toward the stairs before I'd even had a chance to put down my handbag and drop the keys in a round ceramic midcentury dish by the front door.

"Not a chance," I said.

Alex turned around. "What?"

"We need to talk. Now." I pointed toward the living room. Alex reluctantly obeyed. We sat across from one another, Alex on the couch, me on a chair. Alex looked tired. She was pale, and there were dark circles under her eyes. "I don't know if you noticed, but that didn't go well today."

"Scott said he thought it did," Alex said.

"I'm pretty sure that Scott's an idiot. He should never have allowed you to talk to the police. Not without knowing what they knew."

"I can't believe they think I was involved," Alex said, nudging the tip of her running shoe against the carpet.

"That's just it. Those detectives don't know you. They don't care about you. They can place you at the scene of the crime. You wiped out all of the data on your electronic devices. The only reason they haven't arrested you yet is because they're still waiting on the medical examiner's report."

I realized my voice was raising with each word. Alex was staring at me, her eyes wide and startled. I forced myself to lower my voice. "Alex, if that report concludes that Callie's death was a homicide and not an accidental death, they're probably going to arrest you. Do you understand that?"

"I didn't kill Callie!" Alex protested.

"I know you didn't!"

"Then why are you so mad at me?"

"I'm not angry. I'm scared," I said quietly.

This admission got Alex's attention more than my raising my voice had. She nodded and said, "I'm scared too."

"I know." I inhaled deeply. "Why did you wipe everything off of your electronics? That looks bad. Really bad. It looks like you're hiding something."

Alex stared at the patterned carpet, as if it held the answer to my questions.

"Why haven't the detectives interviewed Daphne and Shae?" Alex asked.

"I don't know if they spoke to the girls or not, but Detective Reddick said they both have alibis. Their parents said that both girls were home that night."

"They're lying," Alex said.

"How do you know that?" I asked.

"I just do. Isn't that enough?"

"No," I said, shaking my head. "It's not enough. If you know something, you need to tell me. Now."

Alex stared at me with a level gaze. "What if I can prove Daphne and Shae were there at the beach that night?"

"They were at the beach? How can you prove that?"

"I just can. But it might get me in trouble."

"What trouble is worse than being arrested and tried for murder?" I exclaimed. "Tell me what you know, and we'll go from there."

Alex shook her head. "I can't tell you. I have to show you."

She stood and headed upstairs. A moment later, she rushed back down.

"Here," she said. She was holding out something in her hand.

"What's that?"

"It's proof that I didn't kill Callie."

CHAPTER FORTY-TWO

KATE

The object Alex handed me was a USB flash drive. It was small and silver, and it had a ringed hoop so you could keep it on a key chain. I wasn't the most tech-savvy person, but I knew that it basically functioned as something you store data on. Files, pictures, videos.

"What's on this?" I asked.

"My video diary. All of it. It's the only copy I have. I deleted it everywhere else."

"I didn't know you kept a diary. When did you start doing that?"

"Just before we moved here. It's supposed to be private. That's actually the whole point. Beatrice thought that it might help me work through stuff."

I nodded. I'd liked Beatrice, Alex's therapist back in Buffalo. She was young, probably no older than thirty, and had been both intuitive and kind. I was glad Alex had had her to talk to during the tough months after Ed's death.

"I don't know what a video diary is exactly. Is it just you talking to a camera?" I asked.

"Mostly, but I also started videoing things," Alex said. "I don't know why. It just became kind of a weird habit. I'd take a video of a cute dog I'd see while I was out running or someone doing something funny at school. I just got in the habit of keeping my phone out, ready to go."

And then I knew. I could even picture it. Daphne and the coach having sex, Alex seeing them from the doorway and pulling out her phone. Her capturing the intimate and yet very illegal encounter on video.

I closed my eyes, inhaled deeply, and then looked at my daughter and said, "The video of Coach and Daphne? You took that, didn't you?"

Alex caved forward, her slight shoulders drooping and her face a sickly white. She nodded her head once. "I didn't mean to," she whispered. "I don't know why I did. I hadn't planned on it."

"Of course you didn't," I said automatically. But my mind was racing. I wondered whether the video was on the USB stick I was holding in my hands, and I suddenly felt as sick as Alex looked. Daphne was a minor, so taking a video of her having sex might be considered child pornography. Was that what Alex had meant when she said that it would get her in trouble? "How did the video get leaked?"

"I made a mistake. A bad one."

"Oh, no. Please tell me you didn't text it to everyone."

"No! God, I would never do that! But I gave it to Callie, and she was angry at Daphne for sleeping with the coach, so she sent it out to everyone."

"Wait. Callie's the one who texted the video to everyone at your school? Why would she do that? I thought she and Daphne were best friends," I said. But then I remembered the chill between Ingrid and Emma at the last homecoming dance committee meeting I'd attended. Emma had mentioned the girls were fighting. At the time, I assumed it was normal teen drama. But there was nothing normal about Daphne having a sexual relationship with their adult tennis coach, nor Callie texting out a sexually explicit video of the two of them together to their classmates.

"I think Callie was in love with Coach Townsend," Alex explained. "She didn't tell me that. It's just a guess. But I think I'm right."

My head was swimming. "Was Callie having a relationship with Coach Townsend too?"

"I don't think so," Alex said. "I think that's why she was so angry. Callie was in love with him, and Daphne knew. And that's why Daphne pursued him, or at least, that's what Callie thought. It was like the ultimate screw-you to Callie, you know?"

"Callie sent out the video in revenge?" I asked, my stomach curdling at the thought.

Alex nodded. "And the weird thing is she didn't even seem to care that Coach is going to jail. It's like she thought he deserved it. And not because he was having sex with a teenager. But because he'd chosen Daphne over her. Or, at least, that's my theory. Callie didn't exactly confide in me, and now . . ." Alex stopped and swallowed.

And now Callie was dead. And we would never truly know her motives.

"What else is on here?" I asked, waving the stick.

"You need to watch it and see for yourself," Alex said.

I flinched. I hadn't seen the video of Daphne and Coach Taylor, and I certainly didn't want to. "Why?"

"Oh, no!" Alex suddenly flushed red. "I don't mean the sex part."

"Oh, thank God."

"God, Mom!" Alex looked shocked.

"Well, I don't know what else is on here!"

"There's more. A lot more. Trust me."

"How am I supposed to watch it? We don't have a tablet or anything I can plug it into."

"You can watch it on the TV," Alex said. "There's a port on the side."

We both looked at the large flat-screen television. It had cost a fortune when we bought it years ago, but Ed had insisted that we get the most expensive model. He had said he needed a high-definition picture to watch and critique films of Alex's tennis matches.

"Do you know how to do that?" I asked.

"Yep." Alex took the USB stick over to the television and, after some fiddling, stepped back. "Where's the remote?"

I handed it to her. "How do you even have this? I thought the police took everything."

"It was in my backpack," Alex said. "And the detective didn't search it, he just asked for my electronics."

"A USB stick doesn't count as electronics?" I asked doubtfully.

"I don't know. Maybe technically it does," Alex admitted. "But I didn't want to give it to him. There's a lot of private stuff on here. And I thought they could figure out what really happened that night without it. I thought they'd talk to Daphne and Shae and, like you said, look at the doorbell cameras in their neighborhood or at the GPS data on their phones. I thought they could solve it without me. But I guess I don't have a choice now. They're going to have to see this."

"I guess you'd better show me what's on there," I said.

Alex picked up the remote and clicked a few times until she got to a screen where she could access the USB drive. She glanced at me. "Ready?"

I nodded. "Go ahead."

CHAPTER FORTY-THREE

VIDEO DIARY OF ALEX TURNER

OCTOBER 13

Alex stood at the end of the boardwalk that led to the beach. She looked serious and resolute. There was a strong wind blowing up off the water, and it riffled her hair. Behind her, a full bright moon hung low in the sky.

Let me just check and make sure this is set to record at night and that the flashlight is off. *Alex fumbled with her camera, causing her face to go off screen for a moment.*

Okay, it's all set. I think this is where Callie said she was meeting Daphne, but they're not here. Wait. *Alex turned and looked down the beach.* Is that a fire? *She turned back toward the camera.* Someone's having a bonfire just down the beach next to the lifeguard tower. I'm going to try to get a little closer to see if it's them. I don't think they'll be able to see me if I stay up in the dunes where the grass is tall.

Alex scrambled up the dunes behind the beach, and as she did, the camera pointed downward, filming a blurred shaky image of sand and vegetation. Alex suddenly appeared back on screen. She hunched down.

I hear voices. I think it's them.

She turned the camera to point it at the beach. The picture was focused on a small group gathered there. Alex zoomed in on the group. There were three teenage girls standing around a small bonfire drinking from red plastic cups, their faces lit by the fire and the reflection of the moon on the ocean.

Daphne Hudson. Shae Thacker. Callie Nord. All three girls wore long-sleeved T-shirts and cutoff denim shorts, and they all had their hair tied back in ponytails.

I have a clear picture, but I can't hear them. I think I'm going to need to get closer. But if I get too close, they'll see me. Maybe if I can climb up on the lifeguard tower.

Alex turned her camera toward a lifeguard tower a short distance from where the girls had built the bonfire. It was a large fiberglass structure on a steel base. It had a cabin with open windows on three sides.

Now the only question is, How do I get up there without them seeing me?

Alex waited. The sound of her breath, rapid and shallow, was picked up by the microphone.

"I'm going to do a handstand!" Shae yelled loudly.

Daphne and Callie both turned toward Shae, their backs to the lifeguard tower.

Okay, I'm going now.

The picture turned shaky and unfocused while Alex moved quickly toward the lifeguard tower and scaled the steel ladder on the side. Her breath was loud and jagged. The laughter of the three girls by the bonfire could be heard off camera. Alex's face appeared in the picture again, and then the camera focused back on the three girls. This time, the picture was closer, and the girls' voices could be heard clearly. Shae attempted—and failed—to complete a handstand.

"You're way too drunk to handstand," Daphne said.

"Seriously, Shae. You're going to fall into the fire," Callie said.

"It's the wind. It keeps blowing me over." Shae laughed and made another attempt at a handstand. This time she held it for a few seconds before falling over. Shae clambered back to her feet and held her hands triumphantly up over her head.

"I can handstand," she yelled.

"You are such a dork," Daphne said. "Do we have more vodka?"

"I think so." Shae bent down to rummage through a bag, from which she retrieved a glass liquor bottle. "You want some OJ too?"

"Nah, I'll just guzzle it straight, like our moms. Of course I want OJ."

"My mom doesn't guzzle vodka," Shae said.

"What do you think a martini is?" Callie asked.

"I don't know. What is it?" Shae replied.

"It's like straight vodka with a little vermouth in it," Daphne said. "I had one once. It was so gross. But I looked amazing holding the glass."

"That's what I love about you, D. You're so modest," Callie said sarcastically.

"I know, I'm awesome," Daphne said. "That's why you want to be just like me."

"Who said I want to be like you?" Callie asked. She folded her arms over her chest.

"You always copy me. I had a French-themed sweet sixteen party, and then you had a Parisian-themed party. I got a Louis Vuitton cross-body for Christmas, and then you asked for the identical one for your birthday. I decide to go into prelaw at UF, and suddenly you start talking about wanting to go to law school."

"You knew I wanted that cross-body when you asked your mom for it!" Callie said angrily. "And the French-themed party was my idea first. You stole that. Like you steal everything."

"Then why am I always first-court singles, and you're always second court?" Daphne asked.

"You're not always first court," Callie said. "Alex has first court now. And you didn't even fight her for it. You just quit."

"Whatever. I was done with the team," Daphne said. "And Seth was always all over me. I mean, it was getting pathetic. I thought we were just hooking up, and he thought we were, like, going to get married and have lots of babies. It was really kind of sad."

"Trust me, he did not want to marry you," Callie snapped. "You were just an easy lay for him. Convenient and disposable."

"Really? Then why was he always telling me he loved me?"

"It doesn't count if he only said it while he was fucking you."

"Did it ever occur to you that I was the one fucking him?"

"Why him?" Callie asked. She braced her hands on her waist, her elbows sharply angled. "You could have gone after any other guy. Why did you target Seth?"

"Because I wanted to," Daphne said. She stepped closer to Callie. "Because I could."

The two girls stared at one another, squaring off.

"Who blasted out the video of us? Was it that loser new girl?"

"No," Callie said. "It wasn't her."

"I know you wouldn't have done it," Daphne said. "You don't have the balls for it."

Callie took a step closer toward Daphne. "Then you don't know me as well as you think you do. Because it was me. I sent it to everyone you know, and they sent it to everyone they know, and now everyone's seen it."

The two girls stared at one another, their expressions lit by the flickering fire. Callie looked triumphant, Daphne coldly furious.

"Come on, you guys, I thought we were here to make up. Not just get into another fight," Shae said. "Who wants more vodka?"

Callie held out her cup. Shae poured more vodka and orange juice into it. Callie turned away from the other two girls and tipped her chin up to drink the vodka in one gulp, a long drink.

"Anyway, you did me a favor," Daphne said. She tossed her ponytail back.

"What do you mean?"

"I was getting tired of Seth. I mean, I think having him arrested was a little extreme, but at least I don't have to deal with him anymore. And my mom thinks I'm traumatized, so she's taking me to the Bahamas in a few weeks for a vacay. Really, I should be thanking you."

"I thought you'd be pissed off."

"Not even a little bit."

Shae looked uncertainly from Daphne to Callie. "I thought we were going to do something fun tonight?"

"Okay, let's do something fun." Daphne peeled off her T-shirt and discarded it on the sand near the bonfire. "Let's go for a swim."

"No way," Callie said. "It's too cold."

"It's, like, seventy-five degrees out," Daphne replied.

"I meant the water is too cold. I stuck my feet in when we got here. It's freezing."

"Are you chicken?" Daphne asked in a mocking tone.

"Are you seriously going to try that? Yeah, okay, I'm chicken," Callie said.

"Come on, Shae. I want to go for a swim," Daphne said.

Daphne and Shae stripped off their clothes, which they left in a pile by the fire. They ran naked toward the ocean, squealing as soon as the water lapped over their feet. Undaunted, they both dove into a wave. Callie stood on the beach watching Daphne and Shae while they bobbed in the water, shrieking to one another, their faces silvery in the moonlight.

"Come on, C!" Shae yelled. "The water isn't that cold!"

"Yeah, stop being such a lame ass," Daphne called.

Callie hesitated. Finally, she set down her cup and slowly and deliberately pulled her T-shirt off over her head and dropped it on the sand beside her. Once she was naked, she ran toward the ocean, where her friends were cavorting in the waves.

"Oh, shit," Alex said off camera, her voice soft. "This is a bad idea."

Callie dove into the surf and then broke back up through the surface, yelling, "It's freezing!"

All three girls bobbed in the water, moving constantly to stay warm. They chatted and laughed, although their words were lost in the wind and the thrum of the surf. Alex zoomed in the picture. The three girls appeared to be play fighting, splashing one another and dunking one another under the waves.

Suddenly, Daphne jumped up on Callie, her hands pressing down on Callie's shoulders. Callie disappeared under the water. Daphne struggled to keep a grip on Callie, who suddenly broke the surface of the water, coughing violently. Daphne lunged at her, and Callie flailed, trying to strike Daphne, although Daphne evaded her. Daphne looked at Shae, who had gone still while she watched. Daphne said something inaudible, and Shae moved toward her. Together, Shae and Daphne pushed Callie back down under the water.

They held her there as first seconds, then minutes ticked past. When they finally stepped back, Callie's body was floating facedown on the water.

CHAPTER FORTY-FOUR

KATE

The video ended. I stared at the blank screen, my hands cupped over my mouth in horror.

"They killed her," I gasped. "Daphne and Shae killed Callie. The two of them together."

I had wanted something bad to happen to those girls. I had wished for it. But the reality of it was more awful than I could have possibly imagined. I thought of how terrified Callie must have been in those final moments, and shame burned through me.

I glanced at Alex, who sat next to me on the sectional sofa. Tears were streaming down her face.

"What happened next?"

"I don't know. I left right after the video ended." Alex clutched the throw pillow she was holding closer to her chest. "I was afraid Daphne and Shae would see me if I stayed where I was. I climbed down off the lifeguard tower while they were dragging Callie's body up on shore. They didn't see me."

"Why didn't you call for help? The police, or an ambulance, or me?"

"I don't know," Alex said again. "I wasn't thinking. I panicked. I just wanted to get away from there, and . . ." She stopped, and a terrible sob ripped out of her. " I shouldn't have left. I should've stopped them. She'd be alive if I had."

I was already shaking my head. "You don't know that. You might not have been able to stop them in time. And if they knew you were there, they might have turned on you." The thought sent a chill through me. "They could have killed you too."

"I still should have tried to help." Alex drew her knees up, hugging them tightly to her chest. "First Dad, then Callie. People keep dying because of me. It's why I didn't want anyone to see this. To know that I was there and that I ran away. Like a coward."

I put my arm around her and held her while she began to cry. Her sobs were loud and ragged, and she sagged against me. I couldn't remember the last time she'd allowed me to hold her.

"What happened to Callie wasn't your fault," I said into her hair, which smelled faintly floral.

"I'm the one who took the video of Daphne and the coach together. I'm the one who gave it to Callie. In a way, I set everything in motion. If I hadn't, Callie might still be alive."

"Why did you give it to her?"

Alex shrugged helplessly. "I don't know. I showed it to them that day they hung the doll in my locker. I was so mad. It was like something had snapped inside of me, and I just wanted to hurt Daphne back. To make her stop laughing. So I played the video and held it up for the three of them to see. That's when Daphne smashed my phone into pieces. Then, a few days later, Callie asked if she could have a copy. I didn't know she was going to text it to everyone at school, but honestly? At that moment, I didn't care. I was angry."

"Understandably. But we're going to have to give the data stick to the police," I said. "And you're going to have to tell them everything."

Alex nodded resignedly. "I know. I was hoping that they would find out that Daphne and Shae were lying about being home that night and then find out that it was Callie who texted out the video. Because I'm pretty sure that's why Daphne killed her."

"But what was Shae's motive? Why did she help Daphne?" I would never forget the chilling almost black-and-white image of the two girls holding Callie down under the surf. It hadn't been a quick death. They'd had to keep her there, pushed down under the water, for long moments. And although I couldn't see Callie at that point, I knew by the way Daphne and Shae had struggled to keep Callie submerged that she'd been fighting back.

"Shae does whatever Daphne tells her to," Alex said quietly.

"But there must be more to it than that. No one would kill someone just because their friend told them to." But even as I spoke, I remembered Emma telling me the story about the girls going to dance classes when they were in middle school. How Shae had been the best dancer, and in return, Daphne had shunned Shae until she agreed to drop out of dance classes. Maybe Daphne had been grooming Shae to follow her orders for years.

"Callie talked about it with me once. She said that Daphne has a way of making you do things you don't want to do. That it's like this power she has. I guess Callie was right."

"We have to go to the police," I said. "They need to arrest those two girls before they can hurt anyone else."

Alex hesitated. "I think there's probably one more thing you should see before we go to the police."

"I really think we should leave now. The police are just waiting on the coroner's report. If it shows that Callie was killed—and after seeing how much she struggled, I have to imagine it will—they're going to arrest you for her murder."

Alex nodded. "I know, but there's more. I need to show you one more video."

My stomach curdled. How much worse could this get?

"I screwed up," Alex continues. "I didn't mean to, but I did. The law of unintended consequences, I guess."

"What are you talking about? What's the law of unintended consequences?"

"We learned about it in my economics class. It's when someone passes a law hoping to accomplish something and something unexpected and unintended happens instead. Like when they banned alcohol and it resulted in the formation of organized crime."

I wondered whether Alex could be in shock. She'd been fragile even before she witnessed a murder. "I don't know what you're talking about, sweetheart."

"I was trying to get Daphne and Shae to admit to what they'd done. But instead, I warned them."

"What did you warn them about?" I asked. "Something else happened on the beach that night?"

"Do you know how I was just telling you that Daphne has a weird effect on her friends? That people do things because she tells them to?"

I nodded, impatient to get this data stick to the police. Alex wouldn't be safe until they saw it.

"I think Daphne has the reverse effect on me," Alex said. "She just makes me so angry. And I end up acting before I think through the consequences."

Suddenly, she had my attention. "What did you do?"

Alex picked up the television remote and selected another video from the data stick.

"Just watch this," she said.

CHAPTER FORTY-FIVE

Video Diary of Alex Turner

October 17

Alex stood in the school courtyard, holding her phone up in front of her.

Daphne and Shae are over there. I'm going to see if I can get them to confess. I want to make sure I get a recording of this. Hold on.

The picture shifted from selfie to camera mode. There were throngs of students hanging out in the courtyard. Some sat at tables, others stood in groups. Daphne Hudson and Shae Thacker were off to one side, standing close together near a palm tree. They were whispering angrily to one another. Daphne's arms were crossed, and her cheeks were flushed with anger. Shae's face was creased with worry. Alex moved closer to them. She lowered her phone so they wouldn't notice she was taking a video, checking first to make sure that Daphne and Shae were on camera.

"This is seriously bad," Shae said.

Daphne shook her head. "Just forget about it, Shae!"

"How am I supposed to forget what happened?"

"Hi," Alex said, her voice off camera.

Daphne looked up. When she saw Alex, her eyes narrowed. "What do you want, freak?"

"We're having a private conversation," Shae said.

"About Callie?" Alex asked.

"Um, yeah? She was our best friend. We're upset. Obviously," Shae said.

"And it's none of your business." Daphne waved her hand in Alex's direction. "Go on. Get lost."

"I know what you did," Alex said.

Daphne and Shae both turned to stare at her.

"What did you say?" Daphne asked.

"I know what you did," Alex said again.

Daphne stared at Alex for a long moment. Her pretty face twisted into an ugly sneer, and she laughed dismissively. "You're such a liar."

"I was there," Alex said. "I was at the beach that night. I saw what you did."

Shae blanched. She turned to Daphne. "You said there wasn't anyone else there! You said you checked everywhere!"

"Ignore her. She's obviously lying."

"I don't lie," Alex said. "I was on the lifeguard tower. You didn't check there, did you?"

Shae's eyes widened, and she turned to Daphne. "Oh, my God, Daph. We're going to get into so much trouble."

"Shut up, Shae," Daphne hissed at her. "She doesn't know anything."

"Are you so sure about that? Because you couldn't see me, but I saw you. I saw all three of you. I know what you did to Callie."

Shae started to cry. She covered her face with her hands, but her sobs were loud and her shoulders shaking. Other students standing nearby looked over at her.

"Shae, get your shit together," Daphne said. She glared at Alex. "What the fuck is your problem?"

"You're my problem," Alex said. "You've been my problem since the first day we met. And now I'm going to make sure you go down for what you did."

"I have no idea what you're talking about," Daphne said. "But everyone knows you're a mental case, so no one's ever going to believe anything you say anyway."

"You remember that video of you and Coach? The one I took?" Alex asked. "The one Callie sent out to everyone you know just to humiliate you? That wasn't the only video I took."

"Oh, my God. She has a video?" Shae exclaimed.

"You're both very photogenic. You look great in close up," Alex said. "I think it might even go viral."

"Are you filming us right now?" Daphne asked, looking at the phone in Alex's hand.

"What if I am?"

"Give me your phone." Daphne took a sudden step toward Alex. There was a murmur among the other students in the courtyard. Daphne looked around, apparently just noticing that their argument had attracted an audience.

"Are you going to break my phone again? In front of everyone?" Alex asked. "That's going to be hard to explain to the police."

Daphne took a step back. "Come on, Shae. Let's go to class."

"But what are we going to do about her?"

"Don't say another word." Daphne grabbed Shae's arm and pulled her away from where Alex was standing. "Not one more word."

CHAPTER FORTY-SIX

KATE

"When did this happen?" I asked once the video had stopped.

"Yesterday morning, right when I got to school. That's why I left. I mean, everyone was looking at me and talking about me, I wasn't lying about that. But it was partly because this happened." Alex gestured at the now-blank screen. "I left and went to a Starbucks. While I was there, I downloaded all of the videos to the USB stick, and then I wiped my tablet and phone. I even wiped the cloud."

"They don't admit they killed Callie," I said.

"I know," Alex said. "Shae almost did, but Daphne stopped her. If one of them was going to crack, it would have been Shae. It's too bad, I would have liked to have had that on tape."

"But we have solid proof that they killed Callie." I was confused. "The police will be able to make a case without your having gotten Daphne and Shae to confess on camera."

"I know. That's not why I wanted you to see it," Alex said.

"Okay. Why then?"

"Callie and Shae *know* I made a video of them killing Callie," Alex said. "I told them I did. They might come after me."

I considered this. It sounded dramatic, the idea that these two lip-glossed and ponytailed suburban teenage girls would be a physical threat to Alex. But after seeing the video of Daphne and Shae drowning Callie, I understood my daughter's concern.

"We need to go to the police station. You're not going to be safe until the police have that video."

"That detective said they might be able to retrieve the data off of my phone and tablet," Alex pointed out.

"I suppose it's possible, but we can't count on that." I frowned as something occurred to me. "Why did you erase everything? Were you trying to protect Daphne and Shae for some reason?"

"No way." Alex shook her head. "That wasn't why. At first, I was just going to delete the video I took of Daphne and Coach having sex, because I was afraid it would get traced back to me. I was worried I'd get in trouble for having taken it. But then I realized there's a lot of other private stuff in my video diary. Things I don't want anyone to listen to. Not the police, not you, not anyone. The entire point was that I was supposed to be able to say what I was feeling in the moment, no matter what it was." Alex's eyes filled with tears. "Sometimes it wasn't very nice. Everyone who sees it is going to think I'm a terrible person."

It reminded me of the constant worry I had that my bad thoughts made me a bad person. Maybe Joe was right . . . maybe everyone had dark thoughts. The important thing was not acting on them.

I reached over and squeezed Alex's hand. "You're going to find out that one of the nicer parts about getting older is that you stop caring so much about what people think. Or so they tell me."

Alex smiled faintly. "Can I speed up to that part?"

"Don't wish away time," I said. "No matter how hard it is right now. It passes by quickly enough on its own."

I couldn't help remembering Ingrid's doctoral thesis, arguing that we should teach our daughters to stop being people pleasers. To teach them how to be bold and ruthless. To fearlessly take up room. And looking at my worried, tearful daughter, I wanted all those things for Alex.

Just not how Genevieve had gone about it. She had taught Daphne about power and domination but had neglected to temper those lessons with the importance of grace and kindness. By doing so, she had, day by day, year by year, turned Daphne into a monster. The sort of girl who takes what she wants, no matter whom she destroys in the process. And Ingrid and Emma had allowed Daphne influence over their daughters, even though they must have had some idea how poisonous she was.

And now one girl was dead, and two others were most likely going to jail, probably for the better part of the rest of their lives. Three futures were gone, just like that. Daphne and Shae were certainly guilty. But what would happen to Genevieve, Emma, and Ingrid? Didn't they share some of the blame for the death? For the part they played in destroying three lives?

"Alex, I really think we should get going." My nerves were jangling, and I instinctively knew we needed to act quickly. I stood and looked around for my handbag before remembering I'd left it by the front door.

"Do you think we'll be at the police station for a long time?"

"Yes, I imagine they're going to have questions," I said.

"I'm going to go up to my room and grab a hoodie. It was freezing in there earlier."

I nodded. "Good idea. Will you get me a sweater too? My black cardigan is on the back of the chair in my room."

Alex ran up the stairs, and I headed into the kitchen to get us each a bottle of water from the fridge. And then I stopped suddenly and gasped.

Emma was standing in the middle of our kitchen. She was dressed for yoga class in a long light-pink tank top and cropped black leggings.

Her long wavy hair was loose around her shoulders. But something was off. Her face was oddly blank, with the exception of her eyes. They were unusually bright.

She raised her hand, and I saw it then. A flash of metal that made my entire body go cold.

Emma was holding a knife.

CHAPTER FORTY-SEVEN

KATE

"Emma?" I asked, staring at the knife in her hand. It was long and sharp looking and not one that I recognized. She must have brought it with her. "What are you doing here? Why are you in my house? How did you even get in here?"

But even as I asked this last question, I glanced at the back door. I must have forgotten to lock it earlier after I'd gone out to water the pots of flowers on the back patio. Before we went to the police station.

"Where's Alex? I need to see her. Now," Emma demanded.

She was standing just next to the kitchen table where I'd sat with her two days earlier, drinking a glass of wine. On that visit, she'd been pretending we were still friends. That pretense was clearly over.

"She's not here," I said automatically, hoping that Alex would sense the danger and stay upstairs.

"Bullshit. I just heard her voice. I heard the two of you talking." Emma raised the hand holding the knife so that the sharp tip was pointing straight at me. "I don't want to hurt you, Kate. But I will if I have to."

"What do you want?" I asked.

"I know Alex took a video of Daphne and Shae that night on the beach. I want it."

I stared at her, horrified by both the knife she was wielding and her admission. "You know what Shae and Daphne did? You know they killed Callie?"

Emma took a step toward me. The knife she was holding looked terrifyingly sharp as it flashed in the light. It was long too. The blade was at least seven inches and curved to a sharp, deadly point. I tried not to think about the searing pain it would cause if it pierced my skin.

"Shae didn't do anything," Emma said. "She came to me after school yesterday and told me everything that happened. She told me Daphne killed Callie. Shae was there, but she couldn't stop it from happening. And she told me that Alex took a video that makes it look like Shae was involved. I'm going to need every copy you have of that video. I don't care what happens to Daphne, but Shae is not going to have her life ruined for something she didn't do."

"Your daughter lied to you," I said. "It's all on the video. Daphne and Shae drowned Callie together. Callie was fighting to get free, so it took the two of them to hold her under the water."

"Shut up," Emma snarled.

I wasn't sure whether telling her about the video was a good idea. I didn't have a plan. I just wanted to keep Emma away from Alex for as long as I could without getting stabbed in the process. Talking was the only delay tactic I could think of. My hope was that Alex would overhear us and she'd be able to get out of the house safely.

Emma's eyes were flashing dangerously, and her mouth was pressed in a tight line. I remembered the first time I'd met her, and she'd seemed so breezy and upbeat, a glamorous version of the girl next door. Now she looked like a cornered animal, frightened and feral and ready to attack.

"I want every copy of that video," Emma said. "Get your daughter in here *now*."

My heart was pounding, and my mouth had gone dry. I tried to listen for Alex, but I didn't hear anything. Not the floor creaking as she walked overhead or her footsteps pounding down the stairs.

Get out, Alex, I thought desperately. Run as far away as possible. And bring the USB stick with you.

"We already gave it to the police," I said, stalling.

Emma laughed, an ugly barking sound devoid of humor. "Liar," she said. "I told you, I heard you talking. You haven't given it to them yet."

I tried to remember exactly what Alex and I had said. What Emma could have overheard.

"Then you know the police already have it. They took Alex's tablet and her phone, which she used to make the videos."

"You're still lying. Mark's younger brother is a deputy sheriff. He told us that all of the data had been wiped off Alex's electronics."

This town, I thought. Even the policemen gossip.

"The detectives we met with today assured us they'd still be able to retrieve the data. We were just going to give them the copy we have to make their job easier. But the final result will be the same." I had no idea whether this was true. I hoped it was. "Shae is going to be charged with murder. There's nothing you can do to stop that. Hurting me will only make things worse for you and your family."

"Shut up! You don't know what you're talking about!" Emma took a sudden step in my direction, decreasing the distance between us. She flicked her wrist, waving the knife at me.

My heart lurched as I stared at the weapon. The fact that she'd brought it with her was even more terrifying. This wasn't some wild, erratic moment of madness. Emma had come here planning to hurt me. To hurt my daughter.

I forced myself to lift my gaze from the knife to meet Emma's hostile glare. "It is true. I saw the video. Callie, Daphne, and Shae were all at the beach that night. Callie admitted that she was the one who sent the video of Daphne and Coach Townsend having sex to all of their classmates. I think that's when Daphne decided to kill her. She and Shae lured Callie into the water. And then, they attacked her. The two of them, together, held her under the water while she fought to get free. And it wasn't a few seconds, Emma. It lasted for five or six minutes. I can't imagine how terrified Callie must have been before she died."

"Callie wasn't an innocent." Emma practically spat out the words. "You just admitted that she's the one who blasted that video out to everyone the girls knew. That was a terrible thing to do!"

"And you think she deserved to die for that?"

"I didn't say that," Emma said angrily. "But if Callie had been more loyal, none of this would have happened. She shouldn't have sent out the video, and Ingrid shouldn't have sent out the texts, and—" She stopped suddenly, her lips pursing into a startled *O*.

"What texts?" I asked.

Emma shook her head. "That's not what I said."

"You said Ingrid shouldn't have sent those texts," I repeated. Then I realized what she was saying. "Wait. *Ingrid* was the one who sent those awful texts to Daphne? The ones calling her a slut and telling her to kill herself? But . . . why? Why would she do that? That doesn't make sense."

"You don't know her," Emma said. "Just because you hung out with us a few times doesn't mean that you really got to know any of us. You were never one of us."

If not for the fact that Emma had broken into my house and was brandishing a knife, I would have laughed at this. It was so childish and petty.

"Then tell me," I suggested. "Explain why your good friend Ingrid sent nasty anonymous texts to the daughter of your other good friend Genevieve?"

"I know Ingrid seems calm and poised on the surface. But the reality is she's always been a very jealous person. She was jealous of me, of Genevieve. That we were both happily married, while she was single and alone. That's the thing about Ingrid. Having the picture-perfect life has always been important to her. She wanted all of it—the perfect marriage, the accomplished career, the high-achieving daughter. When her husband cheated on her and blew up her perfect family, she never recovered from that. She's always viewed the end of her marriage as a failure."

"If she was jealous of you and Genevieve, why would she target Daphne?"

Emma let out a humorless laugh. "Because Genevieve has never missed the opportunity to rub her perfect life in Ingrid's face. Her rich, successful husband. Her beautiful and gifted children. Her house that could have been featured in a magazine. And it got to Ingrid. It was like a pebble in her shoe, a constant irritation that she couldn't get rid of. And she couldn't confront Genevieve because that would have been the end of their friendship. But she could take her frustrations out on Daphne."

"But those texts were awful. They were ugly and mean. What kind of an adult would go after a teenage kid like that?" I asked.

"I think it was Ingrid's way of taunting Genevieve that her family wasn't as perfect as she likes to pretend."

I wondered how Ingrid would feel when she learned that Daphne had murdered her daughter. Would she question whether the texts she'd sent Daphne had inflamed a conflict that ended in her daughter's death?

"It's all so toxic," I murmured. And it was. The clique of mothers and their murderous clique of daughters.

"Yes. Daphne *is* toxic," Emma said, missing my larger point. "I've always wondered if there's something fundamentally wrong with her. Like if she has borderline personality disorder or malignant narcissism. That's probably what happened. It wasn't Shae at all."

Emma was suddenly earnest, as though she were trying to convince us both that Shae was just another one of Daphne's victims. And maybe I would have believed her. If I hadn't seen the video. Shae hadn't hesitated when Daphne demanded that she help her kill Callie. Shae had jumped right in.

"Emma. Listen to me." I held up my hands, and Emma hesitated, lowering the knife. "I know you're upset. I know it's a lot to process. But your being here isn't going to change anything. The truth is going to come out about what happened that night."

Emma shook her head dazedly, as if continued denial was enough to stop the truth.

"Shae would never hurt anyone. It's not in her nature," she said quietly.

"Shae always does what Daphne tells her to."

Emma took another step toward me, the hand holding the knife rising up again. I skittered backward until I hit the wall next to the entrance to the kitchen. My head banged against the framed Ellsworth Kelly poster I'd bought at the Albright-Knox museum back in Buffalo. It swayed back and forth. I wondered whether it would fall off its hook and crash to the ground—and hoped it would, because that might alert Alex to the present danger—but it stayed put.

"I need to see Alex now," Emma said, biting out each word.

"Absolutely not."

"I'm not asking. I want every copy of that video, and I'm not leaving until I have them."

Emma lifted the knife again and took another step toward me. The blade was now dangerously close.

"I'll kill you if I have to," Emma said with such quiet determination, I believed her.

My heart drummed with terror as I stared at the lethal weapon in Emma's hand. I could see the resolve in her eyes. She really was prepared to kill me and Alex in order to save her daughter.

I looked around, wondering whether I could make a run for it. It was possible I could get out of the kitchen and into the front hallway before Emma could catch up to me. But what then? Would I be able to get out of the front door before she had time to plunge the knife into my back? Or make it to a neighbor's house to call for help? Maybe, but I wasn't sure. And I still didn't know whether Alex was aware that Emma was in the house, threatening to hurt us. I could hardly leave her here alone, even to go for help. Emma would find Alex. And I would not let that happen.

Emma took another step toward me. She was now only a few feet away from me. So close, I could see the green in her hazel eyes, the tiny mole above her right eyebrow. Emma seemed to be readying herself to commit the violence she was threatening. Her eyes were oddly blank, her mouth set in a grim line. She didn't look sane. Was it possible that she'd experienced a psychotic break? That learning that her daughter was a murderer had been too much for her to bear?

"Emma, please think this through. More violence isn't going to fix anything," I said. My voice was thin and high pitched. "It's only going to make everything worse."

Emma shook her head once. "Once I destroy every copy of that video, this will be over. At least it will be for Shae."

"But you can't. The police will still be able to recover the video off Alex's tablet or phone."

"Maybe they will and maybe they won't," Emma countered. "But I can make sure they don't get it from you."

She drew in a deep breath, raised the knife up to shoulder height, and braced herself. Terror flooded through me. I put my hands up, already anticipating the pain from that deadly sharp blade piercing my skin.

Should I scream? I wondered wildly. And alert Alex? Or would that just cause her to run downstairs and make herself a target for Emma? I decided it was better to warn her.

I filled my lungs with air, and then, as loud as I could, I screamed, "Alex, get out of the house!"

Emma stepped forward and plunged the knife into my chest.

CHAPTER FORTY-EIGHT

KATE

The pain was unlike anything I had ever experienced. It was hot and searing, and I suddenly couldn't draw in a breath. I stared down at the knife sticking out of my chest, like a prop in a Halloween haunted house. Only this wasn't make believe. I could feel something dripping down the front of me, and I distantly realized that it was blood. There was a dark-red circle on my T-shirt that was expanding outward.

I'm going to die, I thought as my feet slowly slid out from under me. I fell into a seated position, leaning against the wall.

I looked up at Emma, who stared down at me in stunned horror. The pain worsened, an unbearable throbbing that I didn't think I would be able to withstand much longer. I desperately wanted to pull the knife out of me, thinking that might stop the pain. But I remembered vaguely that you weren't supposed to do that. That removing it could cause the blood to flow out even faster. But did it matter? I wondered. Wouldn't it be better to die faster than suffer the slower painful death I was now enduring?

"I stabbed you," Emma said in an odd high-pitched voice. She stared down at me with wide eyes, her hands twisting in front of her. "I just wanted the video. It didn't have to be like this."

Just then there was a loud crack followed by the sound of glass shattering. Emma shrieked and turned toward the source of the noise.

The vase of roses Joe had brought lay in pieces on the counter. Water poured from the fractured vase, off the counter, pooling on the floor.

Just as I was trying to process how the vase had broken, Alex ran into the kitchen and tackled Emma. Emma let out a grunt as she was knocked down to the floor, Alex on top of her, the two of them struggling. Emma was taller, but Alex was stronger and more athletic. She rolled on top of Emma, grabbing hold of her wrists. Emma twisted from side to side, trying—and failing—to dislodge Alex, but to no avail.

"Get off me!" Emma yelled, struggling to get free.

I tried to pay attention, but it was like the struggle was happening at a distance.

"The police are on their way," Alex told me. "I called them from the phone in your room."

I could hear sirens then, faint but growing closer.

"Oh, thank God." I closed my eyes for a moment and then looked at my daughter. She was so strong, so brave. Whatever happened to me now, she'd be okay. And in that moment, I felt something close to peace engulf me.

Emma heard the sirens too. She stopped fighting Alex and went perfectly still. Alex let go of her wrists, and Emma covered her face with her hands. Then she started to cry.

"I'm going to go to prison," Emma said.

"Mom? Mom! Are you okay?"

As soon as she realized Emma had given up the fight, Alex scrambled across the floor toward me. She knelt beside me, her eyes round with horror. I looked down at myself and noticed hazily that my shirt was now completely soaked through with blood. And I was so cold, so very cold.

"Don't die," Alex said, taking my hand and squeezing it in hers. "Don't die, don't die, don't die."

Her words were like a chant. I wanted to tell her not to worry, that I wasn't scared. It just hurt so much, I couldn't stay much longer. And

I wanted to tell her that I loved her and wanted her to go on and have the most wonderful life. But when I tried to speak, the words didn't come. My vision was starting to fade, the edges turning spotty, like an old-fashioned television tuned to the wrong channel. I tried to draw in a breath and realized I couldn't inhale.

"Mom!" Alex yelled.

And then everything went dark.

CHAPTER FORTY-NINE

Kate

I could hear voices and sense people moving around. A hand briefly rested on my arm, warm and reassuring. Someone nearby was crying. No, not just crying but wailing in horror. It was Alex, I realized. Alex was more upset than I'd ever heard her.

"One, two, three, go," a voice I didn't recognize said. And then I felt my body lifted up and then gently set down. Wherever I was lying now, it was softer and cushioned. Straps were fastened over me.

I tried to open my eyes. I had to find out what was wrong with Alex. But then the pain returned, the unbearable throbbing engulfing me. I couldn't bear it.

When the darkness fell again, I didn't fight it.

The next time I swam up, I could feel myself being moved swiftly down a corridor. I wasn't in my house anymore. I was somewhere larger, where the noises echoed off hard walls and floors. It smelled like industrial cleanser.

I still couldn't open my eyes, but I had the sensation that I was on wheels. There were people nearby, both the ones pushing me and others we were passing by.

"Hold the elevator," a voice from above me called out. There was a slight bump, and then I was rolled into a new, smaller space.

"Where are you going?"

"Third floor. Surgery."

"Oh, my God. Is that a knife?"

"Yeah, she was stabbed."

"Jesus, that looks bad. Is she going to make it?"

I didn't hear the reply. The overwhelming pain returned. I wanted to scream, I wanted it out of me, but I couldn't lift my arms. I couldn't even move.

Make it stop, I thought. I can't bear it anymore.

The merciful darkness came again. This time I intended to stay there.

I opened my eyes.

Where am I? I wondered, but just as quickly, my thoughts answered me. I'm in a hospital room.

I was lying in a bed, hooked up to monitors that were letting out soft regular beeps. There was a needle taped to my arm that connected to an IV rack next to the bed. Directly across from the bed, there was a cabinet upon which a beautiful vase of white roses sat. There was a whiteboard on the wall above it, which, strangely, had my name written on it. I turned my head to the side and saw an empty chair.

Where is everyone? I wondered.

Then, suddenly, Alex was there, walking into the room. She was wearing an oversize black T-shirt that had **Surfside Grill** screen printed on the front. She saw me, and her eyes widened. "Mom? You're awake!"

"What's happening?" I asked. My voice sounded creaky.

"Hold on, I have to get the nurse."

Alex rushed from the room, and when she was back, she was accompanied by both a nurse and Detective Gavin Reddick.

"You're going to have to wait to speak to her until we've had a chance to assess her," the nurse told the detective. She was around my age and had blonde hair cut in a short spiked-up style. She smiled at me, and her face softened. "How are you feeling, Kate?"

I considered this. I was tired, very tired, and the pain was still there. But it was muted compared to how it had been. I looked down at my chest. The knife was gone, and so were my blood-soaked clothes. I was wearing a clean blue hospital gown.

Detective Reddick and Alex both stood back while the nurse bustled around, checking my vital signs on the machine I was hooked up to, asking me whether I wanted to sit up, and then helping me sip some water through a straw. She set the plastic mug on a side table that she rolled over, closer to me.

"Take small sips when you're up to it. Not too much all at once," she said.

"I can help her," Alex offered.

"Good girl," the nurse said. She eyed Reddick warily. She didn't seem to like the detective any more than I did. "Don't tire her out," she ordered him. "I'll be back with the doctor."

"Emma?" I asked, my eyes moving from the detective to Alex and back again.

"She was arrested," the detective said. "She's facing charges of attempted murder and assault with a deadly weapon, along with breaking and entering." He shook his head. "You got lucky. The doctor said that when Emma Thacker stabbed you, she missed your lungs by millimeters."

"I feel lucky," I joked, although as soon as I spoke, I was hit by another wave of pain. I had to close my eyes for a moment.

"Mom!" Alex drew closer. "Are you okay?"

I opened my eyes and nodded. "It just hurts a little."

"You were in surgery, but the doctor said you'll make a full recovery," Alex assured me. "But you lost a lot of blood. She said you're going to feel weak for a while."

"The USB stick," I said suddenly.

"It's okay. I gave it to the police," Alex assured me.

"Thank God," I said. It was over. Alex was safe. I turned to the detective. "Did you watch the videos?"

Detective Reddick nodded. "Daphne Hudson and Shae Thacker have both been arrested."

"That's good. At least I didn't get stabbed for nothing," I said with a faint smile.

"Mom, it's not funny." Alex looked shocked. "You almost died."

"The vase broke," I said. My thoughts started to feel hazy.

"I threw that decorative bowl at it. The one you keep by the front door for keys. I wanted to distract her."

"Good thinking."

"I thought she was going to kill you. There was so much blood. It was all over the kitchen."

My smile faded, and I nodded. I remembered the blood, remembered how warm and sticky it had felt dripping down me. I felt a wave of fatigue, and then the pain grew more intense.

"I'm tired," I said. "I think I'm going to close my eyes for a minute."

The next time I woke, Joe was sitting in the chair next to my bed, holding a paperback book in one hand.

"I've never seen you wearing glasses before," I said.

Joe looked up, startled, but then he grinned at me. "I'm secretly incredibly vain." He set down his book and reading glasses and reached for my hand. "How are you feeling, sweetheart?"

"I feel a lot like I was stabbed in the chest with a chef's knife."

Joe grimaced. "Don't remind me."

"Where's Alex?"

"She went to the cafeteria to grab something to eat. I said I'd sit with you while she's there."

"Where is she staying while I'm here? Is she still at home?" I asked.

Joe nodded. "She insisted on it. That detective . . . the suspicious-looking guy with the squinty eyes?"

"Gavin Reddick," I said.

"He wanted to arrange for a family member to come stay with her. Your mom, I think. But Alex absolutely refused."

"Smart girl," I said. "My mom is a handful."

"He's posting a police detail at the house to make sure she's safe. And I'll keep my eye on her. Make sure she has food, all that good stuff. They said you'll be discharged in a few days."

"Good," I said. I was feeling sleepy again. "Knowing you, you'll bring her an entire luau feast, including a roast suckling pig."

Joe's eyes softened as he looked down at me. He stroked my brow with his fingers, which was surprisingly relaxing. "Don't worry. I'll take care of everything. You just rest and get better."

CHAPTER FIFTY

KATE

“That looks absolutely terrifying,” I said, staring up at the giant roller coaster. Joe hadn’t been kidding. The track went straight up in the air at a ninety-degree angle from the ground and then plunged back down again, the passengers on board screaming the whole time. Just looking at it made me queasy. “Are you sure you want to ride that?”

“Absolutely,” Alex said.

“It’s fun!” Sean said with the enthusiasm of a roller coaster fanatic. “You should try it.”

I shook my head. “I think I’ll pass.”

I thought it would probably hurt like hell to be strapped into a roller coaster. A month had passed since Emma stabbed me, and I had mostly recovered. But there was lingering pain.

“You don’t know what you’re missing,” Sean said.

Joe’s son looked just like him. They had the same kind brown eyes and full mouths. They even stood the same way, their backs straight and weight shifted to their heels, arms folded in front of their chests. Sean was an easygoing kid, and he and Alex had gotten on surprisingly well.

In fact, our Thanksgiving trip to Universal Studios had gone better than I would have imagined. Alex and Joe had bonded over jokes and a shared love of junk food. In the weeks since Daphne and Shae had been arrested, Alex had been slowly unwinding. She wasn’t quite back to the untroubled girl she'd been before her father died, but she had lost her brittle, fragile veneer.

"Dad, you're coming, right?" Sean asked Joe.

"No, you kids go ahead. I'll stay and keep Kate company on the ground," Joe said.

"Come on," Sean said to Alex. "I'm going to see if we can ride in the front row."

The two teens headed off toward the roller coaster. Joe and I watched them, both smiling.

"They're getting along well," I said.

"I think Sean is like the annoying little brother Alex never wanted," Joe said.

"Are you sure you don't want to ride with them? I'm okay hanging out on my own."

"Can I tell you a secret? The last time I rode that roller coaster, I almost threw up afterward. It's a little too intense, even for me."

I laughed. "I hope the kids won't get sick."

"They're kids. They're built for roller coasters." Joe gestured toward an empty bench. "Do you want to sit down? You must be getting tired."

"I'm fine," I said reflexively. If I kept telling everyone I was fine, maybe I would convince myself. But he was right; I was tired. I still fatigued quickly.

We sat, and Joe slipped his arm around my shoulders. It was a beautiful day, warm and sunny. The park had been decorated for the holidays, and so there were Christmas trees and wreaths and festive red bows wherever we looked. It smelled like popcorn and coconut-scented sunscreen.

"This has been a nice break," I said. "I think Alex and I both needed it."

"She seems like she's doing well."

"I think so too. I thought that with all the media frenzy surrounding the murder case, she'd get overwhelmed. But it's been just the opposite.

It seems like the more the truth gets out about what happened, the more grounded she is." I shook my head. "Especially considering how crazy it's all getting."

Almost as soon as Daphne and Shae were taken into custody, their arrests had become a national news story. I shouldn't have been surprised. Daphne and Shae were photogenic, privileged, and, on the surface, unlikely murderers. Their victim was an honors student with a bright future ahead of her. When you added in the inappropriate sexual relationship between Coach Townsend and Daphne, which had been the first domino that was tipped over in the events leading up to Callie's murder, and Shae's mother stabbing me, it was a pretty salacious story. All the major news channels had covered it, and Lita had told me—when she'd cornered me at Target in the paper towel aisle—that there was a production team in town working on a documentary about Callie's murder and the upcoming trials.

I'd been contacted by television producers, reporters, and podcasters, all eager to offer me a platform to tell my story. I had gotten into the habit of leaving my phone turned off.

It wasn't even a given that there would be trials. Emma had already agreed to a plea deal for the charges of attempted murder, assault, and breaking and entering. She would spend fifteen years in prison, which was a much lesser sentence than she would have been facing had she gone to trial. The state's attorney had contacted me before they inked the plea deal with Emma. Apparently, if I had objected to it, that might have had some effect on how her case was disposed. But I agreed. I didn't think Emma was going to commit any further crimes. The one she had committed had been to protect her daughter. I didn't condone it, but I understood it.

Mothers did what we needed to do to keep our children safe.

Lita had also told me there was rampant speculation that Shae and Daphne might take similar plea deals. That they'd each been offered a deal to turn on the other in order to secure a lesser sentence. I doubted it was true. Daphne was far too sharp to pass up a good deal if one was offered to her. And besides, Lita also told me the state's attorney had political ambitions and so wouldn't want to miss the chance to prosecute a nationally televised trial and become a media star.

But I hoped the girls would take plea deals, especially if it gave them a chance for a somewhat normal life at some point in the future. They deserved prison sentences for what they had done, but they were so young. If they cooperated with the prosecution, they might have a chance to someday be released and rejoin society. Hopefully, at a point when they were too old to have daughters of their own.

And I didn't want Alex to have to testify at their trials. She was on her way to getting better, but I didn't think being the star witness in two murder trials would help her move on. The internet really was forever. I didn't want every job she interviewed for, every new friend she met, to end up as a Google search that led back to Daphne and Shae and what they did to Callie that night on the beach. I didn't want the story to follow her.

There were already too many victims.

"I heard a rumor that Genevieve and Richard are going to move to Miami once Daphne's case concludes," Joe said.

"Really? I'm surprised they'd want to make big decisions like that right now."

"Jonathan's in the same grade as Sean. Sean said he isn't doing well. I guess the other kids are giving him a hard time over Daphne's arrest. I think the Hudsons want to move him somewhere he'll be more anonymous."

"I'm sorry to hear that," I said. And I was. Jon was yet another victim. Then I remembered what Alex had said when I'd suggested she move to a different school. "But he probably won't be able to get away from it. The kids at his new school will find out at some point. It's all one internet search away."

"I think life was easier when we were kids. Before social media and selfies," Joe said.

"It definitely was," I agreed. "After all, if Alex hadn't taken the video of Daphne and Coach Townsend and Callie hadn't texted it to everyone in her contacts, she might still be alive."

"I don't think you can look at it that way," Joe said. "Technology didn't make Daphne and Shae lure Callie to the beach that night, and it didn't make them kill her. There's something wrong with them on a fundamental level."

"You're definitely right about Daphne. I'm not as sure about Shae. I think she was conditioned over the years to do whatever Daphne wanted. If she'd never met Daphne, she might never have hurt anyone. But I guess we'll never know."

"Peer pressured into committing murder." Joe shook his head. "Poor Callie."

"I wonder how Ingrid is doing. First, she lost her daughter, which is just about the worst thing a parent can experience. Then she finds out that her best friends' daughters were the murderers. It must be like a nightmare she can't wake up from."

I shivered at the thought. Joe, sensing my discomfort, held me a little closer.

The roller coaster swooped by overhead on its curving track, its passengers screaming. It was moving too fast to see whether Alex and Sean were on board, but I hoped they were. I hoped my daughter was flying above us, without a care in the world.

CHAPTER FIFTY-ONE

Video Diary of Alex Turner

December 1

Alex was on a screen-in-screen video chat with an attractive woman in her early thirties. The woman had kind blue eyes and long light-brown hair that fell around her shoulders. She was wearing oversize glasses with round tortoiseshell frames. Alex looked relaxed and alert.

"It's good to see you, Alex," Beatrice Malone said. "How have you been since we last spoke?"

"Good. Really good actually," Alex said brightly.

"Have you been playing tennis?"

"No. After everything that happened, the school board decided to cancel the rest of the season. But I joined the cross-country team, which has been fun. I like running, and I've made some friends. Well, a friend. But it's a start. At least I have someone to eat lunch with."

"That's definitely progress. What's your friend's name?"

"Isabel. She's nice. And her friends are pretty cool too. None of them seem to care that I was a murder suspect, like, five minutes ago." Alex waved her hand. "Now everyone's talking about Daphne and Shae. There's a rumor going around that Shae may take a plea deal to testify against Daphne."

"If she did, you'd only have to testify at one trial, instead of two."

"It doesn't seem right. Shae is just as guilty of killing Callie as Daphne is. And everyone's acting like she's a victim, just because Daphne's so terrible."

Beatrice nodded sympathetically. "It's probably easier for people to see Daphne as the leader in the relationship, and Shae as the subordinate who was following orders, than to acknowledge that two girls could both be that destructive. And it's human nature to make excuses for behavior we can't understand. I can see why that would be frustrating for you, especially considering that you were there. And you saw what they did."

"They're both evil," Alex said flatly. "No one should make excuses for either one of them. Shae and Daphne both deserve to rot in jail for the rest of their lives."

"Maybe," Beatrice replied. "But I like to think that people can change. That those two girls could still turn their lives around and become productive members of society."

"You sound like my mom," Alex said.

"You don't agree?"

"No. I think they should be locked up somewhere where they can't ever hurt anyone ever again."

"It's okay that you feel that way. And it's okay if you change your mind over time."

Alex shrugged. "It's not like it's up to me whether or not they go to prison."

"How are things going with your mom?"

"We've been getting along. I guess in the end all we needed was for someone to break into the house and try to kill her to bring us together."

Alex smiled, but Bridget did not return it. Her brow creased with concern, and Alex's smile faded.

"Sorry, bad joke," Alex said.

Beatrice dipped her head. "How is she feeling?"

"She's better. Some of her movement is still limited, but the doctor said that's normal. She decided to open a consignment store here, and she's still dating that guy."

"How do you feel about her dating?" Beatrice asked.

"Actually, it's fine. It doesn't bother me as much as I thought it would. Joe's nice. He's been helping out."

"It's good that you're open to the change," Beatrice commented.

"Well, I'm going off to college next year. My mom's going to be on her own, so I can't exactly tell her not to have a life, right? I don't know." *Alex shrugged and lifted her hands in front of her.* "I'm just rolling with it."

"Have you thought any more about what we talked about during our last session? We were discussing that you might talk to your mom about what happened on the day of the car accident."

Alex's smile vanished. She leaned back in her seat and crossed her arms in front of her.

"I don't think that's a good idea. Especially after everything that's happened the past few months. She's still recovering from being stabbed."

"I think you should give her a chance," Beatrice said. "She might surprise you."

"I know my mom wants the best for me. But she also wants me to just be a normal teen doing normal teen things. She doesn't need to know what happened that day."

"When I spoke to your mom, back when you first started seeing me, she was hoping your memory would come back. She thought it would help you heal and move on from the accident," Beatrice reminded Alex.

"I do remember. I just haven't told her."

"Maybe it would help her understand what happened."

But Alex shook her head resolutely. "She doesn't need to hear that my dad screamed at me until there was spittle flying out of his mouth. That he ranted that I would never have what it takes to be a professional tennis player. That he was ashamed of me." *Alex's voice grew louder and sharper. She stopped and shook her head once.* "No, she doesn't need to hear any of that."

Beatrice tipped her head to one side, her expression sympathetic. "I'm sorry that's your last memory of him. I'm sure he didn't mean what he said. That he was just speaking in anger."

"I think he meant every word. I was a disappointment to him. But he disappointed me too."

"Your father was a very troubled man. I keep telling you, no one is all good or all bad. Everyone's a shade of gray."

"I screamed back at him. I told him I wished he were dead. And I meant it." *Alex looked down, her expression troubled.*

"You're not the first teenager to say that to a parent," Beatrice said gently.

"Yeah? And how many teenagers watch a traffic light turn red, and instead of stopping, they speed up? Because that's exactly what I did that day."

"It's not that simple," Beatrice said. "You're framing it as though you were acting out a violent impulse. I think you were trying to self-harm that day."

"I saw the truck," Alex said flatly. "I knew I was driving into its path. I knew it was going to hit the passenger side of the car."

"We're talking about a split-second decision made in a moment of extreme emotion," Beatrice said.

"And in that split second, I killed my father."

Alex and Beatrice looked at one another.

Beatrice sighed. "Then that's where we have to start. We need to figure out why you made that decision. I don't think you're a violent person, Alex."

"You don't think there are some people who are fundamentally damaged? Who are just born wrong? I do. I think Daphne and Shae were. I think I might be too."

"No, I don't think a baby comes into the world born evil. Everyone is shaped by their life experiences."

"What's my excuse?"

"Your father was abusive. Verbally, emotionally, even physically. Those times he made you train when you were hurt. That's abusive, Alex. It affected you profoundly. You had one bad moment. Everyone has them. It's just your bad moment had a terrible consequence. You can't let that define who you are."

Alex was quiet for a few moments, her fingers twisting the end of her long braid.

"The thing that scares me is . . . what if it wasn't just one bad moment? I meant what I said that day. I wanted my dad to die. And then I killed him. What if that happens again? What if I get mad at my mom and end up hurting her?"

Beatrice hesitated, looking unsure for the first time. "Are you having fantasies about hurting someone?"

"No, I'm not. It's just . . ." *Alex stopped and looked directly at the camera.* "Sometimes I worry that it's just a matter of time before it happens again. I'll snap and lose control. And I'll end up like Daphne and Shae, sitting in prison for the rest of my life."

"Then we'll start there," Beatrice said. "I can help you learn how to manage your emotions. Teach you some techniques to stop your anger before it gets out of control."

Alex hesitated but then finally nodded. Her wide eyes were luminous against her pale skin, and her expression was uncertain.

"So you think you can fix me?"

Beatrice smiled kindly. "I don't think you're broken, Alex."

"I hope you're right," Alex said. "But I don't think you are. I think I'm one of those people who were just born bad. Like Daphne. We're really just two sides of the same coin."

"I disagree. You and Daphne are nothing alike. You're kind and empathetic and want to be a better person. You're willing to work on yourself."

Alex lifted one shoulder and then let it fall. "I think the only real difference between us is that Daphne's going to jail for what she did. And I'm not."

"I think that's a good thing," Beatrice said.

"I guess we'll find out." *Alex sighed and shook her head.* "One way or another, we'll find out."

ABOUT THE AUTHOR

Photo © 2017 by Robert Holland

Margot Hunt is the *USA Today* bestselling author of *Best Friends Forever*, *For Better and Worse*, and *The Last Affair*. Her work has been praised by Book of the Month, and her Audible Original *Buried Deep* was a number one bestseller. You can stay up to date on Margot's books and upcoming projects on her website, www.margothunt.com.